THE REDEMPTION OF ROAN

KATHY COOPMANS

Copyright

This is a work of fiction. Names, characters, places, organizations, and events portrayed in this novel either are the product of the author's imagination or are used fictitiously, and any resemblance to actual persons, living or dead, business establishments, events, or locales is entirely coincidental.

First edition: December 2015

Editor: Julia Goda Editing Services
https://www.facebook.com/juliagodaeditingservices/?fref=ts

Formatting: Affordable Formatting
https://www.facebook.com/AffordableFormatting74135/

To my son Aaron.
The reason, I'm called MOM.

Prologue

I watch her closely as she sways her small 5'4 frame back and forth to the music like it's absorbing into her skin, her long blond hair swinging to the beat of the music as seductively as her hips. This woman masters a pair of five-inch heels with the compulsion of a runway model. And her dress. Fuck me hard! That has got to be the sexiest and classiest dress I have ever seen. Green as the fresh spring grass, shiny as the dew on a bright sunny morning. High neckline. Low cut back. I cannot take my eyes off of her.

I never thought I could be attracted to a woman who's almost a foot shorter than I am. I've always gone for the taller ones. But her, Christ. She's all legs. With a slim, curvy body. An ass made to spank. Tight and ripe. And her breasts; I've fantasized about how they would feel in my large hands or the way her nipples would perk right up when I'd run the tip of my dick over them. I picture my name coming out of her sweet mouth at the same time she comes inside of mine. The desire to taste her runs so deep it's surreal. I've fantasized over her for months now. She's in every dream, day or night. She denied me once, when I asked her out a few months ago. I'm going to make her mine, not for the purpose I had months ago when I found out about her and my brother. It has nothing to do with that anymore. It has everything to do with the fact she fascinates me.

It's more than wanting her in my bed. The need to know everything there is to know about her far outweighs everything else. Why did she choose to be a Pediatrician? Why doesn't she date? My list of questions is endless when it comes to her. The rest is an added bonus. She deserves to be on a pedestal. Held high, cherished while at the same time independent. Fuck, I sound like a crazy man.

"I have an addiction and you're my cure," I whisper.

Alina Solokov rules this dance floor at ROCK, the newest nightclub in Manhattan, and she doesn't even realize it. She commands it. Dominates it even. Prowling in her own little world while those around her wish to be in her circle. She's fucking beautiful. Especially when she laughs at something her girlfriend says to her. I'm not the only one who's attached himself to his spot, caught up in the elegance of this woman. She has absolutely no god damn clue she'll be the bull's eye for a hell of a lot of sperm when we all go home and grip, jerk, and pull the trigger on our guns, wishing to god it was her instead of Rosie fucking Palmer!

I've been with no one since my eyes landed on her. My hands have callouses to prove it. I've come more times to images of her face alone than I've fucked other women. And Christ, I'm not proud to admit it, but it's more women than I can count. More faces than I can remember. But her... I would never forget her. Do I sound crazy? Absolutely. Am I crazy? Most definitely not. This woman defines the meaning of the total package. Something I never thought I would ever want.

Once I found out who she was, I wanted to use her to lure my brother out of hiding. Now, I want to protect her. Turn her world upside down the same way she's done mine.

Alina is not who I thought she was when I first started following her. I've learned as much as any one person can know about her. From her shoe size to her weight to everywhere in between. She's a riddle, one that has not been solved yet. You would think a beautiful woman who lacks for nothing, the daughter of Ivan and Charlotte Solokov, the Russian mob princess, the only daughter out of seven children would be a bitch. This intriguing creature is nothing like that. She's soft spoken. Kind hearted. And she has consumed and occupied my mind for way too long. I need to get to her. I need her to see me for a man who wants and craves and worships her. Not the brother of Royal "Scarface" Diamond. The killer. I want her to see me. The real me. No games. No rules. Just her and me!

I've fallen in love with a woman who wants nothing to do with me because of who I am. I'm Roan Diamond, the younger brother of a man who she used to date ten years ago. A man who for some reason she walked away from. I'm nothing like my brother and I'm going to give it my all to prove it.

Chapter One

Alina

My eyes skim the nightclub as I sip on my glass of merlot. The lighting is dim, the dance floor lit up only by the lights adorning the perimeter. Bodies mingle, mesh, sweat pouring out of them as they grind against each other. Hoping they've found the one they will be taking home with them for the night.

My roommate Deidre is no exception. She's lurking around Mr. Fuck-Me-Right-Now-All-Night-Long. How any of these people can do this is beyond me. It's as if they have no self-respect. You're disloyal mind has tricked you into thinking it's okay to sleep with a stranger. That it's not degrading to yourself to do the good ole walk of shame in the morning. Or to slip out before he wakes. Some of these jackasses who call themselves men get what they want from you and go as far as kick you out the moment they've satisfied their dicks. Women do the same. Then the next night they move on to their next victim. How a woman or a man can use and be used like that for their own personal satisfaction will continue on forever.

As I stare at all the people making out in the booths and in the corners, I wonder why I didn't study the human mind instead of the body. I'm curious as to how it works. Does the mind actually send a shocking nerve wave down to a man's dick or a woman's pussy and say he or she is the one? Make them twitch. Wet? He or she is the one? My heart pulses with this one more than it does with that one? It makes me truly wonder if we as humans really only think with our personal body parts when it comes to the opposite sex.

I thought that way once. With the desire to give myself over to a man, to give him as much pleasure as he gave me. To fall apart in his arms. Although, it wasn't casual sex for me. That man became the biggest mistake of my life. At the age of eighteen, I thought for sure I was in love and he was in love with me too; this strange young man with a jagged scar down his face, one eye covered with a black patch. He intrigued me. Those flaws had stories behind them. None of that mattered to me. I was captivated, eager to see him every chance I got

My dad took him in, trained him and treated him just like he did my brothers. Being the only daughter, I was sheltered from dating. And who wanted to date Ivan Solokov's daughter anyway? This entire city knows who my dad is. People tend to run the other way at the mere mention of his name, scared to have any association with us at all. I've hated it my entire life. Until he showed up. He told me he felt my pain. Knew what it was like to feel helpless, to be the black sheep of your family. Only Royal was just like my dad and his army of killing soldiers. Worse. It took me four months to realize just how unhinged he really was.

He was family in the eyes of my dad, so the two of us dating made him very happy. He took it as a sign that my heart might change and I would finally accept the things our family did. And I did, all over a man who lied and then turned out to be one of the biggest monsters a person will ever meet. He played off of my innocence, my sympathy for others. So many lies poured out of his mouth. He would tell me how his family disowned him.

Claimed they banished him because he was stupid, not smart like his younger brother. They said he was reckless and I believed everything he told me because I had overheard my dad several times talk about Salvatore Diamond, Royal's dad. An enemy to our family. Not wanting to start a war between the two, both my dad and Salvatore made a treaty with one another: you stay out of my business and I stay out of yours. I believed Royal because nothing happened when he came to work for my dad, no one came looking for him. No war had been started. His family did nothing. Said nothing. No blood was shed over him crossing that unethical line. And when my brother Anton told me the truth about Royal, I was devastated. Here I thought my dad was training him the same way my brothers were learning. What they were doing, I had no clue. I never thought he was being trained to be a killer. And I sure as hell did not know he was addicted to heroin. Poison. The young, naïve woman I was, was blinded by it all.

I knew I had to find a way to get away from him. I left my family no choice but to accept the fact I was leaving. They all knew how important becoming a doctor was for me. With their blessing and the promise from Anton he would kill Royal if he didn't let me go, I was scheduled to leave, with only one thing left to do and that was to tell Royal. He never once showed his temper to me. Treated me with respect, love, almost to the point of being obsessive. I ignored it all because I thought I loved him. I know now I should have never gone to his apartment by myself. That night changed me towards men. I promised myself I would never give my heart away again, and for ten years I have kept to myself. Not once bringing a man home with me. Not once longing for a touch, a kiss, or the feeling of a man moving inside of me. It is better for me to be alone for the rest of my life than to be in bed with bad company. Men are unscrupulous assholes.

I take another sip of my wine, my thoughts still going back to my past.

Royal Diamond. I hate him. Just the mention of the word *diamond* makes my skin turn inside out. I remember that day ten years ago when I finally broke it off with him. He knew I was going to England to study. The lying asshole that he is, he told me he would follow me there, the thought of being separated from me was too much for him to handle. He could work for my dad over there. Fly back to New York when needed. That night I told him I was leaving the country earlier than expected to further my education in Pre-Med at Cambridge University in England was the night I saw the real Royal Diamond. Evil. The prodigy of the devil.

I've told one person of that horrible night when he beat me with a belt, leaving one long scar across my butt from the prong. My college roommate, Joelle. She stayed in her country of England after we both graduated from medical school. Joelle was a godsend. I believe her and I were meant to be friends for so many reasons. I owe her everything. Our weekly skype talks keep me from missing her more than I do. It's not the same as seeing her in the flesh though.

Royal drugged me after he beat me, tied me up, and then continued to get himself high on heroin. My heart beat faster than a rocker beating on his drums. I hated the feeling of not having any control over my body. I fought as hard and as long as I could not to succumb to the feeling of those drugs slamming through my veins. He laughed in my face. Punched holes in the wall. Destroyed anything he could get his hands on. I feared for my life.

Then he shoved a needle into my arm again. I tried to fight him, but he overpowered me in every way. I began to drift, my head full of fog. It wasn't until hours later when I woke up to a sore body and a constant dull pain in between my legs that I knew he had raped me, the open condom wrapper on the floor was even more proof. I cried for hours at the loss of my innocence, wondering why and how this could happen to me. How I could have been so naïve. How he brain washed my entire family into believing anything he said. When I felt myself starting to gag, vomit coming up my throat only to have to swallow it back down for fear I would choke, I remembered that I'm an expert at weaseling my way out of a knot. Growing up with six older brothers who thought it was fun to practice the skills they were taught on their younger sister makes you either fend for yourself or tattle on them. I chose the latter. Don't get me wrong, I did my fair share of being mean to them. I'm close with all of my brothers now that we are older. Especially my brother Anton, who is only eighteen months older than me. I'm twenty-eight, he's almost thirty. All of my brothers work for my dad in one way or another. All of them are killers. Drug pushers. Pimps. You name it; every single one of them has done it. And I hate it.

I left the next morning for England. A bruised, battered shell of a gutless woman. My family saw me off. I proclaimed being tired and nervous for my newfound adventure being the reason why I looked like hell. The marks left on my body from the night before were hidden under my clothes. Somehow, I had managed to clean myself up and bandage my bottom. That part of me hurrying to escape is vague. I just knew I had to leave. My lifeless hair was pulled back into a haphazard ponytail. No make-up. I cried and cried in my parents' arms. Both of them believing it was because I was leaving, me knowing it was for something I would never be able to tell them. I was afraid. Not out of guilt or shame, but scared a war would start amongst the families. Not just The Solokovs vs. the Diamonds, but all of them. Innocent lives would be slain. Children. I couldn't let that happen. It's been years since mafia families have fought against one another. I had no idea at the time that Royal had lied to me about why he really had no connection with his family at all. As a woman who was about to start her journey into training to be a doctor there was no way I would be able to live with myself. So I bared the burden of being raped. Went to bed every night and thanked my God for having been drugged so my heart wasn't a constant open wound, reliving those horrid memories over and over again. Even though I was pretty sure he used a condom, I still went to a clinic in England and had testing done for every disease out there. My entire flight I worried to the point of dry heaving, chewing my nails to nubs and thinking he may have given me something.

I take a big gulp of my wine, telling myself not to think about Royal anymore. For some reason, though, my mind drifts back to my family.

Growing up I thought we were a modern Russian-American family. I was taught two different languages. Went to public schools. All my brothers played football. I was on the soccer team. On the outside, we were as normal as any other American family. On the inside, we lived a very different life. Many men and women traveled the short path down the foyer to my dad's office. I thought nothing of it. I played with my dolls, kept to myself, unless I was being picked on or teased by one of my brothers, then I plotted as best as a young little girl's mind would let her to find a way to get them back.

It wasn't until I was old enough to understand that my life wasn't all full of those bright colors you see in a gumball machine. It was one solid color. The color Red. The boldest color on the wheel. Bright as blood. It can be angry, mysterious, and ever since the day I found out exactly who my family was, I've hated the color red. I'm a Doctor and I hate the color red. The only way I stomach seeing that color is knowing I may be saving the life of another.

My dad met my mother after his family moved here from Saint Petersburg, the second largest city in Russia. They never went back, choosing to re-enlist their use of organized crime in the States.

I haven't spoken to my parents in years. I want no part of that life. If any member of my family wants to see or talk to me, then they come to me. I will never step foot in their home again. My dad is the root of it all. How my mother with her pretty smile and her soft-spoken voice can stand by and ignore her surroundings is something I will never comprehend. I miss her like crazy, but she's either scared or stupid. Or both. There was only one time I brought it up to her. Asked her how she could do it. How she could sleep next to a man who, when he left in the morning and then came home at night, she knew could very well have had that vibrant color of red on his hands while he was gone. Her response was quick and to the point. "There are no correct words to describe love, Alina. You feel it here." She pointed to her chest. "You have every right to not want to be a part of what this family does. But as long as you live under this roof, you will respect me and the love your dad and I have for one another and never bring it up again."

That day distanced me from my mother too. I love her and I love my dad. I often tell myself I'm such a hypocrite for having a relationship with my brothers but not my parents. It's a catch-22 sort of thing. I've searched long and hard for answers and come up with only one. My dad started this and my mother helped him grow. He was the first bud on a tree; then came her and the rest of us. Now that tree is fully grown. And yet I miss them both terribly.

There are times like this when I feel so alone that I wish I could pick up the phone and call them. Ask them to forgive me, but I won't. I choose to live my life in the dark of my family's business. The less I know, the better. One thing I do know is my dad still has me being protected. I'm constantly watched, guarded by a man named Hugo, who reports to my dad daily, this I'm sure of. Yeah, I know. I've gotten to know my bodyguard quite well over the years. Especially these past few years since Royal Diamond has gone missing after his failed attempt to try and kill his brother Roan and his cousin Calla.

Calla and I have become very close in the past few months. She herself has been through a lot. Her family is mafia too. Her dad and her mother as well as her husband. Calla found out about her family a few years ago. She's now one of their attorneys. I admire her ability to be brave and accept them for who they are. It's so hard for me to think about the things they all do when I'm a doctor who would run and try to save one of those lives that my family can so easily snuff out.

Why do I judge my parents and not anyone else? I'm not sure, I just do. Maybe because if it weren't for them, I would feel normal. My life would be different, my heart wouldn't be so bitter and angry toward every male I come across. I wouldn't feel so alone and I would not be standing here right now staring up into the green eyes of Roan Diamond. A man I met a few months ago when out to lunch with Deidre and Calla. A man who looks a lot like his brother Royal. A man who tried to get me to go out with him, and a man who has no idea I know he has been following me. Another trait I picked up from Hugo. "Always watch your back, Alina, even when I'm around. And never let your guard down." Those were Hugo's exact words. "I've had my guard up for years," I told him. He just doesn't know why. Hugo thinks I'm bitter and angry because of who we are. Of course that's part of it, but most certainly not all of it. I've had my eyes wide open out of fear that one day Royal would find me, and a repeat of the things he did to me would happen. I am certain he would kill me.

Roan Immanuel Diamond is an impossibility. We would be like mixing Ammonia with Bleach. We would explode; if he didn't kill me first. He has the same blood pumping through his veins as his brother.

Lifting my glass of wine in acknowledgement, I deprive my eyes from how ruggedly handsome he really is, reminding myself he is just like every other man.

Rumor has it he is the opposite of his brother. Everyone says he's a protector of the ones he loves. I have a high regard for him and his loyalty to his family. Rumors are just that though, they're rumors. Most of them are lies. Unless I see things with my own eyes or hear them with my own ears, I believe nothing. God, I sound like a bitch. All that aside, tonight for some reason, he has piqued my curiosity. We've spoken few words to each other. Right now though, the way he's looking at me, it's as if he's reaching into my chest, tugging on my heartstrings, and pulling me towards him. What is it about him that has me wanting to gravitate to him right now?

He's the enemy, Alina, even though he may appear to be kind. He has an agenda. I know he does. He wants revenge on his brother. The question is, what does he want with me? Am I part of the plan to lure Royal out or does Roan simply want in my panties like every other dick-fuck in this town? The way he watches me though, it's as if he's put me on some sort of a pedestal. And he doesn't even know me. I've stared at him just like he has stared at me. I may not need a man, but I'm not blind when it comes to checking out a good-looking male. Roan has got to be the best looking man I have ever seen. He stands at least a foot taller than me. His legs are long and lean. His arms and shoulders are thick and muscular. His entire body speaks power. The man is definitely built like a boxer. His dark hair is cropped short. And the scruff he wears on his face would be a turn on for me if I didn't hate men like I do. God, he's as handsome as any one person can be.

I've had enough wine to make me daring enough to go talk to him, to let him know I know he stalks me like some crazy serial killer waiting for the right time to pounce and attack. This is the first time I've acknowledged him since the day I met him. He needs to know I'm not interested. That I want nothing to do with him.

I sit my glass on a nearby table and slowly make my way through the crowd. I can feel his eyes on me the entire time. They never once leave my face. There's something in the way he looks at me. Roan, such a beautiful name for a man. Bracing my hands on the banister, I begin to climb the stairs that lead to the upper level. My legs start to wobble when I get close to him, my chest growing tighter, my brain struggling for the right thing to say. Better yet, the right words to get him to stop following me.

I stop just a few feet short of where he's standing, and still his gaze never wavers. He isn't looking at me like a piece of meat he wants to pound until it's tender and abused. No, he's picking my brain. Or trying to at least. *Have at it, buddy. Pick away.*

"We meet again." His deep voice commands attention while at the same time speaks with authority.

"We do." I try to make a conscious effort to pitch mine back just as strong. I don't think it worked when his brow quirks up as he shifts his body to where his back is now leaning against the half wall. Damn, my deceiving little body goes up in flames. I tingle everywhere. My nipples harden underneath my little pasties. Sweat forms in between my breasts. What in the ever loving hell is wrong with me? *Ignore your body, Alina. Say what needs to be said and leave.*

"Although," I say, taking the few steps to stand directly in front of him. *Crap, wrong move*. I should back away because, holy hell, he smells so good. Not from cologne. Not from alcohol. He smells like a man. A real man.

"You've been following me for quite some time now, never showing your face. So why tonight are you finally allowing me to see you?" My entire body is shaking. I want to know why. I want this conversation over. I don't like the feelings I'm getting inside of me by staring into his penetrating eyes. I could get lost in them and never find my way out.

I wonder if his eyes naturally sparkle or if it's the different shades of light coming from the dance floor downstairs. He's intriguing, this individual standing before me. And I'm so mad at myself right now for drifting away from the real reason I've approached him. *Get back on track, Alina.*

"When in doubt, just ask." My smartass remark seems to amuse him when he reaches up and runs a hand across the scruff on his chin.

"I find you fascinating, Alina Solokov. I'm a man. You turned me down for a date. That has never sat well with me." Reaching down for his drink on the table, those long fingers circle around the glass. I watch him and he watches me as he finishes it off, his Adams apple bobbing just so. *Why am I not frightened of him right now? Why do I feel safe standing here talking to the enemy?*

"Still doesn't answer my question, Roan Diamond. Why are you following me? I already have one man following me around. I sure as hell do not need two."

"Ah. Hugo. Yes. What an interesting man. Did you know he used to be an NFL football player?" He speaks as if he knows Hugo. Of course he knows him. Hugo wouldn't be doing his job if he didn't. Which leads me to marvel as to why Hugo has never mentioned him to me.

"Listen, Roan. Cut the shit. You and I know nothing about each other. So here's your first lesson about the type of woman I am. I hate being lied to. I hate secrets and I'm not particularly fond of you or anyone else in your family, except Calla. The lives you lead, I want no part of. I'm going to ask you one last time. Why are you following me?" This time I step into his personal space. A few inches separate the two of us. I can smell him again. The warm sensual flow of amber and musk mixed with his scent of all man, light enough to send a divine chill all the way up my body.

"Go out with me and I promise to tell you why?" he smugly asks.

"I told you no before and I meant it," I say trying to catch my breath.

He tilts his head. I swear I can see his pulse quicken in the veins of his neck. He knows he's breaking me down. There's amusement in his expression. Whatever it is about him that has me drawn to him right now, it's a damn magnetic force and I cannot seem to pull away. Every thought I had of telling him no, to stay as far away from him as I can, went tumbling down the stairs I just climbed.

"One date. That's all." There is no sexual innuendo behind his words. He seems to really want to talk to me. Either that or he's just as good of an actor as his brother was. Either way, I will give in to this one date.

"Fine. One date. I promise you though, if you try anything on me, if you're playing some kind of game with me, you'll be sorry," I say, throwing him a stern look.

"No games, Alina. I will pick you up tomorrow morning at ten. And wear something comfortable." He leans into me and grazes his lips across my cheek, sending an unaccustomed breath of anticipation rocketing its way throughout my shield.

Not even ten minutes ago I told myself he was a dangerous man. What the hell did I just agree to? I just said yes when I wanted to say no. When I should have said no. Shit. I have a date with the brother of the devil.

Chapter Two

Roan

Tonight couldn't have worked out any better. I wanted Alina to see me. To know I was watching her. She threw me for an unexpected loop when she said she's known all along I've been following her. Though it really doesn't surprise me the more I think about it. Growing up the way she did, she was trained to always watch her back. That was one of the first things my dad taught me. Always have your eyes trained in every direction, keep your guard up, and watch people around you. Trust very few.

The protective part of me is downright happy as hell she watches her back, since no one knows where Royal is or when he will surface again.

She's been back for several months now, and not a word from him. I know she left in a hurry to study in England. What I don't know is why. Why did she leave him? Did he do something to her? I have dug around into every hole I can think of, talked to so many people, but keep getting the same answer: it was because she found out he was being trained to be a killer.

They all say he was lost when she left. Became even angrier and bitterer than he already was. How that could be possible blows my fucking mind. He was already teetering on the edge of insanity. Whatever happened between the two of them pushed him over the ledge.

I leave the bar a few minutes after she leaves with Deidre. I've known Deidre a long time. Her father is one of our family attorneys. A good man. Loyal. He's the one who helped me convince Calla to befriend Alina in the first place. It did not do me any good at the time. What it did do is give my cousin a friend.

I'm grateful they have a friendship. Even though Calla works her ass off and she spends most of her spare time with Cain, her husband, or her parents, she has found the time to have lunch a few times with Alina.

Locking the door to my penthouse behind me, I toss my keys in the dish on the small table in the foyer before I, make my way into the kitchen. I down a bottle of water and turn off all the lights, then retreat down the hall to my bedroom, strip myself down to my boxers, and climb into my bed. The New York skyline is vibrant through my floor-to-ceiling windows. Propping up against the headboard, I look in the far out distance in the direction of Alina's apartment.

I cannot seem to get her or the fact she agreed to go out with me out of my head. I know she agreed to one date. One I plan to make damn good, leaving her no choice but to want to know me better. This woman fascinates me. For several reasons, I like her without knowing her personally. She strikes me as a caring woman. One who respects herself as well as others. She never goes home with a man. Hell, she has never even been linked to anyone but my brother. I need to find the missing pieces here. Bond them all together and figure out exactly why a woman as open yet mysterious, independent, driven, and outright beautiful as her is all alone. Which she won't be any more if I can help it.

She seemed different tonight, troubled. Something was brewing through her mind after she stopped dancing and stood off to the back of the club. She was disturbed. I know that nothing happened in the club to make her upset. My eyes never left her face.

I close my eyes with images of her face. She has it all: the looks, the body, the mind. Lying down in my bed, I drift to sleep thinking about all three of those things. Knowing damn well when you mix them all together the result could lead me into a disastrous situation. I look forward to the challenge.

I'm anxious when I wake, it's only been a few months since this woman has caught me in her web or beauty and grace, at the same time it feels like forever.

I shoot a quick text to Cain to let him know I won't be working out this morning, hop out of bed and make my way to the shower. In a little over a half hour, I'm on my bike, weaving through the New York traffic. To see beauty, to breathe in Alina Solokov and her very existence.

A thin layer of sweat drapes down my back when I stop and park my bike along the curb of Alina's apartment on 61st Street, close to Central Park. The closer I get to her place, the more nervous I become. Sure, I've taken women on dates before. Usually the first date is about getting to know one another, to see if you hit it off, to feel if there's any type of chemistry between the two of you. That shit never mattered to me before. Now it scares the fuck out of me. I know there's chemistry between us. I felt its power last night the closer she got to me. And it wasn't just my dick that felt it. It was my entire body. I fought within myself not to haul her closer to me. To breathe in her scent. To drag my tongue across her satin skin.

Her view has to be immaculate from here. The park is one of New York's most beautiful places. It's a little bit of a drive for me.

Hell, just getting around this town is a drive. Though I'm used to the traffic after living back here for a few years now, doesn't mean I like it.

Pulling my helmet off my head, I swing my leg over my bike, inhaling the crisp early spring air, trying to shake off my nerves. Why the hell I'm nervous I have no idea.

It's warm for early April, I tell myself. Yeah right, asshole. It wouldn't be because you're about to take the woman you've been gunning for on an actual date. I run my hand through my hair and begin to climb the stairs to the building. And there she is, standing in all of her glorious perfection in a pair of jeans, a pink hooded sweatshirt, and matching pink converse. Her hair is pulled back into a ponytail. I fucking love it. She looks stunning. She's still the same woman from last night, except today her blue eyes are brighter. She looks carefree. Christ almighty, she's remarkable.

"Is this casual enough?" she rasps out. Oh, baby, you have no idea how fucking sexy I find you right now.

"It's perfect. Have you ever ridden on the back of a bike?" I ask, hitching my thumb over my back towards my Harley.

"I haven't," she replies, as she is walking down the steps to greet me. Damn. She looks so fresh and natural. She has a minimal amount of makeup on. So much different than last night when she was all dressed up. Seeing her up close like this with the morning sun shining down, making her hair beam like little golden rays of light, her eyes shining, I can honestly say I love the natural-looking Alina so much better than the made-up one. She's one of those women who stands out in a crowd no matter what she is wearing.

"Here, lets get you one of these." I lift my helmet, both of us taking the few steps back to my bike. Strapping my helmet to the handle bar, I reach into a side bag and pull out the extra one, then turn to hand it to her. With no problem at all, she slips it over her head and fastens it.

"Impressive," I say when I inspect it to make sure it's hooked right, my fingers lightly brushing her chin. God, I've never felt anything so smooth, like the feeling of a velvety leaf.

"My brothers all have bikes," she says enthusiastically.

"I tried to ride with Andre once when I was sixteen. We were all set to go when my mother came running out of the house screaming. "Alina, there is no way in hell you are getting on the back of his bike." To make a long story short, my brothers were very reckless. I'm pretty sure every one of them crashed at one time or another. Being the only girl in the family, I was treated just like that, a girl, so doing something fun like this is an adventure." She smiles shyly.

"I'm glad I brought it then." I grab my own helmet, adjusting it on my head. I then swing my leg over my bike, pat the back, and guide her with my hand in hers to get on.

"Put your arms around me and hold on tight. We don't have far to go." Hell, she looks good on the back of my bike.

"Where are we going anyway? And please don't tell me it's a surprise." I contemplate on whether I tell her the truth or not. Nah. She can sweat it out.

"It's not a surprise, you'll just have to wait and see." Turning away from her, I crank up the engine. A Harley Davidson has a sound like no other. There is nothing like the low rumble of revving the engine to open and close the throttle. And then I feel her hands come around my waist. The delicate softness of her body pressed up against mine has my dick going into a spasm. Shit. Her tight little body behind me feels a hell of a lot better than riding my damn bike.

I take a deep breath, feeling like a pansy ass, make sure no traffic is coming, and pull out onto her street. The ten-minute drive to Sweet Round Donuts doesn't give me enough time to calm down. For one, I've never had anyone on the back of my bike. For two, I can smell her. I've never smelled anything like her unique smell of grapefruit and wild flowers mixed together in my life. It's driving me insane.

I pull up behind the donut shop, cut the engine, and she bursts out laughing. The sound of her laugh does a lot for my raging dick, the fucker gets even harder.

Looking at her through my mirror and seeing her open mouth sniggering has me smiling.

"What's so funny?" I ask as I take her hand and help her off the bike.

"A donut shop?" she questions.

"This isn't just your ordinary donut shop, smart mouth." I take off my helmet, then reach to help her take hers off.

"No, it's not. They only have the best cherry glazed donuts I have ever had." Her tone is growing serious now.

"You're kidding me? Those are my favorite" I say in astonishment. I thought I knew a lot about her. I had no idea she loved the same kind of donut as I do. We both stand there staring at each other for a few beats, our expressions stunned before she turns her head toward the door of the shop, the flush in her cheeks matching the light pink shade of her glossy coated lips.

"Come on." I take her helmet along with mine and guide us to the door.

The place isn't as packed as you would think it would be on a Saturday morning. Jeffrey, the owner, looks up at me after waiting on a customer. I hold up two fingers, indicating two of my usual, then directing us toward an open booth in the back. I wait for her to take a seat first before I slide in on the opposite side of the booth.

"I love this place." She grabs a napkin and starts fiddling with it as if she's all of a sudden nervous. "My dad used to bring these donuts home a lot when I was growing up," She's keeping her eyes focused on the napkin.

"There's something we have in common then. My dad used to bring them home to us too," I say casually. She looks up to me then, her mouth quirking a slight grin.

I place my hands over hers to stop her fidgeting.

"Alina. Relax," I say.

"Sorry. It's just..." She stops and looks back down. I know she doesn't go on dates. Even if I hadn't done my research on her, I would be able to tell just by the scared look on her face.

"I just want to get to know you is all. Today will be fun. I promise." Before I get the chance to tell her where we are going, Jeffrey shows up with two cups of coffee and two cherry glazed donuts.

"How have you been, Alina? I haven't seen you around here in a few weeks." His attention is solely focused on her. I take a sip of my coffee and wait for her response. The two of them start a casual conversation. I'm enthralled with listening to her talk about the children at the hospital. Her entire face lights up when she speaks. Even Jeffrey seems to be enchanted under her spell.

"Well, maybe Diamond will bring you around a little more often." He then turns to me. "Maybe," I say with a mouthful of donut. I shouldn't feel jealous that the two of them know each other, but damn it, I do. "You two have a good day." "You too, Jeffrey," both of us say in unison.

"Where are we going after this?" She takes a bite of her donut and the sweet hum coming from her mouth has me staring.

Clearing my throat and my perverted mind, I finish off the last bite of my donut.

"The zoo."

"Really?" She laughs again, her shoulders bouncing.

"You don't like the zoo?" I ask, sounding shocked.

"In all the years I've lived here, I've never once been to the zoo."

"Never?" I question.

"I'm not sure how you perceive me, Roan, but I've led a very sheltered life growing up. Overprotected by my entire family. I wasn't deprived of love from my parents, don't get me wrong, it's just..." Her eyes lift to mine. "With all the enemies my dad has, he rarely let me out of his sight. I had to beg him to let me play soccer. One of my brothers had to be at every single practice. Every single game. I couldn't go anywhere without one of them."

"Did you have a bodyguard in England?" She doesn't seem pissed when I mention I know about her schooling. "Of course I did. It wasn't Hugo. I... he... Well, let's just say he doesn't work for my family anymore." Her eyes divert to a spot on the other side of the shop. I'm not pushing the issue any further. I know her old bodyguard Troy was killed shortly after she came home. I also know everyone suspects my brother did it. Which is why she is so heavily guarded. If he did kill Troy, then that means Royal is or has been in New York. Knowing him like I do, he's targeted her. Hell, he may even know I've been following her. Which is a good thing for me. I want him to know. I want him to come after me. This time I will be ready for him. I have one sub-sonic bullet in my 9 mm pistol. That's all it's going to take for me to snuff the life out of him, then make him disappear like he never existed. Done wasting time on him for today, I look up into her sad blue eyes, knowing full well she had to have been close to Troy. For almost ten years, he protected her with his own life, only to have it be taken from him the minute he stepped foot back into the United States.

I cannot relive her childhood for her, but I sure as hell can give her the time of her life today.

I pull a fifty-dollar bill out of my pocket, tossing it on the table. It's over double what I owe. I'm not one to flaunt my money, but when I love a place as much as I do this donut shop, I do everything I can to help it thrive.

We arrive at the zoo a little before eleven. After paying, I place my hand at the small of her back and lead us to the sea lions by way of the map she has.

"We can feed them," she squeals.

This is how our entire day goes: stopping and feeding the animals. Petting them. Talking casually. I'm waiting for her to ask why I've been following her. She never mentions it once. Both of us enjoy the animals, letting them eat out of the palms of our hands. She talks to them as if they understand her. They look at her as if they do. She laughs when the rough tongue of a giraffe licks the food out of her hand. She's even more stunning when she smiles and laughs. I need to make her do both of them as much as possible. Given the chance, I will be able to take her out again.

Even Hugo has a grin on his face when we acknowledge him a few times throughout the day.

There is so much more to this woman than she lets on. She's like one of those stubborn jars you try to open. Once you pry the lid off it, you can't seem to get enough.

We answer each other's questions about our schooling with enthusiasm, steering away from every topic about our childhood and our teenage years, of growing up the way we both did.

When I stop in front of her apartment, it's then that she shocks the living hell out of me by leaning up and placing a kiss on my cheek.

"Thank you for today. It's been a long time since I've had fun like that. It was refreshing."

"Does this mean you'll go out with me again?" I'm staring at her like an idiot, watching her chew on her bottom lip. Trying not to let my thoughts go straight to the damn gutter.

"Under one condition." She offers me a curious smile.

"What's that?" I ask, trying to fight back my own smile.

"You never told me why you've been following me around, Roan. I'd like you to tell me now."

And here I thought she would never ask me. No such luck.

"Not out here. Have dinner with me tomorrow night and I'll tell you everything."

Chapter Three

Alina

In less than twenty-four hours I have gone from hating men to not being able to tear my thoughts away from Roan. I don't want to be known as one of those indecisive, wavering people who cannot make up their mind. I should have never approached him last night. Now I feel as if I'm stuck between what I want and what I don't want. One thing I know for sure, I enjoyed every bit of my time with him today. It's been way too long since I've let go of the demons of my past, to feel free. To just have fun.

What is it that enables us to be able to see so much in another person's eyes? One look last night and he had me caving when kindness and compassion stared back at me. And then again today. If I were truly honest with myself, I'd have to admit that he's nothing like the man I made him out to be.

I open the door to my apartment expecting Deidre to be sitting on the couch from wherever she ended up going last night. After talking to Roan at the bar, I went and found her to tell her I was leaving. Both her and the guy she hooked up with stood outside with me as we all waited for a cab. They took one and I took another. I should just catch a ride with Hugo since he follows me everywhere I go. How boring his job must be for him. I work then come home during the week. I may go out a few times a month, but otherwise I'm basically a boring homebody. And Hugo goes wherever I go. I know he's only doing the job he was hired for. Today must have been a shocker when I told him I was going to the zoo. He's a hard man to read., He can be playful at times; other times he is stoic and stone cold. He seemed to be enjoying himself today at the zoo. The few times I caught his eye, his smile turned up. I'm glad I made at least one day of many fun for the guy.

"Deidre," I call out after closing and locking the door. I make my way into the kitchen, where she's making a mess.

"Where have you been?" she scolds me like a child. Her dark brown hair is piled on top of her head while she mixes away on what I know to be her chocolate brownies.

We have an inside joke about me never dating. Deidre has all kinds of names she calls me. Jolly Jester, Hummer. My favorite is Bank Vault. She's constantly saying they need the right combination to be able to get into my pussy.

"Well?" she says, stops mixing, and gives me a dirty look. I choke back my laugh.

"I had a date." She gawks at me, then her mouth hangs open. She tries to talk and swallow at the same time, but she ends up choking and sputtering all over the place at my shocking words.

"Are you kidding me?" She finally manages to get out.

"Nope." I'm smiling.

"Did you put out? I mean, because girlfriend, we all know your pussy is like frozen peanut butter and your damn legs are hard to spread?" Her eyes bug out of her head.

"Jesus, you are so nasty. And no, I did not put out. We went to the zoo. It was nice." I reach up, grab a glass, and fill it up with water. Just as I start to take a drink, she screeches.

"Oh, my fucking lord." She sets down the mixer, walks straight to me, and presses her hand to my forehead.

"Quit it." I swat her hand away.

"Well, you don't have a fever, which tells me you're not sick. And the zoo, that's so cute. I haven't been to the zoo in ages." Propping her ass on the barstool next to me, she puts her elbows on the counter with her hands under her chin. I laugh at her.

"Well, tell me all about it. Who is he? What does he look like? What does he do for a living?" The last question instantly puts me in a surly mood. That's the reason I should stay far away from him. Call him and tell him I changed my mind.

"Alina." Deidre snaps her fingers in front of my face.

"You know him. In fact you know him very well." Finishing my water, I place the glass in the sink and twist at my waist to look at her.

"Who?" Her brows furrow.

"Roan Diamond." She nearly falls off her chair. She was with Calla and I when he showed up at the restaurant for lunch. The day I turned him down. She also knows all about him watching me. Her dad works for his family. They all grew up together until Roan moved to Michigan and Royal turned on his entire family.

Deidre leans forward, her expression telling me she's waiting impatiently for more.

"I thought you didn't want anything to do with him?" Her tone is laced with confusion.

"I don't. I didn't. Hell, I don't know." My eyes flick to hers. She has a damn smile on her face that reaches all the way to her eyes.

"You like him?" She winks at me. I walk to go around her. My head is starting to spin. This conversation needs to end, like now.

Deidre has never judged me, nor has she tried to coax out of me the reason behind never dating. She knows as much as everyone else does about Royal. She also tells me the same thing my brothers do. Get out there. Meet someone. Just make sure we approve of him.

Everyone thinks I'm married to my job. That I don't have time to date. This has been my excuse the whole time I was in school. One year bleeds into the next and before you know it, ten damn years have passed.

"Hey." She grabs me gently by my arm.

"Don't shut me out. I was teasing and I'm sorry," she apologizes.

"You have nothing to be sorry about. It's me." I dump myself down on a bar stool.

"He's not what I expected at all. Yes, he's an underboss to his dad. But god, Deidre, he's so nice. I mean, the zoo! Who takes a woman to the zoo? Oh, and get this." I say excitedly. She leans in, all ears and big eyes like I'm about to tell her some big dark secret.

"He took me to The Donut Shop."

"Get out! I suppose his favorite donut is cherry glazed." We both say cherry glazed at the same time.

"Oh, my god. That's... oh, I don't know, like karma or some shit," she says, flinging out her hand.

"Are you going out with him again?" I sit and watch her pick up the bowl of brownie mix, whip it some more, then pour the batter in the pan, while I sit here contemplating on whether I'm going to go out with him or not.

"Alina. You just said he was nice. And whenever we talk about you know who, the one thing you never call him is nice. Besides, I couldn't agree with you more. I've always though Roan was a nice guy. Did he tell you why he's been following you?" She sticks the spoon in her mouth. I reach across the counter and snatch the empty bowl, swirling my finger inside to get the chocolate, then shoving my finger in my mouth.

"Tomorrow night. He's taking me to dinner." My words sound garbled through the delicious taste of chocolate. Without even thinking, I have made up my mind. It looks like I'm going on date number two with Roan Diamond.

We no sooner have the kitchen cleaned up when the buzzer goes off from downstairs.

"Yes?" I say into the intercom.

"Hello, Miss Alina." Keith's, the concierge's, voice echoes throughout the room.

"Hi Keith. What's up?"

"You have a package down here. May I bring it up?" I hesitate for a second, wondering what in the hell it could be.

"Sure. Come on up." I stand in the hall, waiting for the several minutes it takes to get to the thirty-fifth floor where we live. When the doorbell rings, I open the door to Keith. He stands 6'8, with a neck just as large. Well, not really, but he's big.

"Thanks, Keith." I take the pink box from him. "You're welcome. Enjoy your evening, Miss Alina." He tilts his hat. "You as well." Shutting the door, I know what's inside the box before I even open it. I can smell them. And the box is warm. A small note is taped to the top of the box, and when I open it, inhaling the sweet smell of cherry glazed donuts, I beam with excitement.

Carefully, I peel it off the box, my heart soaring when I read what it says.

"These will never be as sweet as the one reading this."

No one has ever done or said anything like this to me before. One date and somehow this man has me wanting to know everything there is to know about him.

"Who was it?" Deidre comes around the corner. The look on her face is priceless when she sees the box in my hands.

"I hope you remember the combination to your vault, because by the looks of it, you're going to need to open it so Mr. Sex On Legs can make a deposit." She seriously did not just say that.

"You know," I say as I walk past her with the sweet aroma swirling through the air. I hope it sails straight up her nose, leaving the witch begging for one of these donuts. "My donuts and I are going to bed." I don't even have to turn around and look at her face. I know all to well, her mouth is gaping wide open.

Sleep has always come easy for me. Not tonight. Tonight, visions of a dark-haired, tall, muscular man invade my thoughts. I'm giddy, ecstatic, and very nervous about tomorrow night. More so than I was about going out with him this morning.

Flipping over onto my stomach, I moan into my pillow loudly. It takes a long time before I finally fall asleep, and when I do, I dream of lips. Lips I crave to taste.

I fidget all morning long. My nerves climbing. My insides twisting. The clock moving slower every time I look at it.

Finally, the time arrives for me to get ready and I swear a dozen butterflies have emerged out of their cocoons in my stomach, learning how to fly, making my stomach flutter.

"Get your damn hands out of my masterpiece." My dear friend comes up behind me inspecting my hair. I look like I'm going out clubbing on a Sunday night with my smoky eyes, tight black dress, and my favorite pair of Brian Atwood Leopard print pumps.

A few hours ago, Roan sent me a text telling me to dress up. It surprised me when I noticed the number said unknown. Then again, he has been following me around. Therefore, it didn't surprise me in the least when I opened it and saw it was from him.

I don't do well with surprises, so when I texted him back to ask where we were going and his reply was *'It's a surprise.'* I wanted to throw my phone across the room.

Now, here I stand in front of my mirror, scared to death about going out with him. *Get a grip Alina. If anything, enjoy yourself.*

The buzzer sounds and Deidre runs in a full-fledged sprint down the hallway while I stand there like a statue knowing it's Keith alerting us that Roan is here. I do the-inhale-and-exhale thing, then grab my clutch walking out of my room with nervousness and excitement still coursing throughout my body.

"Hey, Roan," Deidre answers the door. "Deidre. Looking good as always." He places a kiss on her cheek. "You too, Mr. Banker." He gives her a curious look while my glare just killed her right where she's standing.

"Holy shit. You look...God, I can't even come up with a word to describe how you look, Alina," he says when he notices me standing there. This time, his eyes do travel up and down my body. For the first time in my life, I actually welcome it.

"Thank you," I say.

"She doesn't have a curfew, so any time tomorrow would be great to bring her home," Deidre calls out as he takes my hand and I follow him out the door.

"Good to know. Thanks." Roan chuckles while I'm sure my face is ten shades of that shit color red.

"Are you going to tell me where we're going?" I ask as we wait for the elevator.

"No. However, I'm quite sure you've never been there before," he says quite smoothly.

"Just so you know. I really hate surprises," I say teasingly when he helps me into the front seat of his Dodge Viper. My hands fiddle with the seatbelt while my eyes stay glued to him walking around the front. He's in a black suit and a white crisp shirt with no tie. The top few buttons are undone. All of a sudden, my body turns from chilly to warm just by looking at him. Christ, I'm going to be in big trouble. I consider briefly what my brother Anton told me earlier when he called to ask me how my little date went yesterday. It's the first time in years I actually lost my temper with him. Of course, my entire family would know I went out on a date. I didn't question him as to how he found out. I already know Hugo called my dad, who then called Anton to warn me away from Roan. Try explaining to your brother that you're a grown woman and it's none of his or anyone's damn business what you do. The conversation ended with him just telling me to be careful. And with me basically telling him to fuck off.

We have a light conversation about my job during our drive toward Manhattan; the hours I work and how much I enjoy working with the kids. I so want to ask him about some of the things he does. But the part of me that hates the mafia wins out. Therefore, we keep the topic on me.

"Are we having dinner with Calla and Cain?" I ask when we pull into the parking garage of where they live.

"No. I live here too. I want privacy for what we have to talk about, but if you feel uncomfortable here, we can go somewhere else." He pulls into a parking spot and cuts off the engine.

"I didn't know you live here and it's fine, really." I hope my voice didn't give away the fact that I'm scared out of my mind to be alone with him. It's not that I don't trust him. Well, I don't really. I hardly know the man. But something tells me I can trust him, that if he wanted to hurt me, he would have done it by now.

He helps me out of the car and holds my hand all the way to the elevator. Once we enter and the doors close, I feel my throat start to seize up and my mind taking over with all kinds of crazy scenarios about being in his penthouse alone with him. I mentally slap myself when the elevator pings and we exit on the fortieth floor.

"I just want to talk. I promise," he says after he shuts the door to his place. The view is similar to Calla's, where the entire New York skyline is lit up. The only difference between the two is you can tell this is a bachelor's home with all the black leather furniture, several bare walls, and very little decorations at all.

He guides me into the kitchen and pulls out a bottle of wine and a beer from his fridge.

"Wine or beer?" he asks, holding up both bottles.

"It depends on what we're having for dinner," I answer.

"Well, then it's definitely beer. Because tonight we're having pizza." His face lights up.

"I must say, first donuts, then the zoo, and now pizza. You really know how to impress a girl."

"I do try," he quotes slyly.

"I'm a little overdressed for a night in, having pizza. Don't you think?" I gesture with my hands down my body. He watches my hands. I watch him. His gaze instantly sets me on fire.

"No. I had you dress up for yourself." Is this guy for real? I mean, who is he? I'm still floored at the sly way he compliments me. The way he truly means what it says. The way even something like hearing him say he had me dress up for myself makes my heart want to do jumping jacks.

"You're quite the charmer, aren't you?" I take the beer from his hand.

"I speak the truth, Alina. Always the truth. I won't ever lie to you about anything." We watch each other as we both take a sip of our beer. My heart screams again, reminding me he is nothing like his brother.

"What do you like on your pizza?" Roan pulls out a takeout menu.

"Pepperoni, mushroom, green olives, and pineapple." He asked, so I may as well be honest.

"I've never had pineapple on my pizza. I'm always up for trying things once." There's no sexual innuendo behind his meaning of trying anything once. He just simply states it. *Then tell yourself,*

Alina, why all of a sudden are you staring at his ass, wondering how it would feel in your hands? I'm the one thinking sexually here, and it's downright frustrating as hell!

Taking out his phone, he places the call for the pizza. I receive one hell of a view of his sculpted ass when he reaches into his back pocket, pulls out his wallet, then rattles off his credit card number to pay. Then he calls who I assume is the doorman and tells them to just bring it up when it arrives. I do believe my head tilts to the side to get a better look when he places the wallet back. I quickly set my gaze back to my beer. He shocks me when he switches his phone off, grabs my hand, and I follow him into the living room, where we both sit down on the couch with our legs touching, sending again a delicious spark up my entire body. All kinds of thoughts are running through my head being this close to him. I've never felt anything like this before. Wetness pools between my legs, yearning the feeling of being filled by him so badly my damn pussy starts to hurt. These foreign feelings have me moving away from him, putting enough space in between us to where I feel I can breathe again without sounding like I want to start humping his leg like a dog in heat. The deep grumble of his words has me jerking my head up. He's staring right at me. *Oh fuck! Please don't let my face give myself away. I'm probably red as the fury fires of hell. I don't even know him and he has me thinking thoughts that have never entered my mind before.*

"You wanted me to tell you why I've been following you? Why I know so much about you?" Either it's my imagination or he's looking at me like he knows exactly what I was thinking. The corners of his mouth turn up. I clear my throat. *What the hell is wrong with me?*

"That's a good place to start." The tension in my own little atmosphere pulls tight like a cord wrapped around my throat, my voice sounding raspy.

He runs his hands across the scruff on his chin again. I'm finding this gesture to be a habit for him. I'm staring now at his scruff, wondering if it's soft or bristly to the touch. The look is definitely him. If he were mine, I would tell him to never shave it off. *Shut the heck up! Mine? I should have studied the human mind. Particularly my own. Good lord. I don't even know who I am right now.*

"I was planning on using you, Alina, in hopes it would help us draw out my brother, but when I first laid eyes on you, I knew you were unique, something special. I told myself I wasn't going to like you. You had a past with my brother." I shift slightly in my spot. Roan looks in my direction, his eyes so sincere.

"When you turned me down, I was fucking pissed off. I came home and started digging into your past to the point it became an obsession to me. I had to know everything about you. To see if there was some way I could blackmail you into dating me or at least try and help me out." He pauses. I'm rooted to the spot. His confession has me tongue-tied. There is so much I want to say, yet I can't seem to get any words out.

Exhaling deeply, he continues. "When I discovered who you really were, the way you moved away on your own, not wanting anything to do with the lifestyle of your family, studying to be a doctor, I just couldn't do it. You're way too good of a person for me to ask you to put your life in danger, but I couldn't seem to get myself to stay away from you. I'm drawn to you in a way I can't even explain to myself. We hardly know each other. Well, that's not entirely true. I know a lot about you, and you know nothing about me." He pauses.

My mouth is somewhere crawling along his dark, shiny hardwood floors. This man is honest. He may be the first man I've ever met, including my dad and my brothers, who has ever been truthful with me.

"When you came up to me the other night, I had no intentions whatsoever of asking you out. When you first looked at me, the fear I saw in your eyes, and then the way you demanded for me to tell you why I was following you, I couldn't live with myself thinking you were afraid of me or for you to think I'm anything like my brother. I'm nothing like him." We stare intensely at each other. He has so many points. I have so many questions. Standing up, I move toward the window, gazing at the skyline.

"I was never afraid of you, Roan. I'm a very private woman. I hate the things my family and you do. I will never understand it." Altering my stance so I'm facing him, I carry on.

"I had a feeling all along it had something to do with your brother. That's why I never approached you. I was hoping you would just give up. To just go away. To leave me alone." I'm being honest too.

"And now?" he says, standing up, a concerned look on his face.

"And now I believe you're nothing like him."

"I'm not." He's so precise. So determined. He doesn't have to prove anything to me. I couldn't tell you when I finally came to the conclusion that this man in front of me is unique, genuine. And while the door of honesty is flung wide open, I may as well plow right through it and tell him everything, like I believe he is telling me.

"It still doesn't change the fact that you do things I don't believe in," I say matter of factly.

"I know, Alina. But I won't change what I do. Not for anyone."

"I would never expect you to change, Roan. Listen, "I say, taking a few steps closer to him. My nerves spilt right down the middle. "Yesterday was one of the best days I've had in a long time. The only time I smile like that is when I'm at the hospital. When I see the smiles on my patients' faces. When I tell a parent their child only has the flu when they're scared to death something is terribly wrong. You did that for me. And tonight, you also made me realize something else." He worries his brows into a thick line.

"I've been judging my parents for years. Not only them but so many others, and I have no right to do any of that. If I'm going to stand here in your home and listen to you be completely honest with me, then it's time I'm honest with myself." Through new-found eyes I watch him as he takes what I said in, a quirky smile on his roughish face.

"So, what does all that mean, Alina?" He takes a step towards me.

I clear my throat. "It means I'm going to go talk to my parents," I say nervously. Another step towards me. "It also means I'm willing to get to know you." Another step. I hold out my hand. He stops quickly.

"I have one condition, though," I say, looking him dead square in the eyes.

"Of course. Anything."

"Let me help you find your brother."

Chapter Four

Roan

"Excuse me? What did you just say?" That's the last thing I expected her to say. She's out of her mind if she thinks I'm going to let her help me find him.

"I want to help you. I know better than anyone how dangerous he is." The mere fact that she is offering shows me how strong a woman she is. However, no way will I put her in harm's way. Whatever happened between the two of them all those years ago may not be the reason she went to school in England, but I'd bet both of my balls it's why she never came back until she graduated.

Does she have any idea at all the man he has become? The horrendous things he has done? How many lives he has taken?

"What are you suggesting exactly?" We shouldn't even be having this discussion. It's not ever going to happen. Now that she's agreed to get to know me, I will back off from following her around. It doesn't mean I won't have someone else keeping their eye on her. Besides Cain, there's only one other person I would trust with her life. I'll be giving him a call first thing in the morning. I know damn well he'll drop everything and high tail his ass here the minute I ask him.

My doorbell rings. It takes me less than two minutes to greet Andy, one of our security guards who brought up the pizza. Needing something a little stronger than a damn beer, I head back into the kitchen to find Alina sitting at the counter, picking the label off of her beer.

"You're not going to let me help you, are you?" I don't miss the slight quaver in her voice.

"No," is all I say. Reaching into my freezer, I pull out my bottle of Dalmore. Cain is always ragging on my ass about putting one of the world's most expensive Whiskeys in my freezer. I love the way the cinnamon citrusy taste feels going down my throat when it's nice and cold. He has no room to talk the way he chugs down his Johnny Walker.

I twist open the cap and don't hesitate one bit when I down enough to take the edge off. God, that shit tastes damn good.

"Would you like some?" I offer the bottle to her.

"No thanks." I top it off with another short swig then place the bottle on the counter, my possessive glare caging her in.

"He's a dangerous man. A killer. A monster, Alina. No fucking way. Besides that, I quite like living. If I took you up on your offer, I may as well shoot myself seven times because sure as shit, your dad and all your brothers will each take a turn killing me. I'm a man, not a cat with seven lives."

I flip open the pizza box, take two plates out of the cupboard and grab napkins, placing one of each in front of her. She digs in for a slice. As do I.

"Did you just compare your life to a life of a cat?" I sure as shit did. Her shoulders start to shake. She's laughing. God, that's a beautiful sound, coming out of an even more beautiful mouth. I chuckle at my stupid phrase right along with her.

"You know, Roan," she says with authority after she's collected herself. "I have resources myself. I could help you find him."

I watch her take a bite of her pizza. Jesus Christ. She even eats pizza sexy, her little pink tongue dashing out to lick the sauce off of the side of her lips. Fuck me!

"Alina. I 'd be surprised if he weren't already here in New York. You let me worry about him. I told you I don't lie. When I find him—and I will find him—I'm going to kill him before he even has a chance to look in your direction. I'm not spending any more of my time with you talking about that fucker." My fingers want to dislocate themselves from my body to touch her.

"You're right. I would much rather talk about you." She tosses her napkin on her plate, shifting her body so her legs brush up against mine. I find a hell of a lot of comfort in the fact she agrees with me, though I know we will be discussing this again. Not tonight, though. I've been waiting way too long to be able to just sit back and talk to her.

"Another beer?" Standing up, I walk to the fridge and grab two more, then twist off the cap and hand her one. She takes it. My fingers linger over hers a little too long, skimming slowly down to her fingertips. God, how I wish I could pull her into me. Kiss that fucking idea about Royal right out of her mind. She gasps slightly when I release the bottle. I smirk, knowing I'm affecting her. *Get used to it, beautiful lady, you've been affecting me for two months now.*

"Come on. Let's make this a proper date."

"A proper date?" she asks.

Placing my hand on her back, I lead her back to the living room. Then I dim the lights and grab the remote. The light sound of Eric Clapton's *You Look Wonderful Tonight* starts to play. I toss the remote on the couch.

"Dance with me?"

Her eyes glimmer. The most captivating smile spreads across her face. Taking her beer out of her hand, I set it down on the table next to me. I gently pull her into my arms. Her body presses firmly to mine. Her hands twine around my neck. God, she feels so good. It's as if she was made to be here in my arms. We sway slowly. Clapton's deep velvety voice is speaking the truth. She does look wonderful.

"You surprise me at every turn, Mr. Diamond." Her breath is so close to my ear. I've never danced with a woman before. I have no clue what the hell I'm even doing. All I know is she spears my thoughts. I can't stop thinking about her. I could easily become addicted to this euphoria as much as I'm already addicted to her well-being. I'm in way over my damned head. I know so much about her, yet I feel like there is so much more to learn. I'm turning into one of those fuck-puppets. She has me dangling on a damn string and doesn't even fucking know it. Alina has the upper hand here without knowing much about me. I chastise myself mentally to move slowly, to learn about her more intimately. Not in a sexual way. She needs to know she can trust me. I wonder what's going through her mind right now. My mind is screaming at me to find out things about her I don't know, while my dick is trying to fight its way out of my pants. *Yeah, well forget it, buddy*. She will definitely be worth the wait.

"That's the plan." My voice is gruff.

She squeals slightly when I dip her back, her long naked neck exposed. It's my tongue this time that wants to reach out and run up her graceful neck. Lick her lazily, seductively. I rein him in. Keep my mouth shut. I bring her back up, spinning her slowly then bringing her back into me. I need to tie my dick up with my tongue, this way they'll both shut the hell up.

"Are you a romantic?"

Our mouths are not even an inch apart.

"I've never had anyone to romance before."

I'm speaking the truth. My hand instinctively reaches up and caresses her cheek.

"You are astoundingly beautiful in every way a woman should be."

The music keeps playing. It switched to a different song. I'm so caught up in her I couldn't tell you the name of the song if my life depended on it. It's slow and sensual, exactly the same way we are swaying back and forth. There's no lead and follow between us. We're two people attracted to each other.

We've stopped moving. My hand is still stroking her cheek. Her eyes dart to my lips. My plan was to go slow with her. To not even kiss her tonight before I took her home. To let her know I respect her in every way. But I can't seem to help myself. My face leans in slowly, knowing I only get one first kiss with this woman. I could devour her with my mouth, clue her in and let her know specifically what she does to me. Instead, when my lips brush across her soft lips, a spark ignites in me. I've often wondered if the truth stands behind what happens when two electric currents collide. I feel it. The heat is slowly building up, then vaporizing in an extremely hot explosion.

Darting my tongue out, I slowly glide it across her bottom lip. She exhales, opening wider, clinging her mouth to mine. My plan was to control this kiss, but she takes complete control, which shocks the shit out of me. I'll let her for now. She shows no sign at all of her sweet innocence, her lack of experience. Those tantalizing plump lips feel better than I ever thought they would. She's kissing me like she's never been kissed before. Bringing my other hand up to hold her in place, I tilt her head to the perfect angle. Her tongue darts out first, slowly meshing with mine. I lose all control then, devouring her mouth with mine. Our tongues play war with one another, each one trying to demolish the other. Fuck me all the way back to Michigan. I am so totally screwed. Totally fucked.

I brush my finger over the shell of her ear. I kiss her again. Fuck. I don't even know what to do. I'm more nervous than I've ever been. I'm a grown ass man so full of being overwhelmed right now. Joy creeps to the corners of her mouth when we separate. Those huge universe eyes of hers, so god damn full of excitement. For the first time in my life I feel it too.

"Wow, Roan Diamond." She says breathlessly.

I smile. Definitely a wow, Alina Solokov.

We spend the rest of the night telling each other stories about our childhood. I leave all of the dark stories about Royal out while she tells me about her brothers teasing her all the time; the things she did to pay them back; embarrassing them every time they brought a girl over.

It's past midnight by the time I take her home, kissing her one last time before she walks into her apartment.

"I have a busy week at the hospital," she tells me while digging her keys out of her purse.

"I have to go out of town on business for a few days. I would love to take you out to dinner when I get back if you have the time." I skip the reason as to why I have to leave until the time comes, if ever. I'm going to decline talking to her about the things I do. The people I meet with. I'm a crazy ass fool for getting involved with her. More for her sake than mine. Call her the magnet and me the crazy nut that can't stay the hell away. People can call it whatever the hell they want. Someway, somehow, Alina Solokov is going to become MINE.

"Call me when you return." Taking the keys from her hand, I open her door for her. It kills me to leave her for a few days now that I'm finally getting to spend time with her. We say goodnight, and she slowly disappears behind her door. I wait until I hear the deadbolt click before I leave.

The very first thing I do when I climb into my car is make that much needed phone call.

"This better be good, motherfucker," Beamer yells into the phone.

"It's better than good, asshole. Get your ass to New York."

In three hours, I've went from sweet, to driving my god damn fist into this crazy disloyal fuckers face.

"Fuck you, you piece of shit motherfucker." This lying bastard has the nerve to call me a name. My fist pummels into Mel's face again.

"You really want to go there, Melvin?" I grab him by the throat. "Call me a piece of shit one more time. I dare you, you lying fucker." I glare at this asshole who dared to try and steal guns from us. All I want to do is get back to New York. Wash this filth off of me and call Alina to see if she liked her present I bought for her. But fuck no. Instead, Cain and I have been in some stinky ass town that smells like a damn sewer in Delaware for the past two days, tracking this bloodied thief down. And when I say bloodied, I mean his face looks like it's been smashed with a sledgehammer.

"You've been working for my dad for years, you scum. YEARS! And you try and steal from him? That has to be one of the dumbest things anyone has ever done. And well now, you pay the price, you jackfuck. All you have to do is tell me who you were taking this load to and Cain won't make that phone call I know he's dying to make." I tilt my chin up to Cain, who brings his phone down right in front of Mel's face, his finger hovering over the send button, the word Digger staring him in the face.

"Yeah, I'd piss my pants too if I were you." I step back and watch this tool literally piss himself.

Digger took over for John when he retired last month. The fucker even scares the shit out of me. But damn, is he clean and quick. Reminds us all of John in the way he can take someone out and return home to his wife and kids like he worked nine to five at a damn bank.

"I'm telling you, Roan, I don't know who it is. I swear on my kid's life, man." Blood pours out of his mouth.

"Call him, Cain. I don't know about you, but I'm done here." Releasing his head, I stand there with my arms crossed over my chest. The fear is settling deep in his eyes.

"Come on, you guys. You don't want to do this." The poor bastard's teeth are chattering. He's been around long enough to know once you cross my dad, there's no turning back.

"I'm not going to do a thing. Cain and I are done." I look up to Cain, who now has his back to me talking quietly on the phone.

"He's on his way." Cain comes and stands by my side.

"I'm going to go call my wife. Do you want me to call yours?" Cain asks Mel.

"Fuck you guys. You two think you can come here and rule this entire empire. That everyone will bow down to two little punks. Think again. You may kill me. Do whatever the hell you want, but judgment day is coming, boys, and you will be rotting in hell right along with me." We watch as his face spasms, condemning himself to death.

"Dude. Didn't we hear something along these lines before?" I ask, angling my head in Cain's direction.

"We did. I believe it was right before my father-in-law killed a few people a couple of years back." He scratches his head. He's just as twisted as I am.

I chuckle. "That's right, I remember. It was Calla who said it. She said something like..." I cast my focus back on Mel. "I may be going to hell, but you'll get there first."

"I'll strike a deal with you, Mel. If you tell me who it is, I will tell Digger to kill you quickly. If you don't, we'll be hearing you scream all the way back to New York." He grunts.

"I don't know. That's the god's honest truth."

"Fair enough, Mel. I'll make sure to cry at your funeral."

"Zeke and Milo emptied the truck and left it where Mel told us he was taking it." Cain informs me once we get into my truck to head back home.

"Good. Then whoever this fucker is will know we're on to him when he opens up the back of the truck and discovers he got his shit, all right. Piles of horse shit." My tone is sodden with sarcasm.

"Who do you think it is? Ivan?" Cain asks.

"Nah. Not his style. Besides, why would he start a war all of a sudden? This has my brother written all over it," I hiss.

"You think he's back then?"

"I think he's been back for a very long time. And this is only the beginning. We all need to watch our backs. That includes Calla and Alina."

"He's a dead man if he comes anywhere near my wife again." Fuck. I wrap my hands tighter around the steering wheel, minus one damn finger from that night my brother tortured Calla and I.

I cringe thinking about it.

"You sure about this thing with Alina?" Cain asks me the minute we get back into my car after burning our bloodied clothes. We're on our way back to New York. Finally.

We stopped at the run-down motel we stayed at last night, both of us going to our rooms to shower. I fucking hate staying in these shit holes. The minute you walk in the door, all you smell is piss and stale cigarettes flowing through the air. Mix that with the smell of the cheap ass floral spray they use and you got a fucking trash dump. How half of those places can meet codes in their townships is beyond me. My guess is money talks just like it does with us. You pay someone enough money and they keep their mouth shut. Sign on the dotted line and keep on moving.

"I've never been surer of anything in my life. She's wonderful, man. A little piece of heaven right here on earth." It's quiet for several moments. I feel his eyes on me.

"I know what you mean," he finally says.

"It's like after years of living in the dark, you finally walk straight into nothing but light. Bright, beautiful light all around you. You wonder what the hell you ever did in your fucked up life to deserve someone like her." This shit just pours out of his mouth.

"I don't have her, yet. Fucker," I snap.

"Just let her make her own choices and you will." His tone is light.

"Thanks, Dr. Phil.' I start to laugh.

"Mark my words, asshole. You'll be whipped. But having her up against you every night, knowing that she chose you over every fucker in this world, is more than worth it. Trust me, I know what I'm saying." He then gets out his phone and starts texting who I can only assume is Calla.

I'm thinking to myself I'm already there and all I've done is kiss her. *You're fucked, fucker!*

Chapter Five

Alina

Missing someone severely is an exhausting mental process I'm not accustomed to. It's been two days and I miss him. Each and every thought I have is followed by another thought of him. It's like a circle. Once you figure out a way to get inside, appreciating your surroundings, you don't bother to try and find a way to get out.

I feel a distinguished vacancy behind me, knowing he's not following me home tonight. Even though I never saw him, I knew he was there. Instead, tonight I take the ten-block hike home in my scrubs from the hospital with Hugo by my side. Now, don't get me wrong, I enjoy his company very much. Tonight is a rare treat to be walking with him, listening to him talk about growing up in Russia. How his family right alongside mine made the trek to the States decades ago. Crazy when you live in the city because, yes, it's true what they say. You can get to places in downtown New York faster by walking than you can in a car. It's a beautiful spring day. This morning as I walked along, passing by the tall buildings, there were flowers blooming everywhere; duds on the trees; birds chirping. The smell of spring mixed in with the smell of everyday life gave my step a pep.

Tonight, not so much. I haven't heard from him since he left. Not that I expected to. I hoped to, I guess. This right here is why one part of me is so damn mad for acknowledging him at the club, while the other part of me is crying just to hear his voice. Make sure he's all right. I hate this life. I have tried to distance myself from it for as long as I can remember. And now what am I doing? I'm jumping in head first into the same thing I promised myself I would avoid.

"Well, here you go, Miss Alina," Hugo says in his thick Russian accent, reminding me so much of my dad. "Thank you," I say pleasantly.

"Alina," he calls out just as I'm ready to grab the door to enter.

"Yes?"

"Your dad is really looking forward to dinner with you tonight. He really has missed you," he declares profoundly. I called both of my parents from work today, my fingers shaking uncontrollably dialing their numbers. I couldn't talk to them for as long as I had hoped, but to hear their voices was enough to get me through the day. It's been a great day, and it will be even better when I feel my dad's arms around me; smell the jasmine of my mom when she folds me into her arms.

"I am too," I speak out honestly.

And I am. It may take a while to get to know my parents and for them to get to know me, even though I know they know every little detail of my outside life. The truth is we don't know each other personally anymore. While riding the elevator up to my apartment, I retrieve my phone out of my bag, texting Anton, reminding him to pick me up in an hour as I step off and walk down the hall. Laughing out loud at his response of *'No Shit. That's all I've heard dad talk about all damn day,'* ending with a smiley face. He's such a child in a grown man's body.

"Deidre," I call out, locking the door behind me, then tossing my purse on the kitchen counter. I exhale. She's not home.

Piling my hair on top of my head, I strip out of my scrubs, adjust the water in the shower, and make what I would love to be a relaxing shower to ease my tension the closer it gets to seeing my parents a five-minute one. The minute I step out, a weary sensation envelops me. Something in my bathroom seems off. Scanning the entire room, I notice nothing out of place. I shake it off, chalking it up to my nerves over worrying about my parents and Roan. I apply lotion, freshen up my makeup, pull my hair out of my clip so it falls freely down my back, and enter my bedroom. The minute I do, I am hit with a blast of freezing cold air, my naked body oversensitive from stepping out of a warm bathroom into a freezing cold room. "What the hell?" I holler out. "Deidre, are you here?" I reach for my robe, the silk freezing on my skin. Still no answer. When I enter the hallway, I check the thermostat, and sure as hell, it's set as low as it will go and the button is cold.

"I'm going to kick her ass." The little bitch is always pulling shit like this. I adjust it to where we normally keep it. A shiver runs through me when I get back to my room. I slip on a pair of navy blue panties and a matching bra, a casual pair of jeans, and a blue cashmere V-neck sweater along with a pair of chunky heeled boots. Geez, I'm still cold.

By the time Anton shows up, the apartment is back to normal. I write Deidre a quick note, chewing her a new asshole for the central air joke, telling her I'm out with my brother. Lord only knows she would show up if she knew I was also with my parents, just to make sure I was ok. I forego that part, saving it for when I get home.

"You nervous?" My brother asks, guiding me into the restaurant. "A little." I shrug. "I mean, I'm their daughter, so I know they would never hate me. But it's been a long time since we've spoken. I feel like I'm meeting strangers."

"Don't be. We're family. Everything will be fine." He gives my arm a little squeeze.

"Alina." Ivan Solokov, the man known as my dad, stands, as does my mother.

"Privet, papa. Privet, mama." The gleam in my dad's eyes does not go unnoticed from my greeting in Russian.

"Моё сердце парит высоко в небесах, каждый раз, когда я вижу мою красивую девочку". He touches my face with both of his hands. His gentle term of endearment brings sudden tears to my eyes. I remember all too well how he would tell me his heart soars highly up into the heavens when looking at his beautiful girl.

"I've missed you." He converts to English now.

"I've missed you too, dad. More than you know." My arms go around him. He holds me tightly against him. His familiar cigar smell smells like home, security, and safety.

"Mom." My eyes flit to hers. Tears are streaming down her face. As soon as my dad releases me I'm drawn into the comfort of my mother's arms. Her floral scent is the same, her warm, loving embrace lasting long until she finally lets me go.

"We don't want to overwhelm you, Alina. However, I must say this. I'm very proud of you for following through with your dreams. For becoming a doctor. Healing children who cannot take care of themselves. You're a good woman."

"Thank you, dad. I couldn't have done it without the two of you paying for it in spite of."

"No. Stop right there." My mom holds her hand up.

"You're our daughter. We paid for your education. And as far as the past goes, it stays right there. We only move forward from here. Understand?" Those words coming from her rip me to my very core. I'm fighting back years of unwept tears. Years of anger. Years of hurt because neither one of them reached out to their young daughter to try and reason with me. I hurt them as much as they hurt me. Forgiveness is such a plentiful thing. Up until this moment, I blamed them. The way they live, the things they do. I will never accept it, but I can live with it. The one reason being family.

"You'll come Saturday at five for dinner then?" Mom asks for the tenth time as we part ways. Dinner was great. Both of them listened passionately when I talked about my college days, my job, and everything in between. Not once did we talk about anything negative. Nothing to do with the family business. I tried several times to ask them about things Anton informed me about, like trips they had taken. My mom finally talking my dad into building her a gazebo in the backyard. Both of them brushed me off, telling me tonight was all about me. I feel elated in a way I can only begin to understand.

"Of course I will be there." I'm actually looking forward to it.

"Beautiful girl."

"Yes," I call out, nervous and guarded with my dad hollering out my name just seconds after we said goodbye.

"Bring Roan Saturday night." Without saying anything else, Anton and I stand on the sidewalk and watch the almighty powerful Ivan slide into the backseat of his limo and drive away into the night, leaving his daughter speechless.

I enter my apartment in a state of excitement, the noise from the television in the living room an indication that Deidre is home.

"Hey," I say, plopping down on the opposite end of the couch, bending over to pull off my boots.

"Hey, woman. How was dinner?" she pipes up from where she had her head resting on the arm of the couch.

“It was great. Perfect, actually.” I sigh once my boots are off. “I had dinner with my parents.”

“You what? Oh, Alina. I’m so happy for you. Tell me everything.” Our happiness bounces off of each other. I’m so lucky to have her as a friend, even though she has a mouth on her. She’s true and she cares about me just as much as I care about her.

“They look so good, Deidre. They forgave me just like that. It was incredible. Oh, and get this. They invited me over for dinner Saturday night and my dad told me to bring Roan,” I say with enthusiasm.

“He what? Alina, that’s amazing. You don’t think it’s some kind of trap, though, do you?” Her tone is a tad alarming. Anton and I discussed this all the way home. He assured me dad has good intentions. All he wants is for me to be happy. And how they know Roan is nothing like his brother.

“No. I don’t. Dad would never hurt me like that. No matter the differences he has with Roan’s dad.”

“I’m so happy for you.” Deidre sits up and scoots down the couch bringing her arm around me.

“Look at the week you’ve had. First, you finally go on a date, then you make up with your parents. I wonder what’s going to happen next. If I had to guess, I would say hot sex. Like dirty, hot sex. You know, maybe he will bring out his machine gun and pump you full of his bullets like this.” Removing her arm, she steeples both hands together and starts pointing them all over the room while shouting, “ack.ack. ack.”

“Oh, my god. You are so dramatic.” Both of us start laughing.

“I’m not, either. I’m just happy for you, and something tells me that if he can steal and strip down a gun, clean it all up, then he’s very capable of dirtying up your vagina.”

“You’re sick.”

"Am not."

"Are too."

"Fine. I am. Oh, and by the way, I'm sorry about the air conditioning. I turned it on when I was working out and forgot to shut it off."

"Well shit, that's a relief. It was freezing when I stepped out of the shower today. At first I thought maybe someone had broken in here."

"I'm sorry. I know I'm always forgetting one thing or another. You would have died laughing the other day at the bakery when I left the oven on after baking a cake." Her hands lift in frustration.

"Not you." I tease.

"No one knew, until my uncle opened up the oven and was doused in the face with heat. I swear he scorched his eyelashes off. Anyway I'm sorry once again, especially with." She scrunches up her face and shrugs. I know what she wants to say, without her even saying it.

"Royal's whereabouts unknown." His name taste like the white trash he really is, when it rolls off of my tongue.

She nods. The serious look in her expression letting me know she knew it was hard for me to say. Then in Deidre like fashion her retort has me laughing.

"Your brother has this place locked up tighter than your vagina. No one can get in here." She giggles.

"When I do finally get some, I'm not going to tell you," I huff and cross my arms over my chest, pretending to be mad.

"You won't have to tell me a thing, because something tells me that man of yours is packing a big cock between his legs, which means you won't be walking the next day out of your room, you'll be crawling." My mouth falls open.

"While you're trying to think of a good comeback, I'm heading to bed. Night." She stands then stretches before she reaches down and snaps my mouth shut.

"I almost forgot. There's something on your bed for you," she hollers with her back to me as she retreats down the hallway to her room. What a little bitch!

Jumping up quickly, I set the alarm and make sure the door is locked up tight, flick on the light above the stove, turn off the television. By the time I get to my room, the anticipation is killing me, wondering what it is. More than likely another matching set of lacy undergarments from Deidre. She is constantly buying me lingerie in hopes that one day I will actually use it and get laid.

That's not what I find when I enter my room. What I do find is a big huge pink box. My feet gravitate in the direction of my bed, my hands shaking when I take hold of the box.

"No card." Gently, I lift the cover then tear away the white tissue paper.

"Wow." My shaky hands run across the most beautiful dress and matching shoes I have ever seen.

It's in that unfocused moment that I return to the kitchen on wobbly legs to retrieve my phone. I hear it ringing where I laid it on the counter when I came back from dinner.

My stomach does some kind of fancy little somersault when I see it's Roan.

"Hello." I quickly turn into my room, shutting the door, my lips curling into a huge smile. "Thank you for the dress and shoes." I bite my tongue, because all I want to do is say '*come over*', even though it's so late.

"You're home," he says, sounding more like a question that a statement.

"I am. And by the looks of what's on my bed, so are you."

I brush my fingers across the multi-colored satin dress.

"I'm in New York, but I'm not home."

"Oh," I reply, disappointment etched in my assertion.

"Well, I can let you go then. I... I wanted to thank you for the dress," I express barely above a whisper.

"Thank me in person, Alina. I'm standing right outside your door."

I think I dropped my phone before swinging open my door and darting down the hallway. I punch in the code to release the alarm, my hands shaking yet again. In less than a minute, I have the door open and proclaiming I was tired before has flown out the window the minute my eyes see Roan leaning up against the door, his dark hair a mess, those eyes still gleaming. He's so manly I can't seem to tear my eyes away from him. He moves first, his strong hand reaching up, cupping the side of my face.

"I missed you, beautiful lady."

He pulls me into him gently. He is hard, not just his body. I feel his thick erection up against me. If it were anyone else, I would flinch and demand to be let go, but this hug isn't sexual. Even though his heavy thickness would normally say otherwise. It's the way he's holding me that tells me it isn't. The way he strokes my hair and breathes me in that tells me it's anything but.

"Do you want to come in?" I say into his neck. I can barely breathe, but I don't want to tell him that. A sixth sense tells me he needed to hold me.

"It's late and I know you have to work tomorrow. I just had to see you."

I'm happy he wants to see me as much as I do him. I pull away from him slightly so I can look in his face.

"I'm off tomorrow," I say with a hint of amusement.

"You don't have to work? I thought you said you had a busy week?" Confusion shadows his incredibly sexy stubble.

"I do have a busy week. It's called Doctor's hours. I work four twelve-hour days with Wednesdays and the weekends off. It's the perk of working in an actual office inside the hospital instead of actually working for the hospital."

He all but growls. My head is jerked forward before Roan lifts me completely off of the ground, walking us backward into the apartment. I have no clue why, but my legs automatically go around his waist. I hear the thud of the door closing, and then his mouth is on mine.

My lips yield to him. This kiss is so different from the other night. It's demanding, controlling, and desperate all in one. Roan is owning my mouth, his tongue twining with mine. I deepen my breath and suck on his tongue and oh god, he moans. Deliciously loud. We're both panting by the time he pulls away from my mouth. I want to cry out for him to put his lips back on mine.

"Spend the day with me tomorrow?" he says with a small smile.

"Under one condition."

"These conditions are becoming a little habit between us, I see."

Roan leans his forehead up against mine.

"I like conditions."

Unwrapping my legs from around his waist, I take his hand, walking backwards towards the kitchen.

I open the fridge, handing him the one and only beer we have in the apartment. I didn't tell him, but hell, I don't even know where it came from. I had to check for an expiration date just to make sure.

"Thanks." Tipping the beer back, and draining half the bottle.

"Stay for a while." I whisper, making my way down the hallway. My nerves rattle inside of me when he follows.

"In here? With you? Is that your condition?" he asks while blowing out a breath when we enter my room. He scans my bed. The light blue comforter with white pillows adorns my king size dark cherry four-poster bed.

"You don't have to stay. And yes, that's my condition," I speak softly, then I look down to the floor.

He lifts my chin. "I would love to stay for a while."

"How did you know what size dress and shoes I wore?" I ask curiously. "Let me guess. Deidre?"

Setting my glass of wine on the nightstand, I pull out the dress and gasp.

"Yes. I wanted to get you a dress. I called her at work and hell she was all about helping out. And by the look on your face, she did well. Yeah?"

"It's stunning, Roan."

Gathering the dress in my hands, I turn and stand in front of the mirror, placing the dress up against my front. The multi colors are bold, striking. It's sleeveless, shorter in the front and long in the back. A small circle crystal of sequins gathers the dress in front. The halter-styled top crossing in the back is adorned with the same sequins.

Roan gathers the shoes out of the box before he comes to stand behind me, his reflection parallel with mine.

"Someone told me how you've never been on a proper date before. A woman like you should be shown off. Worshipped, Alina. I want to take you out Friday night."

He runs his free hand up the side of my arm. My skin flares up in flames with his touch. Speechless is what I am for a moment. I cannot seem to take my eyes off of the two of us in the mirror.

The shoes are dangled in front of me. Black Jimmy Choo platform five-inch pumps with tiny delicate crystals. I would know those shoes anywhere. I have eyeballed them for a long time.

"You and Deidre must have had quite the talk," I hint.

He smirks. "A man never tells who his accomplice is, sweetheart. These shoes, the way they sparkle" both of our eyes fall to the shoes, "remind me of the way your eyes lit up so brightly when they fell upon me tonight when you greeted me at the door. I have never had anyone look at me like you did tonight. You were just as happy to see me on the other side of that door as I was you. You've captivated me, Alina."

I see desire, yearning, and a man who captivates me too. His breath ghosts my ear. It takes every bit of my composure not to turn around and kiss him, to hide the fact this man enlivens me. Makes me desire things I never thought I would.

"So about that date, will you go? Will you let me show you how a man should treat a lady?" His eyes are pleading.

"I would let you take me anywhere."

And by god, I mean it too.

Chapter Six

Roan

The minute I saw her tonight, the haunting from the past couple of days dissipated into thin air. This part of my job is the part I hate the most. The fact I've partaken in the death of a man I once knew. A man whose family is now mourning his death.

The one thing my dad has drilled into my head is to trust very few people in this world. And to love even less. But her...I could easily love her. Walk through the door every night if I could see her face light up like the moon and stars illuminate the sky.

Alina looked at me like Calla looks at Cain, like my mother still looks at my dad. She sees the real me. Not the dark man whose life is full of blood; a man who will reign over my family's empire one day. Most importantly, she doesn't see the brother of a man who hurt her.

It took every ounce of my strength to not take her back to her bed tonight when she kissed me goodbye, to lay her down and strip her bare, then have her beneath me. My hands where clenched so tight around her delicate frame, I could have easily been drawing my own blood the way it zipped straight to my dick.

I don't even give a shit anymore that I don't fear what a woman can do to a man when you care about her and she cares about you. Falling for a chick is the only thing I've ever feared, afraid I would be less of a man if I let her tug me around by my heartstrings. Fuck no. With her it's a two-way street. Fuck, it's a god damned straight highway where you are able to accelerate, feel your pulse quicken, the rush of zooming down an open road, feeling free. That's how she makes me feel. Free. Free to be the man I want to be. Free to soar. To escape from the fucked up shit that's my so-called life.

After I found out she has tomorrow off—or should I say today as I check the time on my clock when I turn over on my side in bed—I instantly asked her to spend the day with me. Up until now, I had no clue what we would do, but I know. I want to be free with her and I know exactly what it is that we can do.

"Where are we going?"

Alina bounds down the sidewalk towards me where I rest up against my bike. She's just as stubborn as she is beautiful and independent. I sent her a text to let her know I was on my way, that I would come up to her apartment and get her. She full on refused. Told me she would wait in the lobby. And Christ, now she stands in front of me in skin tight black jeans, leather boots all the way up to her knees, and the sexiest leather jacket I have ever seen zipped tight across those luscious tits.

Fuck me clear from here to the damn Catskills.

I hook my finger around the strap of her backpack, pinning her in my arms, and kiss the living hell out of her. My palms grip her tight ass. It's the first time I've had my hands on her ass. God, it feels good.

"Good morning to you too," I growl against her neck.

"Good Morning." Her breathing is labored.

"Hop on. I'll tell you on the way." I release her and hand over her helmet.

Out of nowhere her hand cradles mine. She leans and kisses the stub on my finger where Roan cut it off when he held Calla and I captive.

"I'm sorry," she says, then swings those long legs over my bike like a fucking pro. What the hell was that?

"You look fucking hot straddling my bike," I say, praying like a motherfucker she doesn't miss my sexual innuendo. And hell, she doesn't either when her pupils dilate, her mouth parts, opening and closing and then snapping shut. *Yeah baby*, I think to myself. *You're well on your way to becoming mine*.

"Are you going to tell me where we're going?" she yells in my ear at a stop light about forty-five minutes into our drive.

"Zip lining in the Catskills," I holler back.

"Hell yeah!" her high-pitched voice screams in my ear.

"That a girl." I gradually open up the throttle with a smile on my face.

This is being free. The wind in your face. The beauty of nature. The feeling of Alina's hands holding me around my waist. Her laughter echoes all around when I accelerate. She loves it. God, I'm a lucky man.

"Are you nervous?" I ask her when we put our boots, her backpack, and our helmets in the locker provided for us. It took a little over two hours to get here. Her messed up hair is now pulled back into a ponytail. She's stunning.

"Nope. Excited. Are you?" Her face is beaming.

"Fuck, no. I'm stoked. Let's go."

I grab her by the hand and lead her to the room where we were instructed to go for our lesson about safety along with instructions.

"You two are all set."

Our instructor Claude finishes buckling Alina in. I'm about ready to knock his eyes up his ass if he doesn't put them back in his fucking head and quit staring at my girl's tits. Fucking pervert.

"You ready, baby?"

I take her hand, not giving two fucks if I'm showing this beefed up shit face I'm staking my claim. I wonder how he'd like it if my elbow connected with his fucking nose.

"I think so."

She leans up and kisses me. We line up side by side, each connected to our own line. She doesn't even hesitate when he tells us to go. She's gone, screaming as she goes. I take off close behind her, feeling like a bird flying freely, taking in all the beauty below me. The view is incredible from up here.

"Oh, my god. I could do that again."

Her rosy cheeks along with her bright smile send me soaring even higher by the time we get back to my bike after walking around and having a light late lunch. I love the fact that with the combination of her re-uniting with her parents—which she told me all about with a happiness I've never seen radiate off of her before, not even when she talked about her job.

"Then we'll do it again. We can do anything you want, all you have to do is ask." That's the honest truth, especially seeing her smile. "I've never thought about doing things like this, Roan. Trust me, now that you've shown me there is more to life than school and work, I may take you up on that." Shit. She can take me up on anything she damn well pleases. Alina is a gift.

The woman didn't even blink an eye when I told her Beamer was now her bodyguard on my account. She actually laughed, her comment being, "That doesn't surprise me." I felt like I was losing my touch a little when she said she hasn't even noticed him, nor has Hugo said a word to her about him. Subconsciously, I wanted her to see me, be aware, if only to notice me. Some may call me a stalker in disguise. I could give a fuck. She's here with me now. Right where she belongs, right where I believe she was meant to be.

I'm not too happy about going to dinner at her parents' house on Saturday. She's assured me her dad's intentions are not to make any threats. He wants her to be happy. Me on the other hand, I trust very few people, and the fact that Royal is out there somewhere and he worked for Ivan, makes me trust him even less. The man has been nothing but helpful in trying to find him. But how the hell do any of us know if it's a farce or not? A way to lure me in? Have me trapped and then ambush me the minute I walk through the fucking door? I only hope he loves his daughter enough to not hurt her in that way.

"You're all kinds of fun, Roan Diamond." She grabs me roughly by the collar of my coat, tugging me into her. "Now what?" she asks.

"Now, I'm going to kiss you." My lips imprison hers. She moans when she surrenders her mouth to my demanding tongue, tangling her hands in my hair.

"Let's go watch the sunset from my place," I tell her once I let go of her mouth.

"I'd love that."

She darts her eyes back and forth between my mouth and my eyes. Images of her flash in front of me, of seeing the same glowed look as she has right now when I make her come with my tongue dipped inside her sweet pussy. I know she's going to taste sweeter than anything that has ever gone inside my mouth before. I need us to leave before she notices I'm nearly foaming at the mouth like a rabid dog that wants to take a damn chunk out of her ass.

I park my bike next to my truck and my viper and help her off by grabbing her hand. I don't let go of her, not during the entire walk through the parking garage, not during the ride up in the elevator.

The minute I have her in my penthouse is the moment I let go only to spin her around up against the door. I pull that damn ponytail holder out of her hair so I can plunge my throbbing fingers in her messed up hair. I need her to feel closely what she does to me. My dick is harder than titanium right now. I want her to know she's wanted, desired, and I'm lucky as fuck to even know her.

"I'm going to kiss you now. I may never stop kissing you," I say, dropping my mouth slowly to hers. She watches my lips fade down to hers with those huge eyes. One touch and I'm overpowered by a sudden urge to melt into her. To have her open up wide. She complies and gives just as good as she gets. My hands palm her head through her thick mass of hair. I cannot wait to see all that hair spread out on my bed while I'm buried so far inside her she's begging me to take her hard or gentle. Damn, I want her to feel what she does to me so bad. She has to know. Her innocence doesn't scare me. I don't want her to feel ambushed by this intense connection I feel towards her.

Our sexual chemistry is so damn passionate, it's nuts.

"You are intoxicating, beautiful lady. If I'm coming on too strong, please tell me."

Our foreheads are pressed together.

"You're not. In fact, I want more."

She unzips her coat, taking it off and tossing it onto the table. I do the same.

This time, it's her who initiates our kiss. Showing no indiscreetness when she grabs my ass. I want to scream *'Halle-fucking-lujah! Grab it, pinch it, and bite it'. I don't give a shit, just fucking touch me*. I bite on her lower lip, move to her neck, the smell of fresh air mixed in with her natural smell has me tracing my tongue all the way up to the globe of her ear. Natural instincts kick in, and I press my dick into her stomach. The sounds of her panting, moaning, and tilting her head to the side for me has me lifting her up without any hesitation, carrying her into my living room and placing her on the couch, where she pulls me down on top of her. That hair spread out just how I imagined it would be. I need her mouth more. I need her neck more. I need all of her. We kiss for a few more minutes. Small, tiny, deep breaths in between. I have to stop or I'm going to lose control.

"I've got to stop, Alina. I know you can feel what this is doing to me."

Forcing myself to get up off of her, I sit at the opposite end of the couch, run my fingers through my hair, and take deep breaths to calm my shit down. "Jesus." Leaning back, I lower my hand to readjust myself.

"You have no idea the thoughts that run through my mind when it comes to the things I want to do to you. I want to strip you bare. Attach my mouth to those sensitive nipples of yours while you arch your back, thrusting them farther into my mouth. From there, my tongue trails down the middle of your stomach, while my hands move to your breasts. Palming them, squeezing them together while you writhe underneath me, my name falling from your pert little mouth. But I don't stop there, Alina, I head farther south all the way to that sweet juncture between your thighs and send you to a place you have never been before. That's what I want to do to you. And not just once or twice, but for as long as you'll let me."

Shit. My words wouldn't stop tumbling out of my mouth. I wouldn't be surprised if I didn't scare the living shit out of her and she gets up and leaves. Yours truly sits here and braces himself, ready for her to stand up and demand I take her home.

"Well then, I'm glad our minds think alike. And while we're playing confessions instead of conditions, here's mine. What if I don't want you to stop? I... I mean, I'm not talking sex, but what if I want you to touch me? To let me touch you? To have a fantastic make-out session?"

This woman isn't going to be the death of me. This woman is going to bring me to fucking life. To want to live. To be surrounded in light instead of living in the mixture of black and red.

"Are you asking me to touch you, Alina? I need you to say it."

I flick my gaze over every feature of her gorgeous face. From the needy longing in her eyes to the way her swollen mouth moves.

"No. I'm asking you to touch me because you want to. Because you can't help yourself. And because just like me, you want whatever is happening between us."

"Oh, Alina, you have no fucking idea how bad I want this between us. I don't recall ever wanting anything as much as I want this in my entire life."

Chapter Seven

Alina

I'm so nervous about screwing up. I have no idea what I'm doing. I'm a twenty-eight-year-old woman who has no clue what the hell to do. I'm an always-looks-but-never-touches type of woman. I've given myself plenty of orgasms over the course of the years, but I've never had one given to me by a man. Roan makes me want to lose all control, to do things I've only dreamed about, read about, and seen in movies. Beneath the surface, my body reacts wildly to the way he kisses me. My body melts every damn time his lips brush across mine.

"Come with me."

Roan rises up, curls his body down, and puts one arm under my knees, the other under my neck, lifting me into his arms. We walk down a low-lit hallway to his bedroom. I struggle with the fact I'm in his room. I look around at all the dark, wooden, manly furniture; the very large bed facing all of the floor-to-ceiling windows; the rich black comforter on his bed, where he places me down in the center.

"I've dreamt about seeing you lying in my bed, your blond hair up against my black pillows. You're a vision, Alina."

The serious look in his eyes combined with his kind words puts me somewhat at ease.

"I think we need to get rid of this."

Slowly, he starts to inch my shirt up my body. My stomach is bare. Wasting no time, he trails spine-tingling kisses across my stomach, pushing my shirt up higher until my pink-laced bra is showing.

"Fucking hell. You have the best tits. I can see those dark nipples begging for me through that sexy fucking bra. Take it off," he demands.

With unstable fingers, I reach down and unsnap the front clasp my breasts springing free. My chest is heaving up and down. What he does next startles me. He lifts my shirt over my head, stretches my hands up above me, and secures them with my shirt.

"Don't move. I'm going to indulge on you, bring you so much pleasure. I want to hear you, feel you, and make you feel so good. Don't hold anything back, because I'm telling you right now, I'm not holding back. I've waited for months to see you on my bed. To be able to touch you."

I swallow nervously. And hell, when his hand tweaks one of my nipples and his face is lost as he descends down and pulls one into his mouth, a keening longing sends me into a tailspin of heat and desire.

"Oh, Roan."

I arch my back. His scruff is lightly caressing my breast, his movements light, his sucking deep, causing friction to escape from places I didn't even know existed.

He takes more of me into his mouth, sucks hard, and then swirls his magnificent tongue around my nipple. He repeats this cycle with both breasts, making my mind forgetting all about the fact my hands are tied. All I can focus on is how he feels. How the scruff on his face grazes across my sensitive skin. I've never experienced anything like this, the sensations running throughout my body, the way his mouth alone has me teetering on an unaccustomed edge.

He moves gently up my neck, running his tongue is a zig-zag motion until he reaches my ear, the weight of his body pressing firmly into mine.

"I need to taste all of you, Alina."

"Please do," I beg.

He kisses my neck, my cheek, my jaw. Peppers kisses all the way down my stomach. I'm squirming. My hands break free from the confines of my shirt. They instinctively move to his hair. He says nothing to me about my hands being freed. My voice hitches when he unsnaps my jeans and the sound of my zipper being lowered.

"Lift up, beautiful lady."

Roan's nature is commanding, yet soft. My jeans are gone right along with my panties, and for the first time in my life I'm bare in front of a man. At least from what I can remember. I shove "that thought" away for now. Those horrible memories have no place here. Not with a man who I can feel in my soul truly cares for me.

"Jesus Fucking Christ. Every single thing about you is beautiful."

He runs a finger down the small strip of trimmed hair between my legs. I can feel myself start to tremble slightly. It's not until he dips down and kisses the very top of my pubic bone that I come to the realization of what he wants to do. I swallow. My mouth goes dry. I'm so close to telling him to stop, but the words never come out. The need for him to touch me more overpowers anything right now.

The bed shifts when he stands and removes his shirt, my eyes bulging out of my head at the sight of him. Muscles on top of muscles. Beautifully formed and sculpted abs. An intricate tribal tattoo of some sort runs down his arm.

"You think I'm beautiful," I say. "Have you ever looked at yourself?"

He chuckles and climbs back onto the bed.

"You can look and touch all you want to later, but right now, I have a craving for your pussy, Alina, and I'm going to fulfill my craving."

Again, I gulp. He presses my legs open by my thighs. Starting at the top of my legs, he kisses down one side and then the other, placing both of them over his shoulders, and wastes no time when he grabs ahold of my tiny pebble of nerves and tugs lightly. I Inhale deeply and exhale screaming his name. Either he really does have a craving, or hearing my name encourages him, because he doesn't just suck, lick, and nip my pussy, he devours it.

"I knew you would taste sweeter than anything I have ever had on my tongue before," is all he says before he attacks me again, his face bobbing up and down, side to side, while his hands squeeze and knead my ass. I would describe this as both pain and pleasure. Every nerve ending on my clit and pussy is being jostled around in a way it's never been before, causing the most tangible of pains to pulse, muscles clenching, unclenching. The friction, oh god, the heavenly friction. It's too much. I'm going to...

"Hell, I'm going to come, Roan." My voice is unrecognizable to my own ears.

My head flies off the pillow as an overwhelming tingle spreads throughout my body. My vision goes blurry.

"Then come. Let me taste it. Smear it all over my face."

I do too. I explode like a cannon. This is nothing like a self-induced orgasm. This is needy, perfect Roan Diamond giving me the first orgasm by a man, and my brain zings louder than anything when it screams at me, *I sure as shit don't want it to be the last.*

"I can't move," I tell him after he comes back from the bathroom.

"Then don't. Stay."

He's standing in his boxers, his erection still very visible. He has to be in pain.

"I'm fine, Alina. Don't look at me like that. This wasn't about me. It was about you. Trust me, if I have anything to say about it, then you will have plenty of opportunities to take care of him." He points down to his dick. I imagine what it looks like. By the description outlining his boxers, one thing I know for sure is it's long and thick.

"Well then, ok."

I speak with confidence, even though when the time does come, I will have no damn clue what I'm doing. My heart starts to beat wildly in my chest. I need to be honest with this incredible man and tell him what happened between his brother and I. Guilt hits me too, wondering if I should have told him before we did anything at all. It's too late for me to worry about any of that now. I just need to tell.

"So, will you stay? I can drop you off at work," he says wishfully.

"I supposed I could. I have a locker at work with everything I need."

Roan sets the alarm and pulls the covers back for both of us. The comfort of his warm masculine body next to mine feels a hundred times better than climbing into a cold bed by myself. Resting my head on his shoulder, I stare out into the star-lit sky, the lights from New York City glowing.

"I have something to tell you."

Please god, don't let him hate me.

"Go on," he says while stroking my hair.

"The night before I left for England, I went to break it off with your brother."

I feel his body tense beside me. I don't know where the strength comes from, but I place my arm around his middle and pull myself in closer to him.

"I found out about his drug use. I wanted no part of it. I also found out his drugs were the reason why he left all of you. I knew I was leaving in the fall for England, but when I found all of that out, I had my dad pull some strings. He came back and told me I was leaving in a couple of days. I was so young. I didn't know what to do. All I knew was, I had to at least be honest with Royal and tell him why I was leaving early and hope he would quit doing them."

I hesitate for a moment.

"I hate the kind of life my parents live. The things my dad does. I've never wanted anything to do with any of it. I don't know why I got messed up with him in the first place."

I feel so ashamed now. I told myself I could live without a man. But now that I've met Roan, I know I can't. I don't mean any man. I mean him. I don't want to live without him.

"How did my brother take it when you told him?"

I sit up quickly, my mind remembering exactly what he did to me.

"Alina." Roan's worried voice brings a rush of tears to my eyes.

"Give me a moment," I ask.

Quiet surrounds me until I gather my strength to carry on.

"He... threw me on his bed and beat me. I have a scar across my butt to prove it."

"What the fuck?"

"Yeah. That's what I say now. But then, I was devastated. That's not all, though. Let me get this out or I won't have the strength to say it."

I can feel him at my back, his breathing erratic.

"He held me down and drugged me."

"Jesus Christ."

He jumps out of the bed. I sit there staring into the night. The hardest part is yet to come and he's pacing like a madman, breathing heavy like he's been running for hours.

"I don't remember much after that. When I finally woke up hours later, he was gone. But I knew. I knew my nightmare had only begun. I tried to get up, but he had me tied to the bed. Don't ask me how I got free, I just did. I… I went to sit up, to get the hell out of there and…"

Oh, god. I put my face in my hands, my knees to my chest.

"And what? What did he do?" he whispers from beside me.

"He raped me when I was blacked out. He stole my virginity from me."

"Fucking hell, baby. Come here."

He gathers me in his arms like a baby. I can't explain why, but when I'm in his arms like this, I feel safe. In addition, I have exposed my deepest, darkest secret to him and he's not judging me. He's not screaming. He's comforting me. Holding me like he wants to. Giving me the space I need. My tears fall silently onto his bare chest. Being in his arms gives me the strength I need to finish to tell him the rest.

"I gathered my clothes and left. Went home and showered. The next morning, I lied to my entire family about why I had big puffy eyes from crying. I told them, even though I was excited to go, I was going to miss them all. It was one of the first times I intentionally lied to my parents and my brothers. I was humiliated, distraught. I've told one other person about this, Roan. Two now, including you."

I sigh nervously, not knowing how he's going to respond.

"You've kept this to yourself to protect the people you love, didn't you?"

His words come through gritted teeth. The way his body shifts and stiffens, I can tell he's getting angry. Not at me, at the situation.

"Yes. It didn't matter to me that dad thought the world of him or that he was the son of his nemesis. It would have started a war. Innocent people would have been killed, and I couldn't let that happen."

My stomach bunches up in a bundle of knots full of worry.

"God, Alina. Do you know how much I respect you right now? For you to protect the people you love, even people you don't know, shows me the kind of woman you are. I knew you were an angel. You amaze me."

My heart feels like it's going to pound right out of my chest. I'm no angel. I'm a coward.

"That's not true," I say.

"Don't you see? If I had told my dad, Royal would have never done the things he did to you and Calla. My dad would have killed him."

"We can't change the past, baby. You did what you felt was the right thing to do. Please don't ever let me hear you blame yourself again for his actions. None of the things that sick fucker does are your fault. None. Royal has been fucked up his entire life. I could go on and on about some of the sick things he has done. I promise you I will find him, and when I do, Alina, I'm going to kill him."

I cringe at the word kill. But if anyone deserves to die, it's Royal.

I stare at the alarm clock, counting every second of every minute that ticks by, the two of us lost in our own thoughts. The heavy burden lifted off of my shoulders, I feel lighter. The memories will never completely fade away. That horrible night will haunt me for the rest of my life. Right now, I need him to know one more thing, and then I want to erase this conversation from my mind. Go back to getting to know this man who has somehow broken through my wall of protecting my heart.

"There's one more thing."

I've met a man I can see myself falling in love with. I can only hope that he can see what I'm about to tell him as a good thing, as an incredible beginning to whatever or wherever this relationship between the two of us leads. Without hesitation, I lift off of his lap and reach for the light beside his bed. I need to look into his incredible eyes when I tell him this, to see his reaction and for him to see that I'm truly elated. His eyes blink, as do mine, adjusting to the light that now casts a glowing shadow across us. His features are conflicted. Stormy eyes etched in such a hard line of turmoil, sadness, and revenge gaze back at me; his anger trying hard to steal his self-control. The one thing I'm searching for down to the underlying center is pity. I see none at all. My heart leaps up when I trace the frown on his forehead, wishing it to disappear. The last thing I want to do is add more pain to Roan. Royal is his brother and no matter what he has done to me, to him or anyone else, it has to hurt beyond anything I can begin to imagine.

"I've never been with a man since Royal."

I watch him. The raging storm that filled his eyes dissipates right in front of me, turning into the clear blue skies after that storm.

"Don't you see, Roan?" I ask, yearning for him to understand what I'm trying to tell him. "I remember nothing after he drugged me. My body may not be a virgin, but my mind is. My heart is. And it's been saved for you."

He doesn't seem to be turned off in the slightest by my lack of experience—or none for better terms. Instead, he smiles this all pearly white teeth-baring, body, heart, and soul smile.

"What I see, Alina, is a woman who is even more beautiful on the inside than she is on the outside. A woman who to me is the definition of strength. It had to be hard to tell me what you did. I will never hurt you, not intentionally anyway. I will worship you, beautiful lady. In fact," he draws me to within less of an inch of his mouth, "I'm going to start by worshipping this mouth."

Chapter Eight

Roan

"Are you going to kill that fucking punching bag or are you going to tell me what the fuck crawled up your ass and died there?"

I glance to my right where Cain is standing with a towel draped around his neck from his workout. I haven't moved from this spot in my gym since I dropped Alina off at work over an hour ago. Every muscle in my arms, neck, and back is on fire. I keep pushing myself, blind rage overshadowing my every thought, repeating word for word in my mind what she told me.

My fucking brother is a rapist. He drugged and raped her. Left her there. I knew he was fucked up, but this...this is worse than anything he has ever done. Murdering people who don't deserve to live is one thing, but to rape a woman, my woman, is another. I'm going to find that piece of shit, and when I do, his death will be ten times worse than any kill he has ever done.

"Fuck you, man."

Taking one last punch at the bag, my body stills. I turn my back on my best friend.

"Roan. What the fuck? Talk to me."

Cain hands me a bottle of water. I down it in in a few gulps, then throw the empty bottle up against the wall.

Cain's the only man I can trust with this. We've been through hell and back together. We will ride and die together. He's the only one I can talk to. If word about this gets out to anyone, it will destroy Alina. Not only that, god only knows what the fuck will go down between our two families. The thought of anyone hurting her kills me.

I study my chest heaving up and down in the mirror, my fury from last night unleashing like a torrent inside of me. I didn't sleep at all. Instead, I held her all night. Her soft skin up against mine was the only thing that kept me calm. I knew flipping my shit in front of her would scare her. That's the last thing she needs after trusting me with her worst nightmare. I cannot begin to imagine her only telling one person what happened. She should have been able to go to her family. Instead she held it in. Protecting people. No one should have to carry something so tragic by themselves for so many years. This life we all live holds many sacrifices. One of them should not be a woman being raped by a man who continues to work for her dad after stealing her innocence. If Ivan had known about this when it happened, he would have killed Royal. I cannot get this out of my head. I may never get it out.

My eyes drift over to Cain, who is standing there with his brows furrowed, a worried expression on his face.

"Alina told me something last night. Something that happened between her and my brother."

My eyes never waver from his.

"This something would be what? They had sex and you can't handle it?" he says jokingly. I spin on him like a motherfucking dime. He jerks his head back, holds his hands up in surrender. "Hold the fuck on, Roan. It was as god damn joke. Talk to me, brother."

My temper blazes. I'm aiming it at the wrong person. The only brother I truly have.

"Fuckkkkkkk," I roar. .

Holding my arms out wide, I lift my head up towards the ceiling.

"Jesus, Roan. What the hell did he do?"

His voice seems to trail off into the distance. All I can hear is Alina's soft voice saying *'he raped me,'* over and over in my mind.

"He raped her, man. My brother raped her."

My legs give out, my shoulders tighten, my chest heaves up and down when I spit out those vile words.

"Fuck, man. No."

Cain is kneeling down on the floor in front of me, a firm grip on my shoulders, pain etched across his face.

"Jesus. When did he do this?" he pleads for me to tell him. I roll back onto my legs until I am face to face with my true brother. For over an hour we stay that way while I tell him everything she told me, making plans and discussing how I feel about my own brother being the kind of man he is.

Anger and sadness mixed with helplessness collide with each other. He's out there somewhere. Hiding, plotting, and waiting to strike. I fucking know he is.

"I'm not asking you, man, I'm telling you to not even tell Calla about this." My command is sharp.

"I love my wife, but this... Hell, no. She wouldn't be able to handle something like this. And you know I would never betray you."

"I know. We have to find him. The thought of him doing this to her or to any other woman makes me sick. I don't understand how someone can do such a thing. How the fuck is he even my brother? If my mom found out, it would put an end to her. It would kill her."

My fatigued body falls back. I lie there, nausea rolling in my stomach.

"You need to talk to your dad and tell him to put a halt to his plans on training you to take over the Diamond Empire. Tell him you want to finish this business with finding Royal before you can concentrate on anything else. He's a reasonable man. He'll understand. Besides, he isn't ready to give up his thrown quite yet."

My chest tightens thinking about how many of my loved ones this could destroy. Not only mine, but Alina's too. Her parents, her brothers. And then it hits me. Another person who might be willing to help. Our paths have crossed one another's several times. I have to have faith he will keep this to himself.

"Let's go shower. I have a plan."

A few hours later, the two of us are pulling into the street where Alina's brother Anton lives. After our talk, I took a long hot shower to try and ease the tension building inside of me. That shit didn't work. Nothing will work until I drive a knife straight through Royal's black heart.

"She's walking home tonight, Beamer, do not fucking lose her."

My body twitches, bracing for an argument from him to bitch me out on the phone.

"I got her, man. Trust me," he says.

"I trust you. It's just..."

"It's just you care about her. I get it. I got her back and yours."

His remark is a straight punch to the gut. He needs to know what the hell he's up against if Royal catches on to him.

"Listen, man. There's some shit I found out last night. Shit I don't want to talk to you about over the phone. I'm begging you, man, don't lose her. Don't even blink. Got me?" I clip, then hang up once we set a time to meet.

"You sure about this? I mean, he is her brother and we're showing up at his house unannounced at ten in the fucking morning to tell the dude some shit that is going to fuck him up," Cain asks when I cut the engine on my truck.

"I'm sure. The two of them are close. He won't tell anyone about this." I know I'm going to feel guilty about this. It feels like I'm betraying her trust. But it needs to be done. We need her family's help. I try to reel in my rapid breathing. I'm about as calm as I'm going to get. I reach under the seat for my gun, tucking it into the front of my jeans. Cain widens his eyes in my direction.

"You never fucking know." I cock a brow along with a devious smirk.

"All right, asshole. Let's do this. Control your shit before you get in there." My shit will never be under control until I kill a man who doesn't even deserve to be breathing.

Both of us climb out, my eyes scanning the rural neighborhood. I wonder how all of these people in this residential area like the idea of having the son of Ivan Solokov living right under their noses. He's a family man. Married with the white picket fence. The big ass fancy brick house. A god damn minivan in his drive, for Christ sake. And the brother of the woman I'm not afraid to say I'm falling hard for.

"May I help you?" An incredibly beautiful, petite, dark-haired woman answers the door. I've seen her around with Anton at a few social events. This is his wife Andrea.

"Good morning. I'm—"

"I know who you are. Both of you," she cuts me off.

"Who is it, babe?" Anton steps up behind her.

"Roan. Cain. What the fuck are you doing here?" I watch him clench his jaw, working it back and forth.

"It's personal, Anton. I really think you're going to want to hear me out." A sharp scream pierces from behind them.

"Those kids are at it again. I'm going to kick Brady's ass if he's dragging Olivia around by her hair again." Andrea slides under her husband's arm, which is now gripping the top of the door.

"Meet me out back." He points to the side of his house.

We make our way down the sidewalk leading to the drive and the back of the house, open the latch on the gate, then securing it behind us. Both of us take a seat on chairs the farthest away from the house.

I relocate my gaze from the covered pool to Anton when he passes through a sliding glass door then eases it shut. It's hard as hell to read what is going through his mind. He's one mean-looking son of a bitch, I can tell you that. The two of them look a lot alike, except she's always smiling while this guy looks like he wants to kick our ass.

"What's so important, Roan?" His body is tense. He remains rooted to the spot at least a good two feet away from us.

"Shit, man. You need to sit down for what I'm about to tell you," I state loud and fucking clear.

"So help me god, if you hurt my sister in any mother fucking way—"

"It's not me who's hurt her, fuck-head. It's my lowlife brother. Now sit the fuck down." Both of us raise our voices louder than I want.

"Listen, maybe telling him here isn't such a good idea." Cain stands.

"The fuck? You said Royal. Did you find him? And where's Alina?" He paces forward until the two of us are practically chest-to-chest.

"She's at work. No, I haven't found him. If I did, he would be dead. And yes, I said Royal. Now, I didn't come here to argue with you. I came here to tell you something Alina told me last night about my brother. Fuck!" I look into his eyes that look so much like hers.

"Is he threatening her?" I shake my head, exhale, and spill my fucking guts out.

"Jesus motherfucker! Not her," Anton chants repeatedly while pacing the deck around his pool. Neither Cain nor I say a damn word while he works this shit out in his head. Gravity fucking stops. I swear to Christ it dead fucking stops when he drops to his knees on the fucking ground. He fists his hair with one hand. Places the other over his mouth and screams a rip-roaring, painful scream.

"Anton, man. I'm so fucking sorry. I don't know what else to do. Fuck man, I care about her. You have no idea how much I really care about your sister." We watch him punch his fist into the ground, shaking his head. Anton looks up. His eyes are full of blameless anger.

"I fucking begged her to let me take her when she went to tell him she was leaving. She wouldn't listen. She actually looked at me and said, "You do drugs, Anton. What makes you any better than he is?" She was right. Alina has always been right. I was no better than he was at the time. So I let her go. I let her go to him. My sweet sister. I let her fucking go." Anguished agony is written all over his face.

I have no idea why I turn towards the house. When I do, his wife is standing at the window, her hands pressed up firmly against it. She never once takes her eyes off of him, concern, mixed with love in her features. She knows her place. This I can tell. She will stand there and wait for him to either go to her or beckon her to him. I shoot my gaze back to a man I now respect, the plague of guilt eating him, and am thankful Alina has a family that loves her.

"We need to find him. Work together, that's why you're here? That's why you're telling me this, isn't it? You want our families to come together to find him instead of each of us working separate. That's it, isn't it." The ache in his chest is visible to me with his trembling words. The Diamonds and The Solokovs working side by side to destroy a man who has betrayed us all.

"It's been long enough. He needs to pay for what he has done. Pay in ways he himself has never even thought of. I want him tortured to the verge where he's ready to pass out, then bring that motherfucker back over and over again until we say enough. Until we say it's time for him to die. So, to answer your question, yes, I want our families to come together. Not for me. But for her. For Alina," I say truthfully. My chest is heaving like his. We stare each other down, neither one of us ready to back off, the two of us seeking out each other's trust.

"Do you know he actually had the fucking nerve to act heartbroken when she left?" he whispers to me.

"He hurt my baby sister and he acted heartbroken. My family took that drug addict crazy motherfucker and treated him like one of us. Hell, until he pulled that shit with you and Calla..." he breaks his stare from me and tilts his head to look at Cain. "We all took him in. Even though we knew he used. We knew he bought that shit we fucking sell. Hell, I've seen the lowlife buying the shit myself. I never judged the son of a bitch, how could I when I used to do the shit myself? We all ignored what the mighty Scarface was doing because that fucker could kill. He did our dirty work. The shit jobs none of us wanted to do. Well, I'll tell you this. He is going to pay. I will call a meeting with my brothers, and he is going to fucking pay." Anton stands and digs his hand in his front pocket, dragging out his phone, his fingers moving meticulously over the screen.

"My parents will never learn of this," he rasps.

"Neither will mine," I say.

"Good. I will meet with my brothers. Then we'll be in touch." He shoves his phone back in his pocket.

"Fair enough," I say.

I'm shocked when he steps up to me, nose-to-nose, man to man, and holds his hand out for me to take. I grasp a hold of it firmly.

"This has to be hard for you, Roan. Blood is Blood. Family is family. It took guts for you to show up here and rip my fucking heart out. It shows me how much you care about Alina, where your loyalties lie. This I can promise you. As long as you watch over her, treat her with respect, because brother, you may know this already. She's not cut out for this life. She never has been. Unlike the rest of us, she has a heart. Even though I hoped she would find someone outside this lifestyle to care for her, the way I see it as I stand before you, she found the right man. Because once you find something like what I have right there," he tilts his head towards his wife, "it makes all this fucked-up shit we do worth it when you can come home to a woman who loves you simply for what you have in here and here." Anton points to his head and his heart.

"Ain't that the damn truth?" Cain acknowledges.

"One more thing," Anton declares as we turn to leave.

"She's kept to herself a long time and now I know why. Love her, man. Show her what it's like."

"If anyone deserves to be loved, it's her." His pained expression travels into his affirmation.

"My word belongs to her, Anton. Her alone. If it didn't, I wouldn't be standing here. A man like you can understand that. A woman like Alina deserves everything. I intend to give it to her."

"Let me know what the hell's going on?" Cain calls out when I drop him off in front of our apartment building. "Will do," he nods in agreement.

An hour later, I'm sitting across from my dad in his office trying like hell to come up with an excuse for him to let me ease off. I've known my whole life I've been expected to rule the Diamond empire. He has to know I can't give it my all, to learn everything there is to know, when my loyalties lie elsewhere.

Salvatore Diamond is no fool. He can smell a lie before it's even spoken. I swore to myself I didn't want him to know what Royal did to Alina. But I have to tell him. I have to crush my dad, hurt him more than he's been hurting for years over the loss of one of his sons. He's well aware of my every move. He knows what must be done. I admire this man who is well aware that one of his children will be taking the life of the other. Doesn't make it any easier to speak those words out loud.

"What brings you by, son? Are you here to finally tell me all about you and the mysterious Alina Solokov?" he asks with a polite smile.

"Yes and no," I reply.

"What's troubling you, Roan?" His mouth goes tight.

"How the hell do you do it, dad?"

"Do what exactly? All of this?" he asks, waving his hand throughout his office.

"That, plus keep your emotions in check. Never show weakness. Never let anyone know when you're troubled?"

"Well, I'll be damned." My dad's face calms, a slight smirk of amusement on his mouth.

"What, old man?" I mock his smirk.

"My boy has gone and fallen for a woman." His grin is slightly curved and his eyes are a whole hell of a lot playful, and all I can think about is yes, I'm falling for a woman. And how what I'm about to tell him about her and my brother is going to wipe his happiness clean off his face.

Chapter Nine

Alina

I take a deep breath and open my eyes to examine my appearance in the mirror. Deidre has been fussing over me for the past hour like a mother bird.

"You look remarkable, Alina." Shaking my head, I let my thoughts travel to last night talking to Roan on the phone as well as the other night in his penthouse and the way he made me feel. The sweet things he says and does. He makes me feel alive. Childlike, really. I can honestly sit here and see brightness in my eyes. A happy woman staring back at me when I look at her. I'm looking for the good in people now instead of the bad. I've been surrounded by so much sadness my entire life, shut myself out of living outside of school and work, and as I gaze at my smoky makeup, my smiling lips with a natural gloss on, I feel confident about myself. I owe it all to him. I only hope I'm not making a mistake by going through with all of this and following my heart.

"Am I a fool for giving up my promise to myself to stay clear of men involved in the mafia?" I take my gaze away from my reflection and look at Deidre, who's standing behind me.

"Alina?" She stares at me. I can tell by the way she says my name with annoyance that the serious Deidre is coming out. I haven't told her or anyone what happened the other night between Roan and me. For the first time in a very long time, I lied.

Deidre knew I spent the night with him. Tried like hell to get me to tell her, or should I say got down on her hands and knees and prayed that I finally got laid, only to be sadly disappointed when I told her nothing happened.

She didn't believe me at first. Pestered me for over an hour, driving me insanely nuts, until I finally told her we talked for most of the night. Which wasn't a lie. Finally she relented and gave up after I told her about our date tonight. She begged me to promise her I wouldn't deny myself a good pussy pounding as she called it. Which leads us to now after a very long and sad two days at work. Ones I would much rather forget about.

I love my job, wouldn't give it up for anyone, but when you have a family come in with concerns when their child is all of a sudden bruising easily, sleeping more, and showing a loss of appetite, only to run tests and find out they have leukemia, your spirits fail you. The hardest part is to sit down and tell a family that you are referring them to an oncologist. It's a parent's worst fear. A selfish feeling zips through me, thinking I am heading out for a night of fun, a night to try and help me escape from my thoughts of this family, while they are home trying to cope with the news I delivered to them today.

"Where did you just go?" Concern is stamped in Deidre's voice. I wave her off and stand. "I had a thought about an unpleasant conversation at work today. I'm fine."

"I don't know how you can do it. And I know you can't talk about it. Whatever it is, please don't let it ruin your night, Alina. You're a good woman and an incredible doctor with the biggest heart of any person I know." I balk somewhat, ready to tell her that's not true, that she's the one with a big heart. She's the one who has sacrificed a lot of her time to stay home with a boring person like me when she's been invited out, but I don't get that far because our doorbell rings. That joyous feeling sinks back into my bones while at the same time my nerves become so unsettled I feel as if I could retch.

"Stop fidgeting, you crazy woman. I'll grab the door." She flies out of the room, her hair a flash of all kinds of black strands swishing in the air. Laughing, my mood lightens at watching my bubbly friend. I check my appearance in the mirror one last time. I feel sexy, alive for truly the first time ever. It's as if I've been waiting, subconsciously hoping for a man like Roan to come in and sweep me off my feet my entire life.

Grabbing my clutch, I sigh. I see a woman I barely recognize and fly out of my room like a child on her last day of school, ready to start a summer full of fun, trouble, and memories. I come to a sudden halt. I'm shaking, panting even, when I see the man standing in my doorway talking casually to Deidre. He's... oh hell. He's a modern day bad man, dressed in an all-black suit, a green tie matching the green in my dress. The wall leading into our foyer shadows me. I do that little quaking thing in my shoes. The most lewd flashes of ripping that perfectly fit suit off of his body just so I can bite and touch it anywhere I want to blaze in my thoughts. I don't know what it is about him that separates Roan Diamond from any other man who has asked me out before. His line of work scares me. I hate it, but standing here gawking at him like a looter ready to make her attack and hoard all the good stuff, my heart pounding through this dress, I feel like I have been waiting for him my entire life.

"Hey." His force of power draws me to him. He makes no secret about how much he likes what he sees. My focus is trained on his scruff, which just a few days ago scraped between my legs. Chafing my neck, my face in the most indescribable way.

"Sweet mother of god. You are a fucking vision, Alina. I'm in so much trouble." He is eyeing me up and down with hunger in his eyes. The difference between his hunger and the ways other men look at me are like night and day. Roan looks at me like he would cherish every part me, while when I catch other men looking at me, they look like all they want is whatever they can get to satisfy their hungry needs.

"You sure the hell are, buddy. You packing a gun tonight?" Deidre and her unfiltered mouth break up our sexual tension.

"Always." Bringing his hand out to clasp me by my elbow, he guides me straight into his chest, his eyes never leaving mine once he's made it abundantly clear by his inspection that he likes what he sees.

"Good lord. I'm going to be surprised if the two of you haven't started a fire in here by the way your sparks are flying all over the damned place." I hear her, but I can't take my eyes off of him. His stark ones not leaving my face either. And those sparks she's referring to seem to always be there when I'm around him. He's slowly bringing me to life, a life that had been led around by my mind due to experiencing all the evilness in this world. I've believed my entire life that most men come from evil. There's the good, the bad, and the so very ugly. Roan Diamond may have all those traits in his day job, but for once in my pitiful life, I don't care. The good inside of him outweighs all the rest. That's the trait inside of him I focus on.

"You ready, beautiful lady?" His voice is deep, raspy. Dripping with ungodly amounts of 'I want to show you, make you feel things that neither one of us have ever felt before.' I tweak. I twinge. I want to shove my hands underneath the short part of this dress and stroke myself right here in front of him instead of the confines of my bedroom, which over the past few weeks since he's disrupted my life in a good way, I've been doing more of. I'm a new woman. A woman who's dying to live on the edge tonight. To let him take me wherever he wants. Do whatever he wants as long as when it's all over, the last thing I hear him say is my name, for reasons I'm still trying to figure out. I could so easily see myself placing my timid heart in the hands of this brutally handsome man.

"Don't forget this." Deidre watches me with humor and mischief dancing through her thundering, I'm-so-envious-of-you eyes.

Bashfully, I seize hold of my small overnight bag she took upon herself to pack for me. "Thank you," I say through gritted teeth. I give her an I-will-kill-you-later glare, which in return has her rolling her eyes right back, saying "you'll thank me later." Like hell I will. Embarrassment floods my cheeks.

"I've got it." Roan graciously pulls my bag from my hand the minute we shut the door behind us. Strong fingers snake down the delicate bare skin of my shoulders, gripping my waist to draw me into him.

"God damn, how did I get so lucky? You've sparked something inside of me, Alina Solokov." That one word—spark, the beginning to a fire, a storm brewing, a desirable connection between two people. That spark could easily be doused out with how wet I'm becoming between my legs.

His soft but firm lips take mine by surprise. Needy, greedy for me to open up. I do. My mouth tingles, my mind is in sync with my heart. His impaling gaze locked on mine while his tongue sweeps inside of my mouth, I melt. This man could possess me. There is no mistaking whatsoever when he kisses me, letting me set the pace and then taking over in a dominating way, that he wants me. A woman who has never been with a man. None of that seems to matter anymore. I want him too. I'm slipping, falling into the abyss of an erotic stagger, my mind no longer sleeping, my heart leaping.

"Let's go before I decide to drive us right to my place," he whispers into my ear.

"Where are we going?" I am eager to get our night started. "Dinner at Le Main. Then dancing at Provocateur." A smile taps its way across those lips I will never get enough of.

"Two of my favorite places. How did you ever know?" I tease when he opens his car door, one strong finger scaling down inside of the crisscross of my dress until it rests just above the swell of my ass.

"If I'm going to impress my girl, I need to know the things she likes. The places she likes to go. It's my job to know everything about you, Alina." His girl? His job? Oh, my Lord!

Crossing the street to his car, I cannot help but think I should be scared out of my skin. My head should be doing a freak out dance. My heart should be running down the road, scared to even let anyone come near it, and here I sit, driving through the heavy Friday night traffic, content, excited, and downright giddy as a teenager because he called me his girl.

Roan holds my hand the entire drive to Le Main, stroking his thumb over my heated skin, sending waves of desire down to my toes. He holds my hand as we enter the low-lit romantic setting of the restaurant, never letting me go until I'm seated in my chair by the waiter. The wine he orders is tested and poured into our glasses. The entire conversation is smooth and easy, his questions directed towards my job. He's making the entire night so far all about me. Telling me the one thing he wants to know more about is my passion for the children. I tell him everything. From the good to the bad, leaving out the identities of them all. His compassion runs deep when I touch briefly on the family today. It's as if he has the ability to draw my worries out of me.

To make me see the good inside myself. How it takes a special person to commit their life to taking care of the sick.

This isn't an individual gravity field, the pull between the two of us is shared, I feel it in every fiber of my being. Roan Diamond may live the life I've told myself repeatedly I want no part of, now that I have him in my life, I'm willing to give in, to sacrifice, because the more I get to know him, the more I cannot see my life without him in it.

"Thank you," I say as he helps me out of the car when we park in front of the valet at the club. A place where if you're lucky enough to be here at the right time, you may catch a glimpse of a Hollywood celebrity. Provocateur, is dark, mysterious. You can come alive in the most provocative of ways. The name speaks for itself.

Roan tosses his keys to the valet driver and places his hand on the small of my back, guiding me gently into the club as we pass a line of men and women waiting anxiously to enter. His presence is known by everyone. We're guided to a secluded booth in the back. It's packed. It's gorgeous. It's decorated in every color above and under the rainbow. Deep purples, vibrant greens, bold blues. Music is pumping through everyone's veins, the beat sensual, seductive.

A waitress dressed in a sexy yet classy skin-tight black dress takes our drink order. Her eyes drag up and down Roan. Jealousy tugs at my skin. A remote emotion I've never felt before. "Can she bring us our drinks before you kill her with your looks?" his arrogant but laughing voice whispers in my ear. Heat is rushing to my face from embarrassment.

"Why do woman think it's ok to ogle a man like that?" Bravery and a whole heck of a lot of insecurity leech their way out of my mouth. "Let her look. My eyes didn't even notice her, Alina. My eyes are glued to the woman who I guarantee men are looking at right now, praying to a god most of them don't even believe in, that they were me."

"You're smooth, Mr. Diamond." I place a kiss on his cheek.

"I might be, but I also speak the truth, Miss Solokov. The mere idea that I know you have no clue how captivating you really are, how heads fucking turn when you walk into a room—and believe me, they turn—is the sweet part.

"I noticed you." Instinctively, those three words slip from my mouth.

"And I'm one lucky son of a bitch that you did." He drags me to him. Plants his lips close to mine. "I could care less if every man in this entire building looks at you. As long as I'm the only man who touches you. Who drives you wild tonight when your body rubs up against mine when you dance. When those lips who are begging to be kissed right now seek out only mine when they want to be devoured, and when I'm the one who takes you home and peels this dress off and takes this insanely one of a kind, molded-to-perfection body to bed." Good lord. My breath hitches. Visions swirl in my head as slowly as the steady beat of the bass playing in the background, visions of Roan taking me places I've never been before, of me succumbing to him, of him guiding and teaching me how to please him, drive him as blustery mad as he makes me.

"I'm drawn to you, Roan. It's thrilling and frightening all in one. You make me want to open my heart and feel."

"Then feel me. Feel me everywhere. Feel me here." Right there in the middle of the overly crowded nightclub, he inclines his head, placing a kiss right over my heart. Then without a care in the world, he scoops me onto his lap and devours my aching lips, that god yes, are begging him to kiss me.

"What's the craziest thing you've ever done?" Roan asks out of the blue. We've been screaming over the loud music for the last half hour, talking. It's crazy how much you can learn about another person when you solely focus on them. Of course, my eyes seem to stay glued to his lips whenever he speaks. Once he notices, he stops to take my mouth then carries on. Swirling my finger around the rim of my wine glass, I contemplate his question. He's going to find me rather boring, actually. I haven't done much crazy in my entire life.

"I'm rather boring," I'm speaking truthfully. "However, I guess taking off to England on my own at the age of eighteen."

I stare into his deep eyes. His reaction is quite amusing the way he's smirking.

"We have a lot in common, you and I. You see, I left home at sixteen. Although, my circumstances were different than yours, and I had my Aunt and Uncle around." He smiles cheekily.

I've heard the stories about him moving to Michigan. Training with his uncle, Calla's dad. Roan is a dangerous man. To me he's anything but... he's kind, caring and one hell of a piece of eye candy. I could stay here all night just staring at him.

"Dance with me?" he asks, extending his hand to help me out of the booth. The music turns to slow and sensual with a song I've never heard, the beat reminding me of sex.

Pushing his way through the crowd with his hand firmly holding mine, he finds a tight spot on the dance floor. Bodies are molded to one another. Lovers dancing seductively.

I'm shocked when he pulls my back to his front, his strong hands gripping my waist, his warm breath on my neck, his hard body pressed up against mine. I suck in a breath, my body moving with his.

With a mind of their own, my hands cover his, guiding them up and down my hips as we veer on the edge of physical seduction on the dance floor. Our hands glide up and down my ribs sensually, his large erection pressing into my backside. You would expect me to be nervous, scared, and yet I'm not. The heat radiating off of his body has me in a tailspin of arousal. I want him. And then, oh my god. When he licks up the back of my neck, a chill passes through my body. Wetness collects between my legs. I'm about to pull away when he spins me to face him.

"Let me take you home," he growls into my ear. I nod. Like a man on a mission, he grabs my hand. No words are spoken. He muscles his way up to the bar, catches the eye of the waitress, and hands her a few hundred-dollar bills. And just like that we are in his car and driving in the direction of his place.

Now that we're entirely alone, my mind starts to reel. I'm frightened. I fidget. I cannot sit still.

"As much as I want you, Alina, I would never do anything you're not ready for." God, the raspy way he says my name, like I'm a treasure to be opened when the time is right, makes me want him like I've never wanted anything before. I trust him. It's me and thoughts of my past I don't trust. I bury those vulgar thoughts. They will not destroy the best thing that has happened to me. I won't let them.

"I want you too." I turn to face him. His jaw is flexing. God, he's beautiful and experienced. I have no doubt about that. *Stop it, Alina,* I tell my silly mind.

The rest of the drive is quiet. We pull into his parking garage. He helps me out of his car and as we climb into the elevator, my heart pounding rapidly, I watch the floors tick by when it hits me. In my mind I'm going to lose my virginity tonight. That's where I leave my thoughts when we enter his penthouse. Soft lights are illuminating the hallway.

"Would you like a drink?" he asks, The tenseness leaking out of his voice.

"No, thanks. What I'd like is for you to take me to your bed," I state boldly, a shock to both of us that those words were expelled from me. He slowly turns, his eyes penetrating as dark as the night sky.

"You sure?"

"Positive."

I follow him into his room, swallowing several times.

"You are so damn beautiful." He takes hold of both of my hands, walks backwards, and we tumble on top of his bed with him on the bottom and me splayed out across him.

He flips us so he's on top and stares into my eyes. "Let me love you." I nod. Fascinated, overwhelmed, and becoming aware of what it really feels like to be touched by a man who admires me.

He controls our kiss. I'm panting. My brain takes over. I'm no longer scared but anxious to finally be with a man. To feel for the first time in my life what it truly feels like to be worshipped. To be placed in sexual bliss.

I'm consumed with his mouth seeking out every inch of my exposed skin. Featherlike touches torch my flesh. I miss the warmth of his body when he stands and removes his clothes from the waist up. He's perfect. And the tattoos running up his ribcage are something else. It's difficult to make out exactly what they are. Some kind of tribal pattern maybe. It doesn't matter. I want to run my tongue across that tattoo. To divulge the meaning of it into my mouth. My soul.

Extending his hand, he helps me up, tilts my head, and unclasps the back of my dress. Taking a strap in each of his hands, he drags the dress down my body. My breasts are exposed. He stills when he lowers himself to the floor, my dress falling down with him. "Fuck." His crude word has me chuckling. Hands glide up my legs until he's cupping my naked sex.

"All night long you've had no panties under this dress?" He removes his hand and replaces it with his face, inhaling my sex and blowing right onto my core. I throw my head back. A loud moan escapes my throat. Roan stands, his fingers moving to his pants. I want to remember everything. The way he unzips them, drags them down his legs. Toeing off his shoes. Kicking them to the side. Stepping out of his pants. Seeing them on the floor next to my dress. I travel up his muscular legs. Watch his fingers delve into the waistband of his boxers. My legs give out when I see how truly huge he is. My ass hits the bed. His cock is in my face and if I knew what the hell I was doing, I would take him in my mouth. He chuckles once again, surprising me when he lowers himself to the floor and removes my shoes. Both of us are naked. When he stands, my eyes devour him. My god, I've never seen anything like him. Heat blisters my entire being. The way he looks back at me fondly, as if he's making sure I'm ready for this. And I am. I've never wanted to submit. To feel pleasure, to be pushed beyond boundaries I know absolutely nothing about.

"Let me get the covers." He helps me stand. I'm an inferno of passion when he lightly traces my spine with his finger while pulling back the covers with his free hand.

I reach for him, settling in the center of his bed. The sheets feel fresh and cold against my heated skin. And like an electromagnet, he attaches himself to me. Hard against soft, man against woman. My legs spread, feeling him press up against me.

"Tell me you want me, Alina, because god, I've wanted you since the moment I saw you. You've done something to me, something I cannot explain. It's like you've been sent to me, not only to protect, but to cherish, and I never want to do anything to hurt you." I swallow. His words dampen my eyes, this mystery man who entered my life out of nowhere a few months ago. My heart along with my body wants him.

"Yes, Roan Diamond, I want you."

Chapter Ten

Roan

When I'm with Alina, all the bullshit slips away. Instead of plotting ways to draw my drug addict brother out of hiding, I focus on her. She's so damn beautiful it truly is painful to look at her. Not from her looks but for the fact that I cannot believe a woman like her is here with me. In my bed, eyes glazed over with so much lust and want, and I've barely touched her.

How could any man not want a woman like the one beneath me? She squirms when I run my hands across her perked nipples. Soft, sensual sounds escape her mouth when I take one of her nipples and suck, bite, then sooth with my tongue. She responds to my every touch. And like a moth drawn to light, I respond to her. Fuck, especially when she scrapes her nails down my back. I want to take my cock and pound into her so damn bad. Draw out that bad girl in her. Make her naughty. And I will, but not tonight. Tonight, in her mind, Alina is going to really lose her virginity. To me. A man whose life outside of this bedroom is full of so much crime and death. The very same thing she ran away from. She has morals, values, and respect. Something I never had, unless the circumstance calls for it, which in my line of work is rare. I want to be that kind of man for her.

I want her to know she deserves to have the perfect night. The filth erased from her mind of what my sorry excuse of a brother did to her.

I have never been a selfish lover, always taking care of a woman first before I let myself go. As cliché as it sounds, I'm as safe as they come. Always use a condom. Hell, the women I've been with are just as bad as I am. Looking for a one-night stand. No strings. Just a quick fuck.

This is the first time I'm going to make love. I'm falling for her, and it scares me equally as much as it scares her.

She's so wet. Her pussy is clenching my fingers. Her eyes are pleading with me to make her mine. To claim her in the most intimate way.

I think I fell the first time I laid my eyes on her. The first time she spoke, with class and pride. Our entire lives, we've been intertwined with each other. Knowing who the other person was but never meeting. She's always been the untouchable one. The woman who wanted nothing to do with the way her family operates, and yet here she is, in my bed, ready for me to show her everything I can do to make her fall apart. To show her how good we can be together. To watch her come. God. There isn't a woman out there who could even come close to the one I have beneath me. Her beauty radiates all around her. She's the brightest star in the sky, bringing light into my darkness. Placing her untainted soul into my dirtied life. She makes me want something I've never dreamed of having before. She makes me want to crash right into her. To keep her safe. To protect her. And god help me, she makes me want to be a man who is good enough for her.

My dick has never wanted anyone the way he wants her.

I reach around her, pull open the drawer, pulling out a condom.

"No," she says when she eyes the square packet in my hand. "I'm on birth control. I trust you."

Hell, she just made our first time together mean even more to me. I toss the condom behind my back. Bending down, I kiss her. Long, hard, and deep.

"Tell me if I hurt you, Alina." I say, lining up my dick to the entrance of her heat.

"You won't hurt me, Roan, not unless you stop," she says softly.

"Christ, beautiful lady, I couldn't stop now. Not ever." I slide the head of my dick inside of her. Her breath catches. Her eyes go wide. She's tight. Her mouth lets out a gasp. I still for a moment. When her hips move up trying to take me in further, the last bit of my resistance takes over and I sink myself into her. I will never forget the way her vise-like walls are clenching around my dick as I stretch her out. Jesus Christ. She lets out a small whimper. A shudder escapes her, and I move slowly in and out of her. Taking her mouth, feeling her tiny walls. Filling her. My balls are aching. My cock is twitching and my spine is tingling so damn badly. I need to come inside of her now.

"Oh, my god," she moans out, her hips thrusting up.

"Wrap your legs around me, sweetheart." When she does what I ask, I stare into her eyes, her features telling me she's feeling this. The deep connection between the two of us.

When I reach down and press onto her clit, it's as if I've detonated a bomb the way she shoots off the bed. Her back arches. Her cries full of ecstasy.

"Let go, Alina. Give in. Let me watch you come."

"Do that again," she gasps. I rub her clit in slow lazy circles. Her pussy constricts. My cock is having a hell of a time holding back. Our bodies are covered in sweat, her nipples grazing across my chest each time I slide back into her tight sweet pussy. The smell of her arousal mixed with our sweat sends me so close to drive into her hard and fast. I grasp a hold of one of those perky nipples and suck it deep into my mouth. I have no mercy on these heavenly breasts begging for me to capture and play. The rumbling from her throat, the way my name sounds when it escapes her mouth, has got to be the most beautiful thing I have ever heard. I swirl my tongue around her nipple, my eyes focused on her, when I know she finally comes, her breathing becoming erratic, her glazed eyes looking deeply into mine. She is the most stunning woman I have had the privilege of looking at.

"God. You are so incredible." Picking up the pace for a few more drawn-out strokes, my cock cannot resist slamming into her. I stop mid-stroke, then root inside her as far as I can get, releasing months of pent-up dreams and hopes of finally being inside of her, the feeling of filling her completely. Her eyes are looking up at me with an emotion that tells me she feels the same way I do about her.

"You were worth waiting for, Roan," she whispers. I close my eyes, those six words searing into my brain, my heart, forever. I rest my forehead against hers. Close my eyes and stay inside of her. When I finally pull out, I capture her in my arms. Holding, caressing, and loving the way she feels lying beside me.

"Fuck me, Alina, you're a naughty woman." Her sex drive is insatiable. The light is on beside the bed. Alina is riding my cock like she's starving for it. This is the third time we've had sex. The first two times, I made love to her. This time though, she is fucking me wild, her breast bouncing. Her pussy constricting. My cock finally in heaven and god damn, she feels so good.

"I can't get enough of you," she screams out, picking up her pace. Her hair is all messed up, her eyes large as she is slamming down on my cock. She grips me so hard, my urge to drive into her takes over and I flip us. She squeals. She wants to fuck, then

I'll show her how I can fuck. I pound her tight pussy. Her hands come up and palm her breast. Pinching her nipples. Squirming beneath me. Her mouth parts, moans like I've never heard before escaping those lips. I want those lips on mine. I bite. I nip. I take her tongue and suck it into my mouth. Our teeth gnash. And I fuck her. My secret naughty girl. Her hand slides gracefully down her stomach, ending to where we are connected. My gaze moves down to watch. Jesus, she rubs her clit and cries out my name once again.

"I'm coming," she screams so loud I swear to god they can hear her all the way down to the ground. I don't give a shit. It's me who's making her scream. It's me she will remember when she's so sore she won't be able to sit down for dinner at her parent's house. Exploding inside of her one last time, I drop my dead weight on top of her, no longer able to hold my body up. Not wanting to pull myself out of her either.

She skims her fingers up and down my back. Our breathing is subsiding. We both wince when I finally pull out and let her get herself from under me. I slap her round ass when she stands up and enters the bathroom. Her scar visible to my eyes. I say nothing to her about it. My fist clench at my sides, knowing my brother left that mark on her body. "You'll pay for that," she squeals. "Promise or threat, I'll make sure I do," I say trailing behind her. Her playful tone, the happiness pouring out of her tearing away all thoughts of Royal. He doesn't belong here. Not now, not ever.

I clean both her and myself up, her eyes tracing my every move while I delicately run the warm washcloth between her legs and down her thighs. She doesn't say a word, neither do I. Again, we let our eyes speak. She is thanking me for doing something no one has ever done before, and I am telling her I would do anything to let her know she means so much to me.

Tossing the cloth into the hamper, I leave her to her own thoughts. Entering my room and laughing at the tangled mess of blankets on the floor, I straighten the bed, then pull back the covers and wait for my beauty to grace me.

A few moments later, I hear the flushing of the toilet. She walks out naked. Not ashamed or bashful. My cock twitches once again. I'm thankful she's relaxed after everything we've shared. She snags one of my t-shirts off the chair in the corner, her feet padding across the hardwood floor. By the time she gets to the bed, the shirt is over her head and covering up what is mine.

"Get your ass in here." I lift the covers so she can climb in. The combination of her and me mixed together has me smiling when she lays her head on my chest. My arms instinctively pull her tighter.

"Thank you for tonight. And I don't just mean being gentle with me the first time. I mean dinner, dancing, and just being you." She stares up at me.

"You're welcome. I'll do anything for you, Alina. I mean that." I trace my thumb around her lips.

"I know." Her eyes close. My beautiful lady falls right to sleep, in my arms, where she belongs.

****

"What the hell are you talking about?" I yell into the phone while watching my coffee pot brew a fresh cup for Alina. She's in the shower.

"Cain. God damn it. What is in the fucking package?" *Shit, keep your voice down asshole*, I tell myself. All I need is for Alina to come running out here before I figure out what the hell is happening. The last time Cain sounded so distraught and worried was when Calla left him all those years ago. Something is terribly wrong.

"I don't know, man. All I know is some currier delivered it to Calla at work. I could hardly recognize her voice when she called me screaming and crying. She shouldn't even be working today, god damn it." Wide-ass awake, a slimy feeling slithers down my neck. Cain's voice is strained, on the verge of panic. She's working today because of me. I wanted them working round the clock to get Jackson, one of my men, out of the shit hole he dug for himself; getting hooked up with a damn druggie for a girlfriend and landing his ass in prison, taking the rap for selling cocaine for the dumb bitch just so she wouldn't lose custody of her kids. The bitch doesn't deserve to be a mother anyway. She's right back dealing and spreading her legs for another asshole. But the thing is, I need Jackson out of there. He's one hell of a perfect shot with his gun. Doesn't mind blowing someone's leg off if they try and stop our men from stealing their guns.

"Son of a bitch." Cain's words have me gripping my phone so tight I could crush the fucker in half. My cousin is crying hysterically in the background. Cain is trying to console her. What the fuck is going on?

"Get the fuck over here." He disconnects the call.

"Shit," I mumble. I grab the cup of coffee and make my way to my bathroom. What the hell am I going to tell Alina?

"Oh, hey," she says. Her hair is wet and piled on top of her head. She smells so damn good, all I want to do is bury my head in her neck and inhale.

"What's wrong?" she asks, taking the cup shakily from my hand.

This has my brother written all over it. Fuck, but I'm not going to lie to her. I've already been dishonest by revealing her secret to her brother.

"I don't know for sure, but I have to get dressed and go." Walking past her, I pull out a clean pair of jeans, slip into them, and grab a shirt from my closet, pulling it over my head.

"I want you to stay right here until Beamer comes to get you. Do you understand me?" I reach for her. Kiss her briefly. Wait for her to reply. "Alina?" I question. "Yes, of course. Can you tell me this much? Is anyone hurt? If they are, you need to take me, Roan." Taking a deep breath, I hope I'm doing the right thing here by changing my mind and taking her with me.

"I don't know what's going on, but come on, I will fill you in on the way."

I feel a ball in the pit of my stomach. A nausea-inducing throb of fear. I know this has something to do with my brother. Why he is targeting Calla after the things he put her through is beyond me. I should expect the unexpected from him, though. He cares for no one, not even himself. The sadistic asshole.

"You think it's him, don't you? Whatever was sent to Calla is a warning from Royal." Her breathing hitches. The way she clutches my hand tightly in hers when we ascend in the elevator to Calla's office tells me she is looming on the edge of fear. I should have called Beamer and had him come over to my place. Whatever was sent to Calla has got to be horrendous to have her screaming and Cain yelling for me to get my ass here. And now here we are exiting the elevator. The entire place is in chaos. Amy, Calla's secretary, is crying behind her desk, holding on to Ryan, another attorney, as if they've just witnessed a murder.

"Stay here, baby, please." I hug her. I'm not letting her inside until I see for myself what the hell is going on. Like a dick I leave her standing there. Her hands at her sides. Tears in her eyes amongst the crazed confusion. Making my way down the hall towards Calla's office, I exhale before pushing open the door to be greeted by John, Cain, Calla, and my dad.

"Son." Dad's voice is bursting with a burden so deep I can feel it.

"Take a look." Cain gestures to a box on top of Calla's dark, wooden desk.

"What in the mother fuck?" I look to my dad, Cain, and then John, who is now consoling his daughter. My cousin. She's mumbling incoherently, her shaky little hands curled tightly into her dad's shirt.

This is the work of Royal. Vomit curls in my stomach. I gag at the sight before me. How Calla is even standing upright after seeing this makes it clear she's in shock.

"What is it?" I close my eyes, not wanting to hear her beautiful voice behind me. Alina.

"No... oh god, no." She sags to the floor, her body trembling. I fall to my knees beside her. Holding her. Trying my best to strum up the words to help her. To erase what she has seen. I can't. No one can.

My brother has just declared war. Not just war on my family against him. A war that could destroy us all.

"Call her dad and get Amy and Ryan out of here and make sure they keep their mouths shut," I tell my dad. Christ, the look on his face. The look on everyone's face. How in the hell could Royal do something like this? This is the ultimate betrayal. I hold Alina while she is crying hysterically. Calla is now in Cain's arms. I peer up at John. He has his kill face on. Blank. Emotionless.

I close my eyes and all I can see is the bloodied arm inside that box with the name *Solokov* tattooed down the front, and the words ONE DOWN AND SIX TO GO. WHICH ONE IS NEXT? written on a piece of paper. Royal has killed one of Alina's brothers.

Chapter Eleven

Alina

Grief isn't arranged, it's stifling. Your lungs become airless. Your life seems to have no meaning. You're lifeless. The urge to go on living without the person you have lost can drive someone to the near edge of death themselves.

The loss of my oldest brother Alexei has crushed my family. The sordid life we have all grown accustomed to has hit home. One of us got killed. Murdered in a way I cannot begin to fathom.

It's been a week since my brother's death. My life has gone from the best I have felt in my life to the worst. My parents, my brothers, all of us are confined to the home we grew up in. Grieving. Planning a funeral for a man who didn't deserve to die. Not like this and not because of me. I've told no one I feel as if Royal's resurfacing is because of me. Because I'm back and I'm falling for his brother. He wants revenge on me because I left him. The more I think about this, the more my head spins, my heart aches. My gut tells me not to give in. To not let him win and take away my happiness with Roan. Alexei would want me to be happy. To finally find someone who loves me. He was always our protector. Taking punishment from our parents for something one of us did. Sticking up for us all no matter what the circumstances were. My brother is gone. And I seek revenge.

And my dad. The look on his face when he walked into Calla's office. I have never seen him crumble like he did. If it weren't for Salvatore catching him when his knees went weak, he would have fallen to the floor. You would think the murder of my brother would cause my dad to want to kill Salvatore Diamond. Roan too. Instead, it's the opposite. Our families have finally come together in this nightmare.

Salvatore and Roan and their team of soldiers have put a cease to all of their duties, focusing only on finding that son of a bitch and bringing him to his rightful death. I've never wanted to kill, but today as I stand outside holding a gun in my hand for the first time, Roan by my side showing me exactly how to load and shoot, I want to kill. I want to shoot a hole in every organ and limb in Royal Diamond's body, sending him straight to hell.

"Aim and shoot, baby." We're huddled against each other, his back to my front, my arms straight out, pointing the Glock in the direction of the manmade target. Flashes of my brothers out here practicing on a daily basis seep through my thoughts. Tears threaten to spill. I hold them back, refusing to cry anymore. I've cried enough. After the funeral this morning, all I want is revenge. Vindication.

I'm on leave from work. To grieve. And I will grieve. I will grieve every day for the rest of my life. Today though, I'm here to learn how to kill. How to beat my enemy at this war he has started. A war that has been brewing for years inside of me and has now begun to boil over the top.

"Remember, Alina, a gun is only as good as the person using it. You have control of this gun. It does not have control of you. Kill that motherfucker." My man's sharp, edgy tone sends me into some kind of self-absorbed protection mode. My brothers have protected me my entire life. It's my turn to show them I can be just like them. I'm a Solokov, and I'm training to kill.

"What the hell are the two of you doing? Alina, give me that gun. For fuck's sake, have the two of you lost your minds? If mom sees you with this, she will—"

"She will what, Anton? Cry? Scream? She's been doing that for days now. Besides, who do you think gave this to me?" I jut my chin out. I'm tired of acting like a skittish, scared woman. I hated this lifestyle. Not anymore. Now, I want to be one of them, and I will be damned if my brother tries to stop me.

If there's one thing I learned from growing up in the Solokov home, it's women are treated as equals. Hell, there's even woman bosses, underbosses, and cold-hearted killers, just like Calla's mom used to be.

"Is that mom's gun?" Anton looks from me to the gun. I turn it away from Roan, and he takes it and places it back into the box. Empty. That's right. I emptied the gun into every part of the target I could find.

"Yes, it is and it's about time I learned how to use it." I dust my hands off on my jeans.

"Was this your idea?" Anton cranes his neck in the direction of Roan.

"Nope. All hers. I told you I care about her, and if she wants to learn how to protect herself, then I'm going to show her." Roan stands his ground. The two of them lock into some sort of stare down. Anton caves first. I knew he would. There's no denying Roan cares for me, and he's carrying around his own guilt. We all are. Anton knows Roan has not left my side since I walked in and saw my brother's arm in that box in Calla's office.

And Calla. Poor, sweet woman. Why her has everyone still guessing. She was out of her mind scared when she opened that box. Who wouldn't be? A sick crazy animal seems to target the ones they think are weak. What happened to Roan and Calla a few years ago was unexpected. Calla was just learning about the things our families do. Not anymore, though. He messed with the wrong woman. She's an animal herself in disguise. Only she goes after the throat. She doesn't just taunt, she will kill in an instant. I've heard about the way she is in a courtroom. She can rip even the coldest manipulator in half. Shred him to pieces and spit him out. After what she saw, I can only imagine the raging cyclone churning inside of her.

We've seen no one since the funeral. Everyone is locked away in their homes like a prisoner. It's bullshit, really. I laugh to myself. Everyone is going from one thing to the next. Deidre. She is driving me crazy with her three or four times a day phone calls. Roan has Beamer staying with her. Those two hate each other. I have yet to physically meet the man. Although, Deidre says he is one fine-looking man. But they're complete opposites. And her life has been turned upside down without her even knowing it. Her dad told her to stay put in the apartment until Royal was found. And then hours later, a stranger knocks on her door and takes over said apartment. I can only imagine the uproar she is causing that poor man.

"What's so funny?" Anton nudges my shoulder, his scowl over the gun still lingering on his face.

"I was thinking how I want to go home. I mean, I love mom and dad, but I'm ready to sleep in my own bed," I lie. I do want to go home, but I'm not going to stand here and talk girl gossip with these two.

"Like hell you're going home." Anton startles me with his loud voice.

"Don't tell me what to do." I jab a finger in his chest.

"You can stay with me. I need to get home myself." For the first time in a week, I feel like jumping up and down and actually fist pumping like a little kid when Roan offers me to stay with him.

My smile fades from my lips when yet again these two stare each other down. There's something else going on between them that they're not telling me. I hate secrets.

"What's going on?" I rotate my head from one to the other.

"Nothing," Anton says. "I need to know I can trust him with you."

"Oh, for god's sake." I throw my hands up. "I'm twenty-eight years old."

"You're right. I'm sorry," he concedes. "It's just, I love you so much and he's out there, sis. The thought of you being out of my reach scares me." My chest tightens. Anton is worried about me? I'm worried about us all. If Royal can find a way to get to one of my brothers, tear every limb from his body like he's known to do, then he's capable of getting to any one of us.

"And the thought of you being out of my reach scares me too, Anton. But I'm not going to stop living because that asshole is out there. Roan and I are new. I need to be with him. I know Alexei would want me happy, and this man makes me the happiest I have been in my life." I loop my arm through Roan's and lay my head on his shoulder as the three of us make our way back to the house. Out of respect for my parents, he's slept in one of my brother's old rooms. I'm aching to have his hands on me. To have him make love to me or to fuck me the many ways he told me he wanted to the other night when he ravished both my body and my mind. Stole my heart right out from inside of me. We need each other. It's a need that's bone deep. And we need to talk. I have so many things I want to say. So many things I need to hear. We've spent very little time with each other these past few days. While Roan, Cain, and men I have never seen before hide behind closed doors day and night, digging deep to try and find Royal, I've been trying my best to take care of my mom. Her insufferable pain has gutted me every time I walked into her room. My heart aches for the loss of my brother, but to lose a child is something I cannot even begin to imagine.

"Mom." I tread into her room lightly. If she's sleeping, which I truly hope she is, then I hate to wake her. Reaching her bedside, I find she is sleeping. I look down on her for the longest time. Praying it's a restful sleep and her dreams are as sweet as she is. Not having the heart to wake her, I blow her a kiss before exiting her room. I trail down the hallway, pack my bags, and write my mom a quick note, letting her know my whereabouts and that I will call her soon.

I find my man, say good bye to everyone else, and literally sigh when my head hits the soft interior of his truck when we pull out of the gates of my family home.

"Thank you for everything," I tell Roan the minute we walk into his place, both of us barreled down with suitcases of my things Deidre packed and one of my dad's trusted men dropped off in the lobby. I drop mine by the front door.

"Thank me for what?" I walk into the living room, alone with him at last. He tosses me down on the couch and covers his body with mine.

"I don't know. Everything, I guess." I shrug.

"Alina. You've been through a terrible loss. Like I've been telling you all week, I'm here. I'm not going anywhere." His eyes seek mine. His lips curve into a mischievous smile.

"Take me to bed," I say breathlessly.

"Nah. I think I'll take you somewhere else. Stay right here." He stands, eyes full of mischief, and leaves the room. My mouth hangs wide open.

The sound of him retreating back down the hallway has me sitting up and tilting my head until I see him come around the corner.

"Come here, pretty lady." His eyebrows shoot up, his tone gravelly and deep.

He lifts me into his arms when I reach him, carries me down the hall, and places me on my feet in front of his now running washing machine.

"While those clothes get cleaned, you and I are about to get very dirty, Alina." He reaches behind me and grabs my ass, pulling my body flush with his. God, he's hard. And so incredibly handsome too.

His lips touch mine, and I melt in his arms. God, I've missed his touch. The way he savors my mouth. Biting my lip. His delectable tongue swiping out, licking the spot he just bit. My heart rate increases. My core pulses. After one incredible night with this man, he has me hooked. I want more of him, in a variety of ways: passionately, emotionally, and forever.

He has my shirt off in record time. My bra is next. Gripping the waistband of my gauze skirt, he drags it down my body, along with my panties, until I'm standing there in nothing but my flip-flops. I toe them off, anxious to get my hands on him.

I reach for his shirt, tugging it over his head, my hands searching, seeking out the taunt hard muscles of his chest. His back. His abs. I'm roaming everywhere. He is too. And the entire time, his mouth is lavishing mine. His tongue tasting. Seeking, exploring. The tips of my fingers tracing along his tattoo. I wonder if it has meaning behind it. Casting those thoughts aside, I set sail to continue my exploration of getting to know his body better. I want to know all I can about him. Inside and out.

"Up, baby." He lifts me on top of the washer like I weigh nothing at all. The movement from the washer has me damn near coming. My entire body shimmies and shakes from the vibration under my backside.

"Leave your hands right there," he orders, catching them in his hands, pressing them on the back edge of the washer. Hell, I have no idea what to do or how to act. I still, anticipating his next move.

His eyed darken. "My god, look at you. The mere sight of you on this washing machine with your perfect breasts bouncing, those nipples begging for either my hands or my mouth, has me straining against my own resistance, Alina. You are perfect. A vision I will never erase."

"Touch me." My tone is breathy. Those magnificent hands caress my breasts. I lean into his touch, my body craving him all over. I bite my lip hard to hold back the moan wanting to escape from deep in my throat. It crawls its way out when he trails his tongue down my stomach, releases my heavy breasts, and spreads my legs wide, completely baring myself to him.

"Roan." His name rolls right off my tongue. "I've got you, Alina." Thank god, because I don't even know if I have control of myself.

One swipe of his talented tongue up my center has me bucking against his face with nothing but pure erotic, sensual pleasure.

"Fuck. I've missed this pussy. One night with you in my bed and you have me addicted. I could eat you and fuck you every day for the rest of my life." He attacks me with such a feverish lashing, I'm speaking in a language foreign to my own ears, words flying out of my mouth as fast as he's licking and sucking me. His hands stay firm on my thighs as he thoroughly consumes me. His tongue darting in and out.

"Don't stop." I desperately want to rip my hands off this machine and grip his hair. Shove my pussy as far into his face as I can. I'm falling apart. I come hard on his face, calling out his name once again. "I will never stop." Lifting his head from between my legs, his mouth covered with my juices, Roan has never looked sexier kneeling on the tiled floor, staring deeply into my eyes.

"Hang on, Alina. I'm about to fuck you into the future, sweetheart." He stands, takes his cock into his hands, and strokes. Good lord, I have wanted him so much this past week. For him to take away my pain, if only for a while. Then to hold me in his arms, to soothe me. I have waited years for him and I never knew he was even out there waiting for me just the same. Every time he looks at me, it's nothing short of respect, admiration, and hope. I see hope.

"Ahhhh..." I yell out when he fills me, grips my hips, pulls out, and slams back in again.

I'm moving and shaking, using every muscle in my arms to hold myself up. Beads of sweat trickle down the back of my neck. My breasts bouncing with each thrust he takes. It's as if the washing machine is stuck on the spin cycle the way it's rocking my ass. Rapidly firing sensations straight to my clit. I want to scream, yell, and claim to the world I'm being fucked hard. My thoughts are jumbled up. So many times I've wondered what sex would feel like. To have a man want you as much as you want him. Never did I expect it to be like this. To make me so out of control I lose my mind. The only thing I can think of is how good this feels. How thankful I am that I waited for Roan.

"Oh, god!" falls from my lips. I lay my head back. Clench my pussy muscles to grip him tighter. To feel every rock hard, solid inch of him.

"Fucking hell, beautiful lady. You're already so damn tight. God, when you do that, I want to pound this pussy. Own it. Drive so deep the only thing you feel is my cock inside of you."

"You're a dirty talker." I open my eyes, squeezing my legs tight against his hips.

"And you love it when I talk dirty. In fact, I'm going to dirty you up every way I can. Then turn around and make sweet love to you. I'm yours, Alina. Do you have any idea what you do to me? How crazy I am about you? How much I want to protect you? To tell the whole world I'm falling for you?" My eyes go wide. He smirks, slowing down his pace with a steady swivel of his hips, dragging his cock up against my clit, sending a chill racing down my spine. "You're falling for me?" I whisper.

"I've already fallen." He slams into me hard again. My head jerks back and he fucks me more. Those dark eyes determined to have me how he wants me. To please me in the way only he can. In the way I want him, and only him to. He stills himself as deep inside of me as he can get and grips my ass, his warmth spilling inside of me. I come right along with him. I've also fallen.

Chapter Twelve

Roan

I glance at Cain, who like always, takes a hefty gulp of his expensive scotch, his eyes trained to the floor, deep in thought.

It's been three days since Alina and I left her parents' house. Four damn hours since I dropped her off at her apartment. Beamer is inside going out of his ever-loving mind. I owe that motherfucker big time for the shit he claims his sorry ass has put up with the last week and a half with Deirde. I've never seen two people go at each other's throats the way they do. Christ, I was only there for five minutes, and Deidre was on his ass about having his dirty boots on the table. If I didn't know my buddy as well as I do, I would have pegged him for tagging her ass already, but the way he growls at her like a damn lion wanting to rip someone open by their throat tells me the two of them hate each other.

I study Cain, wondering if he's as worried as I am about the women. Calla insisted on going back to work, which I know pissed him the hell off. Shit, we're all on edge here, waiting to see when Royal will strike again.

My phone buzzes in my pocket. Turning my eyes away, I pull my phone out to see who texted. A sigh of relief washes over me when I see a picture of Alina and Deidre light up my screen, all smiles, her straight white teeth visible. What has me sitting here in the middle of my dad's office, drool forming at the corners of my mouth, is the bright red lipstick painted across those plump lips of hers. Fucking hell, woman, does she have any idea how many times I've dreamed about having her lips wrapped around my cock? Taking me deep into the back of her mouth? She's getting a spanking, god damn it. And then she'll be wearing that lipstick while I make love to her sexy mouth. My dick is hard in an instant.

"Did you hear me, Roan?" Another memory from last night making love to Alina, bowling down the long road mapped out only for her, flashes in my mind.

"No, dad. I didn't. That was Alina, shooting me a text to let me know she's fine." I tuck my phone back into my pocket. My cock instantly goes lax when I look up and eighteen pairs of eyes are all looking at me. My dad's, Ivan's, all five of Alina's brothers', John's, and even Cain's, who now seems to have joined us in this meeting.

"What the hell did you say?" Some sort of indescribable prickle runs up my spine. Whatever the hell he's about to tell me, I'm not going to like.

Dad clears his throat. "Now that we know he's here, we need to make new plans as our leads have gone nowhere. He's smart. He's a killer. Therefore, we need to devise this wisely. And like you, I have no doubt in my mind he's the one who tried to steel all those guns and ammo from us. He's desperate."

My dad is right. Every last Solokov swore up and down they have all talked, beaten, or damn near killed every drug pushing dealer-ass-pimp-motherfuckers they know to see if anyone has seen or heard shit from Royal. They all claim they haven't. Someone is lying. We all know it. I'm going out on my own to find out who it is and they are going to die right alongside my brother.

"What do you suggest? Because if it involves Alina, you can fucking forget it." I stand.

"Do you think we're fucking stupid?" Abram Solokov barks out. Very few people scare me, but I've actually seen this man snap someone's neck, drop him to the ground like a dirty fucking rag. I stand my ground.

"No one's stupid. Everyone's grieving. We can't set a trap for him. He expects that. I know him and he knows how all of this works. I guarantee every one of you he's waiting for us to find him." Darkness flashes throughout everyone's eyes, including my own.

"This is my idea." I whip my head around to the delicate voice of my mother, who is standing in the open doorway.

"That is a definite no then." I turn to look at my dad.

"Have you all lost it? Fuck, no. There is no damn way I'm allowing my mother to be the one who draws him out. If this is what we're going to do, which again I must say I don't agree with, then it will be me. I'm the one he wants. He's so fucked up in his head that he's hurting the woman I care about before he comes at me." My mother moves to stand before me. Those hands that have soothed me so many times when I was growing up cup my face. Her eyes are full of tears and pain. Jesus. The pain and hurt in her features nearly drop me to my knees.

"Listen to me, son." Her sweet voice is tender.

"Mom, no."

"It was my idea for us to try and trap him. It was your dad's idea to be the one. You see, my boy. Many innocent lives have suffered to the hands of a man your dad and I brought into this world. As much as it pains the both of us, this must be done. I will love your brother until my very last breath, but I cannot stand by and watch him destroy the lives of others anymore. You know that saying 'I brought you into this world so I can take you out?' She pauses, her lips trembling. Unshed tears glisten my mother's loving face. I nod. "It has to be this way. It's the right thing to do." Silence is a bitch in this sudden cold room. Turmoil is raging in my blood. Do I stand by my family? Let my dad do this? Or do I go behind their back, find him myself? Either way, this is a decision I will make on my own. For now, I will grant my family with the words they want to hear, even though my mind is already made up. I'm going to find him.

"Then let's plan this." For the first time in years, I've just lied to my broken-hearted mother.

"What the hell is going on with you?" I hustle down the hallway, out the door behind Cain, as soon as he abruptly excused himself after our meeting. He sat stoic during the entire thing. Never said a word. Most likely didn't hear shit either.

Drugs. Everyone kept talking about luring his ass out with drugs.

It's been two damn years since all hell broke loose with Royal. Way too damn long for that fucking scum to still be breathing the same air as any of us. It's time we all get our redemption.

"Just get me the hell out of here," he growls, face full or fury. The moment we both climb in my truck is the first time all damn day I feel the tension leave him. My hand stops mid-air, I reach for my keys. The words he speaks barely registering in my mind.

"Calla's pregnant," he repeats several times, before laying his head back and closing his eyes. I blink, my back slumping against my seat. When my brother kidnapped the two of us, he drugged Calla over and over, causing her to miscarry their baby. A baby she didn't even know she was expecting. It ripped my gut out, knowing I was there in that room with her, my finger cut off, drugged, and nearly beaten half to death, knowing she was scared out of her skin and I couldn't do a damn thing about it. I was barely hanging on myself. But I remember. God, how I remember the way he talked to her. Threatened her. And that slut Emerald using that Taser gun on her. Her laughter crackling in the air while she tortured Calla. Nightmares plagued me for months. I still have them, wake up in a cold sweat. Calla, pale, limp, and lifeless on the floor.

I protected her for years while she was going to school. Watched her every move. That night, I could do nothing to help her. Not a damn thing.

"We have to find him. I don't know why that piece of shit is targeting my wife. I'm not about to let him destroy her again," he says painfully.

"I'm going after him myself. You stay away from it. Your job is to protect her. You get me?" My voice is tight.

"I won't let you do this shit alone, man. I know you. You have a plan and you need help. That's why you're pushing so hard for Jackson to get out of jail, isn't it?"

"For the most part, yes. The fucker's innocent, you know it and so do I." I start my truck and put it in drive, adrenaline spiking through my veins, then hit the gas, wishing like hell I had my car so I could fly down the road, get to Calla's office, and tell her to get the hell out. She's done until this is over. I don't care how much shit she wants to fling my way, how stubborn she can get. She's done.

"I'm going to take her to the house in Michigan. Get her the hell out of here. We can't lose this baby, Roan." His voice is pained, thick with worry.

"You won't, buddy. And congrats. Now, let's get to her office so I can fire her ass." The both of us scoff, our thoughts the same, knowing full well he's going to have to tie her ass up, throw her over his shoulder to get her to leave her job. A job that will be here waiting for her the minute I snuff the last breath out of the fucker who thinks he can walk on water. There will be no water where he's going. Nothing but fire and flames all around him as he burns in the depths of hell.

"How far along is she?" I ask, trying to get him out of his worried funk.

He sighs. "She thinks around six weeks or so. We found out a few days after the funeral. All of a sudden, she started to get sick. At first, she claimed it was her nerves. Stress over what she'd seen. What we all were going through." He pauses. "Then when she couldn't keep any food down, she called her mom, who then showed up a half hour later with a bag full of pregnancy tests. You should have seen the look on her face when she came out of the bathroom holding five of those damn sticks in her hand. God, Roan, she should have come out of there happy. Instead, my wife had fear written all over her face."

Before my mind can take a trip down memory lane, I keep going, trying to make him see the miracle the two of them created. How this news makes me more determined than ever to seek justice on not only Calla, but Alina and everyone else involved.

"Listen. I can't begin to understand how the two of you dealt with your loss before. But hell, man, you're going to be a dad. She's going to be a mom. Don't let him take away what should be the best time of your lives."

"Believe me, I've told her that. And then this morning when she said she wanted to go to work, I agreed to it. She needed out, focus her mind on something else. The thought of her in that office all day has me so fucked up in the head."

I know what he's trying to say without him even saying it. How she could go back there after receiving that horrifying package has me ruffled as much as him. Goes to show how strong of a woman Calla really is.

"She's fine, man. If she weren't, she would have called you."

"The minute I dropped her off, I called her mom. She's been there with her all day. That's why I finally shut my phone off during the meeting. Calla kept sending me texts after Cecily got there. Calling me every name except a nice guy."

I laugh. "Sounds like her. She'll get over it."

"Speaking of the meeting?" I glance his way.

"Dude. I heard. I may not have been all there, but I heard every word. That's how I know you have your own plan. I know there is no way in hell you're going to let Salvatore do this."

And so the drive through the busy streets of New York continues. I drive, while Cain listens to my plan on how to accomplish drawing my brother out. I only hope my team of highly paid lawyers can get Jackson out of the shit he's in. I need that son of a bitch.

"Ha! You two are wacked, because I quit," Calla half laughs the moment I tell her she's fired.

"Good. That means no unemployment then." I give her my goofiest smile, but concern for Cain to get her back to Michigan as safely and swiftly as possible reverberates through my gut.

Cain and Calla exchange a look. A look I'm starting to become familiar with. Admiration, excitement, and love. I'm jealous. Their eyes speak the words I so desperately want to say to Alina. And yet I'm scared at the same time that she's not there, yet. I've known her much longer than she's known me; with my stalking tendencies and all. I stand at the edge of her desk. Watch her attentively make her way to Cain. Envious of the two of them.

"Thanks, baby, for looking out for me and our son here." Clasping her hands with his, she places them on her lower abdomen.

"A son, huh?" Cain leans in and nuzzles her neck, which is my cue to leave. Cecily left with her new bodyguard a few minutes after we got here. Thank Christ, Calla didn't go all ape-shit on my ass when I told her she was done. She agreed without any hesitancy in her voice at all. The baby is more important than anything, anyone of us, really.

"I'm out," I say, pushing myself away from her desk.

"Roan, wait." Calla edges out of Cain's hold.

"Be safe, please." We connect our gazes in a bond that no one can ever break. I know she will worry no matter where she is. She's been through too much not to.

"You know I will." I pull her in for a hug. I nod, closing the door behind me, and make my way towards Ryan's office. I need to know where things stand with Jackson. Not wanting to bother Calla about any of it since she needs to get her ass out of here.

"Hey, man." I knock on his open door. Dropping his cell on top of his messy desk, he leans back in his chair, clasping his hands behind his head with a smug look on his face.

"Well, I'll be damned. I was just about to call you, boss man." Before I can ask him what the hell he is so self-assured about, he stands up, snatches a piece of paper off his desk, and hands it to me.

"You're shitting me?" I ask, re-reading the confession one more time.

"Not a chance in hell. He's getting out as soon as I collect everything I need. The drug addict bitch was busted. Professed guilt ate her alive. Spilled everything. Jackson's free."

"Just like that?" Hell, I have no clue how the law works.

"Just like that. They sobered her ass up, and she took a polygraph. Passed it. I've been on the phone most of the day with the District Attorney's office to convince them to let Jackson go with time served. He lied about the drugs being his, he has, or should I say had, that to deal with. Sixty-two days in jail is long enough for a man to sit with a clean record. He's out." God damn,

I don't know whether to hug Ryan or shake his damn hand. I needed this. This is the best damn news I've had in a long time.

"You need a raise," I say, extending my hand out to him, gripping it firmly.

"Not going to argue with you about a raise. Just doing my job." I hand him back the paper, and he stuffs it in a folder, then stashes it in his briefcase.

"Trust me, you're going to need a raise." For the next half hour I tell Ryan all about the reasoning behind Calla leaving. He knows all about the shit that went down here. He witnessed the whole thing. Held this firm together while we all grieved and tried to find my brother. Fucker deserves a hell of a lot more than he gets.

Two hours later with the night crawling its way through the clouds, the threat of rain on the horizon, I pull up to Jackson's house after hanging up with Alina, letting her know it will be a few more hours before I come and pick her up. God, I miss everything about her. The way she smiles through her hazy morning eyes when she looks at me. The way my bed smells like her. Fresh and clean and so damn innocent. The red tint to her cheeks when she comes while screaming my name. And it's been what? All of ten hours. I'm being ridiculous. A grown man sitting in a truck wishing he could be with his woman. Dumbass. *No, you're a smartass, dude. Don't fuck this up. She's a keeper. If you do fuck this up, then call yourself a dumbass.* "Now I'm talking to myself. Jesus Christ." Snatching my keys, I climb out of my truck and double-click the key fob, making sure the doors are locked. How the hell Jackson can live in this part of New York beats the shit out of me. Murders every damn night of the week on this side of town. Now he's the dumbass.

"Well, it's about time, motherfucker. I thought you'd have a party waiting for me." Jackson throws open the door, bringing me in for a hug.

"Damn. It's good to see you. Don't ever pull that shit on me again and lie for some drug addict bitch." I walk straight into his house, taking a seat on the couch.

"Shut the hell up. Now tell me what the hell you need. Ryan filled me in about the shit that went down these past few weeks. I'm sorry, man." His eyes are full of remorse. Jackson and I go way back to elementary school. He was the bully. Tried to steal my lunch one day. Little did he know, I was bullied at home. No way in hell that shit was happening at school, the only time I was away from getting my ass beat from my brother. I stood up to him. Busted his lip open. End of story. We've been tight ever since. Even when I moved to Michigan at sixteen. Even when I moved to Canada to keep an eye on Calla, we stayed in touch.

"I need your help." He hands me a beer. Twisting the cap off, I guzzle half of it down. The need to get shit-faced grasping strongly the further the cold liquid travels down my throat. A thought of getting shit-faced with Alina hits my thoughts, the idea of drunk sex making my dick twitch.

"Anything you need, Roan. You know this." Jackson swigs his own beer and takes a seat in the chair opposite of me.

"This is some screwed up shit. He killed Alina's brother. No one's safe. I've been at a loss for months, hell, two years trying to find him. Then today, something hit me. Something big, Jackson, and that's where you come in."

And that's what we do, my oldest friend and I. We derive a plan. I make one phone to call to a man I haven't talked to since he landed himself in an upstate New York prison for drugs while Jackson makes a few calls of his own. I need my cousin here. He's the one person I turned to besides my parents when my brother left. The only one who hates him as much as I do. He's been out for six months with very little contact with any one of us. It kills me to ask him for help. To get him involved in the same shit that he was put away for. But if anyone can help me get what I need, it's him.

Jackson and I plot and scheme after my cousin agreed without any hesitation at all to bring my brother out, to make him beg, so he can fucking die; live in hell, where he tries to claw his way out of the darkness, getting nowhere; seeing nothing but black, just like his fucked up soul.

By the time I leave his house, I filled him in on my relationship with Alina, which he knew very little about. Seems catching up with an old friend makes you lose track of time. I reach Alina's apartment at one in the morning after shooting her a text to let her know I was on my way. She never replied. As I pull up to her apartment, I freak the fuck out. *Please let them all be sleeping*. Not a damn one of them is answering their phone.

I run after I park my truck, my heart hammering away in my chest, the early morning security guards gawking at me like I'm a lunatic. I wave them off when they approach me.

When I fling open their door after using the key Alina gave to me earlier to let myself in, I don't say a word for a moment. The site before me has my heart beating rapidly in a whole new way. I'm pissed the hell off.

They're drunk. Alina, Deidre, Beamer, and Hugo are all fucking drunk. Dancing to some techno beat shit. Alina and Deidre are grinding on each other. Jesus Christ.

Some bodyguards these two douche-bags are. Standing off to the side, no rhythm in their fucked up moves.

"What the hell are you guys doing?" All four of them turn to face me. The two girls' eyes go wide. Hugo shrugs and Beamer, whose ass I'm going to kick right now, stalks my way.

"Calm down, asshole. We're fine," he smarts off. Arrogant little prick.

"You sure about that?" They may feel safe in here, but Christ, doesn't he realize my brother is as feeble as a snake? He will slither in here and kill them all if it will get him to Alina. I know he fucking will. And they're all in here like sitting targets. Making it easy for him in their inebriated state. Fuck.

"I've had one beer. One. Your woman needed this, and so did her psycho friend. They're going crazy being cooped up. Nice to know you have faith in me, fucker."

"God damn it, Aidan, I'm sorry." It's the first time I've called him by his real name since the minute he walked through the door at Cain's old club back in Michigan years ago. His eyes go wide.

"I would have to take my last breath before I'd let him get to her. Hugo's fine, too," he whispers, barely loud enough for me to hear over the music.

"I know. This whole situation has me out of my damn mind." I run my fingers through my hair, down my face, across my stubble.

My gaze lands on a carefree Alina. Her hair in two ponytails, a blue tight tank top stretched across those tits I love; a pair of cut-off white shorts, bare feet, and that god damn glorious ass of hers swaying to the music, hips in sync with the beat. Fucking hell. Seeing her smile, her head tipped back, completely ignoring me, laughing with Deidre, hits me right in the gut. She needed this. To let go, have fun, but not without me, damn it.

Being so transfixed on her and what I witnessed when I walked in here, I didn't see the man sitting in the chair. Beer lifted to his lips, decked out in camouflage from head to fucking toe, black combat boots on his feet, steel-looking eyes that match my own pinned on me.

The soft light is coming from the lamp beside him, encasing the tattoos up and down his arms. No doubt many more are hidden underneath his dark green t-shirt.

"You have got to be fucking with me?" I step towards a man I haven't seen in years.

"Dilan." My long lost cousin.

Chapter Thirteen

Alina

"I can walk, you know. I'm not drunk." I squeeze my legs tighter around Roan's waist. When he first stormed into our apartment, my insides froze, unable to get a read on his dark expression. Was he angry because we let loose, had some fun?

My mind needed to unwind. My thoughts of losing my brother drifted away, if only for a few hours. I miss him. I ache everywhere, wondering if he suffered before he died. I thought about his children and my sister-in-law Cora, knowing he wouldn't be around any longer to protect them from harm; to watch his daughters grow up and get married. All the joys of being a parent. A husband. A brother.

"I know you're not drunk, Alina." His hands go to my ass the farther we walk down the dark hallway to my room. I've hardly talked to him since he got here. He found his cousin, who showed up here a few hours before he did, scaring the crap out of me. Not because of the way he was dressed or the fact he has god knows how many tattoos all over his arms. That wasn't it at all. It was the fact that he looks so much like Roan that threw me. Even their voices sound so much alike. It wasn't until he introduced himself as Dilan, Roan's cousin, that I began to breathe again. The genetics of their similarity struck me hard. Christ almighty, their family makes gorgeous men.

I relaxed, got into the groove of the music, ignoring the three men. My sole purpose was to forget how much we were all hurting and to remember the good. I have a man who is falling for me. A man I'm falling for. All I wanted to do was think about how good life feels, to live, knowing there was always someone waiting out there for me.

I cast it all aside as my rock of a man holds me tight with one hand and opens and closes my bedroom door with the other. Even through the dark I feel his eyes piercing through mine.

"I love your outfit, babe, but it has to go." God, I love how his tone changes when he wants sex. It goes from deep to deeper. From rough to rougher. Unwinding my legs from around him, he groans in frustration.

"Sit on the edge of the bed." I steady myself on my own two feet, take a few steps to the bed, flick the bedside lamp on, and spin around to face him.

"What are you doing?" His lids grow heavy, his eyes go dark.

"Sit." I pat the edge of the bed. He moves stealthily across my floor. I'm thankful once again for my room being so far away from the living room and the spare bedroom, where the three men are sleeping. What I'm about to do to Roan will most likely have me screaming and begging for my own damn release. Who cares about Deidre? She had a hell of a lot more to drink than I did. She's passed out cold in her room.

"Relax." I speak with more strength than I feel. Shit, I've never done anything like this before. I've never had the desire to taste a man, to make him feel out of control. To make him lose himself inside of my mouth.

I reach, my god, do I reach into the heavy thickness of this clouded room filled with the sexual tension between the two of us for the courage to do this right.

I drop to the floor, not caring about anything right now except for pleasing him. Encasing him in me. Showing him I can bring him pleasure.

His breath hitches. My hands caress up and down the strong muscled definition of his legs.

"Alina." The way he says my name, so full of love, I cannot even explain how the sound of my name coming from his lips sounds. It gives me courage for some unknown reason. I undo the button of his jeans. Glide down his zipper. He lifts his hips. I tug and pull on his jeans and boxers to free his heavy cock, taking it in my hand and stroking the silky head with my thumb.

"Sweetheart," he calls.

"Shh," I say.

"Fuck," he whimpers when I get the first taste of his musky male scent, my tongue darting out to lick from the base up. I grip him firmly in my hand, watching as his cock jerks. His hands grab my ponytails, tugging hard. The pain, god yes, the pain of desire whips through me.

"Jesus Christ," he growls. I've got him in my mouth. Not all of him. His cock is huge, gloriously huge, and it's mine. Every inch of it belongs to me.

I tease us both for what feels like heavenly eternity. I suck him deep into my throat, weave my way back up by swirling my tongue, pumping the base, and repeating again. He pulls harder. Moans deeper. His taste is consuming me. God, he's infectious. Intoxicatingly delicious.

"Damn, Doc." I smile on the inside. He's never referred to me as doc before. Always Alina, babe, beautiful lady, or other terms of endearment. I love every one of them, but something about doc does me in and I bob up and down, taking more of him in the more I begin to relax. He swears, and I couldn't tell you what words he is saying right now. I'm so beyond gone into what I'm doing, loving the fact I'm pleasing him and pleasing myself.

I'm literally addicted to him. His aroma. His taste. Everything about him.

I feel his balls tighten below my hand, indicating he's close. I swear to god he grows larger in my mouth. The throbbing need to come myself makes the energy between my aching thighs bloom. He cusses louder. Grips tighter. I remove my free hand from wherever the hell I have it, unclenching my fist, palming his balls in my hands.

"I'm about to come." I say nothing to his words. The need to taste more of him when he comes in my mouth urges me on more. I lick, suck, and let him pump his cock into my mouth and fuck me the way he wants. Wild, out of control, mouth-fucking sex.

He swells more, his release filling my mouth. The tinge of his salty, masculine taste on my tongue marks me with uncontrollable desire. I swallow it all, thanking my mind for being consumed by pleasing him.

"Come up here." He releases my hair and possessively drags me up from the floor onto his lap.

"I don't know whether to say thank you or spank your ass." His words startle me.

"What?" Disappointment surges through me. Did he hate it? Oh, no. I feel my face flush with embarrassment.

"Let me rephrase that." His quick response sends my mind reeling.

"Thank you for what you just did. You have no idea how many times I visualized my cock wrapped around those lips of yours. However, the next time you decide to give me pleasure, don't deny me the opportunity to see your body. To bring you the same pleasure that you're bringing me. Now, stand up and take those clothes off." Well then. I see the bossy man is back, his will to please me more powerful than ever.

"Are you going to spank me?" My fingers pull my tank top over my head, letting it drop to the floor. Those dark eyes rake across my navy blue satin and lace bra.

"I'm going to do all kinds of things to you." He stands, and my feet hit the floor. Roan unhooks my bra, glides the straps down my arms, then releases the button of my shorts, coasting them and my panties down the floor.

"God damn, baby. I'm turning that ass the same sweet shade of pink as this wet pussy." He glides a finger through my wet heat all around to the dark hole of my ass. I clench my cheeks together. He glides his finger slowly back to the front, stands and grips me by my waist, bending me over. My stomach hits the mattress, my face planted into the softness of my comforter.

Oh, my god. Hell, yes. Take me now. He doesn't, though. He's waiting. Doing what? What felt like heavenly eternity a few minutes ago, now feels like eternal hell. I'm quivering, the need to come urgent. If he doesn't touch me, I'm going to do it my damn self.

"Roan?" Pulling my head up, I twist to see what exactly it is he's doing. He's looking around the room.

"What on earth are you doing?" My breathing is frantic.

"Looking for a stethoscope." He shrugs with a smile.

"Are you serious?" I pout a little.

"Very." He's serious. The hunger in his eyes tells me how damn serious he is. Our gazes lock.

"There's one in my closet. Inside the box on the floor." A deviant smile creeps over his lips. I watch the muscles in his ass flex when he turns and strolls into my closet. How did I become so preoccupied I didn't even hear him take off his clothes? God, his ass is glorious. His long lean legs, too. He even has sexy feet. Sexy every damn thing. How did I get so lucky?

The light in the closet switches on. I hear him rustling through my medical school box full of items left untouched since I graduated. The light clicks off. He waltzes out, the stethoscope dangling in his hands. I'm not watching it. Oh, no way. Instead, I'm watching his cock bob up and down, his veins growing thick and massive. I had that, all of it, in my pussy, in my mouth. It's mine. The whole damned world needs to be jealous of me right now. His dick is perfection. *People* magazine needs to have the most beautiful dick in the world contest so he could win (without actually showing the world, of course.)

"Fuck, woman. You keep looking at my cock like that and I'm not going to be responsible for what I will do to you." I swallow. I'm not scared. He would never hurt me. He can do whatever the hell his big cock wants to do to me.

Both of us lift our brows. Me challenging. Him asking if I accept whatever it is he's about to do.

"Tell me, Doc. Can you hear the pounding of someone's pulse through their pussy?" Oh hell. I watch in astonishment as he places the ear tips into his ear, then adjusts his body to mine. I yelp, expecting him to place the chest piece on my pussy, but he doesn't.

"Jesus, that's loud." He places it against the bare skin above my heart.

"Oh, god." My eyes roll to the back of my head.

"Your heart's beating mighty fast there, doc," he teases. I relax more.

The warmth of his breath blows softly in my ear. The stethoscope glides smoothly across my scorching skin. Down my spine. He palms my ass and then I feel it. The heat of the chest piece presses against my pounding clit, his finger spreading me wide.

"Strong and steady pulse. Wet pussy. Does that mean you're healthy, Doc? Does this mean you want my cock?" He slaps my ass. I jolt forward and he drags me back, letting go of my ass, slipping his arm around my waist. I can't talk. My breathing is so out of control my pulse is thrumming through my chest.

"You want more?" Not giving me time to answer, he releases me and slaps my other cheek while shoving his finger up inside me. I convulse around him. Clench his finger inside me. He begins to press and circle the stethoscope against my hard clit.

"Roan. It's too much," I beg him to stop, my head thrashing.

"Take it, Alina. Your sweet tight pussy has my finger inside of you. Your clit is on fire. I swear I can feel it pounding in my god damn ears. Let me give me all of you, take you to heaven here on this earth. I'm going to make you scream and beg me to stop, but I won't stop. I want you to come and come often. I want to fuck you hard and then turn right around and kiss the hell out of you. God, baby, you make me fucking crazy with love, crazy with lust, and fucking turn my shit life into something so sweet, so beautiful, and it's mine."

Oh, heaven. He thinks I'm heaven, just like he is to me. Oh god, he starts pumping his finger now. Make that two. I'm stretching, feeling, rocking my hips onto his fingers. The wicked pleasure on my clit is like hot oil sizzling. And then, just like that, it's gone. All of it is gone. I cry out in agony until I feel the passion of his tongue against my hard little bundle of pounding nerves. He bites, and I explode in his mouth. He laps at me with his dirty-talking mouth, and I swear to the master up above who created the man eating me alive I see the moon, the stars, and the infinite deep, dark sky.

The need to beg him to stop lies dormant on my tongue. My chest is heaving. My mind is running amuck. He's torturing me. Ravishing me. And I say nothing, fearful of ruining this monumental time of my life. I feel alive, I feel sexy, but mostly I feel wanted and needed.

Another orgasm is building inside of me. I have no control over my body, my sex clenching once again. His tongue disappears, causing me to lift my head up instinctively off the bed. I turn it just in time to see him line his cock up to my pussy, sliding the head up and down through my drenched heat.

"Roan," I whisper through jagged gasps of breath.

"God, Alina. I can't seem to stay in control with you. You take as good as you give." That thick glorious cock slides into me. His fingers digging into my hips as he thrusts himself into me several times before he grabs my ponytails and positions my head how he wants it. He fucks me like he said he would, his breathing short and loud like mine, our bodies making their own kind of dance music with the sound of them slapping together. He pulls my hair tight, my head snapping back on a whimper. I can feel him gathering it into one hand. Then he's slapping my ass, the pain blending excruciatingly well with the heeding gratification being inflicted on my achy, vibrating pussy.

"I'm coming again." He gives me more, every amazing inch of his blessed girth as he drives violently inside me. "Wait, beautiful lady. God, wait." He's begging. He's pumping. He's grinding while I'm building, higher, farther into that infinity of the dark sky, which unquestioningly is full of so much light.

"Come now, baby." The first soft words he's spoken all night. He bends his body over mine. I tighten around him, let go of another orgasm, glorifying in the way he lets go of his. Wanting the two of us to come together. Too weak to hold myself up anymore, I crash onto my stomach, my arms and legs giving out.

His weight lands on top of me, our legs tangled in a heap of slick sweat, our chests heaving.

, He lifts off of me quickly. My legs are cramped, my inner thighs sting. I'd still think I was flying through the sky if it weren't for the soreness between my legs when I stand shakily.

Roan wraps his arm around my waist, pressing his chest against my back. I'm still on a sex high, but his words bring me back to reality. I gasp. Shocked utterly speechless.

"I love you, Alina Solokov. I can't help myself, nor can I keep it to myself any longer. I fucking love you."

It has to be late morning by the time I open my eyes. I stretch, only to be reminded of early this morning when the tenderness of my sex beckons me wide awake as soon as I move my legs.

"Are you sore?" I smile and rub my hands down that wonderful scruff that was covered with me last night. God, the sad look in his eyes right now nearly breaks me.

"I'm deliciously sore, Roan." I place a kiss on both sides of his face where my hands just were.

"I was rough with you. And these whiskers should go." I sigh loudly, trying to think of the right words to say.

"I love it when you're rough." I kiss his cheek. "I love you gentle too." A kiss on the other cheek. "And don't you dare shave. A trim maybe, but that's all." A small kiss on his lips. My nails lightly scratch his face.

"Now who's being bossy?" He eyes me adoringly.

"This is you. Don't change any part of you, not for me or for anyone. Besides, I love it. Makes you look all kinds of badass."

I shove him onto his back, positioning myself on top of him. God, he has the kind of face that stops you dead in your tracks. Leaves you with the inability to speak. In the late morning light, coupled with being this close to him, I see every angle of his manly face. The specks of gold in his eyes. The weak smile across those lips of his grips my heart and yet… yet that adoring gaze reserved only for me showers his eyes. I'm looking at the most beautiful man I have ever met.

"I never want you to be nothing but the real man you are with me. I don't mean just in the bedroom, Roan, I mean… I don't want you to ever hide who you are from me. Last night meant just as much to me as the first time we made love. It's you, and all I want is the real you." I suck my bottom lip into my mouth. He's crazy if he thinks I want him to change any part of him at all. Our tender gazing continues. A woman who used to be so unsure of herself, sheltering away her life in books and living a fairy tale dream vicariously through fiction, is lying here with a man who loves her. I have yet to say it back, but yes, god yes, I love him.

And there it is. His smile, showing me those perfect white teeth. That roguish gleam in his eyes.

"You drive me out of my mind, Alina. When I'm not with you, I feel lost. I have no idea how I made it to twenty-six years old without you." He circles his arms around my waist.

"I'm in love with a younger man," I say sarcastically. My semi-smirk turns into a full-fledged giggle.

"And she has a sense of humor." He cuts right to the quick.

"Wait? What did you just say?" He flips us over so he's now on top, his erection pressing against my stomach. His eyes are huge. God, I want him so bad again, but I am sore. I feel the chaffing from his stubble on my inner thighs. My legs do spread and I fight back my wince, willing my face to show nothing but the love I have for this man. A man who once again I tell myself is very dangerous on these streets, in the type of world we are both accustomed to. I may have been in denial for years about who I really am, the family I come from, but not him. Roan Diamond stays true to those he cares about. He will protect them with his life. He's not dangerous to me. He's everything to me. And he would never do a damn thing to hurt me.

"I love you, Roan Diamond. My incredibly sexy younger man."

Chapter Fourteen

Roan

I sit here in this sprawled out kitchen of Alina's apartment, the room suffocating my thoughts. Both of us went back to work today after spending an entire week alone in my apartment. Giving, learning, and falling more in love with each other.

A few days after I fucked her so hard I couldn't see straight, she told me she needed to go back to work, even though they told her to take as much time off as she needed. I despised dropping her off this morning, but I'm not the type of guy who doesn't let his woman make her own choices. She's an independent woman, she's been on her own for years, and now that we're together, I wouldn't change a damn thing about her. Just like she asked me not to change anything about myself either. So here I sit after a hell of a long day with her dad and brothers, staring at the door waiting for Hugo to bring her home. Back to me. She sent me several texts in between clients today, letting me know she was all right, but hell, I just need to see her for myself to believe it's true. Not knowing when Royal will strike again has me on high alert. He's up to something. I just know he is. We all know he is. Last night when her dad called, asking me to come over this morning, I thought it had everything to do with this crazy shit my dad has in his head about him being the one to send signals out to the entire underground that he wants to meet with my brother. But fuck no, those sons of bitches sacked me like a quarterback the minute I walked through the door. Every single one of them threatened my life if I did anything to hurt her, while I sat there with a smug, confident look on my face. I respect them for looking out for her. I told them all that, I also told them she's mine, she's not theirs to worry about anymore. That's my job now, and I plan on doing it for a very long time, if she would just walk through the damn door.

"You listening, asshole?" Beamer brings my attention away from the door and to the subject at hand. I heard what they said. I just didn't want to answer.

"Hell, yes, I'm a whipped bitch and it feels fucking fantastic." Both Beamer and Dilan nearly choke on their beer they just took a big gulp of. Beamer knows how I feel about Alina. Dilan and I haven't talked much about her. Our conversations have been about one thing, better yet, one person only. He wants Royal's blood on his hands as much as I do. And for a good damn reason. A reason he shared with me, something I knew nothing about. When he first told me it had my head so damn twisted up and my insides rumbling like a damn train flying through the scariest parts of New York. My brother has deceived every single person in his family, including my cousin, who is sitting across from me at the table in the girls' apartment, asking me a stupid ass question. He set Dilan up. Dilan was getting way too close to some shady shit Royal was doing, and he set him the fuck up with the cops. Got him busted with ten kilos of cocaine. The unlucky bastard was sentenced to six to twenty years. Out in less than he should be. And now, just like me, he wants that kill. He wants it to be his bullet that ends his life. Or his knife that slices his throat as he watches it bleed the man dry.

"Never thought I'd see the day, man. I'm happy for you. How's her old man feel about the two of you? He's never had a decent thing to say about our family. I can't imagine he would start now." My cousin's brows form together and his mouth turns down.

"Like I said, we talked today. Not as much as I'd liked, but he loves Alina. He wants what's best for her, and whether any of them give a shit or not, I know how we feel and that's all that matters. Anyone has a problem with it, they can come to me, which includes her dad." I shrug, knowing damn well he would prefer she were with someone else than a Diamond. But the little bit of talking we have done—or should I say the talking he's done—he knows I'm crazy about her. He also knows the kind of man I am. I protect, uphold my promises. I love her and I will go down dying with shielding her from any harm. If she just walked through that damn door.

"Now that you're here to watch Adolf Hitler's fucking sister, my ass is out of here. I need to get laid." Beamer stands, polishes off his beer, grabs his leather jacket, and strides towards the door.

I'm just about to yell after him to tell him to keep his thoughts to himself when I see him duck as something goes whizzing by his head.

"You bitch," he yells. Dilan and I look at each other with raised brows. He mouths "what the fuck?"

"It's been building for weeks," I mouth back.

"Adolf Hitler's sister? Come on, Beamer, you've got better than that. You... you Skipper Skinny Dick."

I lay my head down on the table. Jesus Christ, not this shit again. Deidre and Beamer hate each other. Thank you, god, for sending Dilan here. It's been a week since I walked into this apartment and found him looking like the king shit he is. I wanted to beat his ass for not telling me he was here when I called him from Jackson's house requesting his help. He was here already. Waiting for me. Found out everything that went down two years ago when Royal decided to try and kill me and left me with one less finger on my hand. I have no damn clue what the hell he's been doing since he got out. He's the type of guy who if he wants you to know his shit, he will tell you. You simply do not ask.

"Those two need to fuck each other, that's what their god damn problem is." We both sit and listen to the two of them go at each other like an angry married couple.

And then he goes and says it. That son of a bitch. I jump out of my chair. I am so damn pissed off. Call a woman anything you want, but do not call her a cunt.

"That's enough. Fuck, man, are you crazy? What the hell is the matter with you?" I grab him by the collar of his shirt.

"It's her. She's fucking nuts. Fuck you, you bitch, and fuck you, too, Roan!" I release him. Stunned my friend would act this way. What's gotten into him? He slams the door behind him, everyone standing there in silence. I break my eyes from the door when I hear a cry escaping Deidre's mouth.

"Don't," she whimpers when I take a step toward her. "That bastard is not allowed in here anymore, Roan. Fuck him." She turns and storms down the hall to her room, leaving me standing there, thinking, *What in the fucking hell*?

The door finally opens just as soon as it was slammed shut. And shit, there she is. More beautiful than when I left her this morning, but the strained look in her eyes tells me all I need to know. She ran into Beamer.

"What's going on?" she asks pensively, her tone worried, her entire body ramrod straight.

"They got into it bad this time." I point toward the hallway where Deidre disappeared.

"Oh, shit. Let me go check on her. You may want to call him. We caught him slamming his fist through the wall when we stepped off the elevator. I asked him if he needed help. He gave me the strangest look, then headed toward the lobby. He was bleeding." I close my eyes and tilt my head to the ceiling. All I wanted to do was hold her in my arms, god damn it. To feel her soft skin against mine. To smell her freshness. To indulge in all things her. And now I have to deal with this shit. What an asshole and what a shit ass motherfucking day.

"Let me knock some sense into the dickhead." Dilan slides up to my side.

"He won't answer his phone. Let him calm down. I'll deal with him in the morning."

"You go get your girl." He pats me on the back. I have no clue what the hell has gotten into Beamer, but hell, he needs to have his head on straight for this shit or he may as well ship his ass right back to Michigan. My brother is too damn smart. If he knows you're showing any kind of weakness or your mind is unfocused, he will sniff you out. Beamer is far from weak. Right now, though, the dude's not focused. Something is tearing him up. I'm bound to find out what the hell is going on with him.

Beamer's mind isn't where it's supposed to be, and right now, he's out there on his own. No telling what could happen to him. I've never seen him lose control this way, and on a woman no less. No. It's not the fact he needs to get laid, or that he wants Deidre. There's more, and I'm going to dig it out of him, even if I have to toss our friendship aside to do so.

"I'm sorry. Do you mind if we stay here tonight? I just don't have the heart to leave her like this. I know she can get on people's nerves. She has a mouth that won't shut up. It's just... I've never seen her so upset before. She is devastated and refuses to talk to me. And for Deidre not to talk is unlike her." I bend down and cup her face between my hands and kiss her firmly on her lips.

"He said some things he shouldn't have. I'll talk to him tomorrow, get him all sorted out. She'll be fine." I feel her relax somewhat against my touch. However, her eyes tell me something else is troubling her and it has nothing to do with what went down before she walked in here.

"Something's bothering you. What is it?" I caress her soft skin. And as she turns her head slightly towards the door, there's a change in her expression when her stare lands on a certain spot, transfixing her there, a tear falling from her eyes.

She drops her gaze to the floor. I cup her chin in my hand, forcing her to look up at me.

"I... I didn't tell you about what happened today because I knew you would come running to the hospital. This was on my desk in my office when I got there this morning." She reaches into her bag she threw on the bed, pulling out a large manila envelope.

My pulse starts racing. Alina is watching me closely, gauging my reaction perhaps. Her hands are shaking. Her voice cracks when she asks me to take it.

"I can't look at those again," she says painfully. "I'm going to take a shower." She stands, my hand slipping from her chin as she moves around me and quietly shuts the bathroom door. I wait. Then I wait some more until I hear the shower running, never once taking my eyes off that envelope, wondering and knowing at the same time what's inside. It's flat. There are pictures inside, of what I don't know. Snatching the envelope off of the bed, I leave her room, give her the privacy she needs, and me, I'm not opening this in here alone. It's from him. I know it is. Whatever the hell is inside had her so upset and worried she didn't even call me. Which makes me think it wasn't a threat.

Still, anger and now remorse seep into my veins. She shouldn't have gone back to work, god damn it.

Reaching the living room, I toss the envelope on Dilan's lap without speaking, take the few steps to reach the mantle on the fireplace where I left a bottle of my scotch, uncork it, and take a hefty swig, welcoming the burn in my throat as it glides down.

"Open that. Tell me what's inside." Dilan looks at me suspiciously. I squeeze the bridge of my nose. My nerves are frayed. I'm feeling like I've been punched in the gut, losing the air in my lungs, and I don't even know yet what the hell is inside of that damn thing.

"That was on her desk this morning. You and I both know it's from him. Just open the damn thing." I exhale loudly. I turn away and place the scotch back on the shelf, leaving my back to him. The ruffling of the envelope being opened sounds like rough sandpaper being scrubbed furiously across my skin.

"Jesus Christ," Dilan exclaims. I spin around. The photos are on the floor in front of his feet. His hands are covering his eyes, the muscles in his arms flexing, constricting like whatever the hell he has seen has burned his mind.

"That sick, lowlife motherfucker," I bellow out when I pick the two photos off of the floor. How in the hell did he get these? She lives so high up this is nearly impossible.

There, in black and white, in front of my damn face, are photos from the other night of Alina and I. One of me with my head between her legs, the other of me on top of her, her legs wrapped around my waist. And written across both of them with what looks like a woman's handwriting are words that have my legs trembling. Words in the color red, the color Alina hates. She told me why she hated the color so much just the other night when we were tucked closely to each other in my bed.

"WHORE."

I'm so transfixed by these photos, remembering how beautiful this night was with her; how desperate I was to be inside of her and make slow, sweet love to the woman who is so deep inside my soul I know I wouldn't want to live without her, that I don't even realize she's standing beside me until I face her. Not one ounce of her being frightened radiates from her. I see anger. I see pain. I see hate and I see the exact same thing in her eyes that I do in my own: the urge to kill.

"I'm fine, Roan." She takes the photos from my hands and retrieves the envelope off the floor, stuffing them back inside.

"I will not let him ruin me. I'm done feeling scared all the time. I want him found and I want him tortured and killed. He will not destruct my courage to stand on my own two feet. And he most certainly will not destroy the beauty of what you and I have. Don't let him take that away from us," she pleads with wondering eyes. A soft-spoken voice full of confidence and sincerity. She's been living in hell because of what he did to her all those years ago, and now she stands before me with her damp hair, her cut-off shorts, and one of my t-shirts, showing me how brave she is.

"He could never take away what you and I share, Alina, but this, this is sick."

"I know, babe," she says quietly.

Dilan clears his throat. Both of us turn his way.

"I don't think you should go back to work," he says matter of factly.

"I have to. Those young patients need me. There's undercover security there, and Hugo sat in the waiting room all day. He can't get to me there." Her eyes narrow.

"He somehow managed to get those into your office without anyone noticing," Dilan makes a valid point.

"There are security tapes in front of every entrance to the hospital. It wasn't him. It was a young boy, couldn't have been more than sixteen years old, who walked up to the registration desk and asked for this to be delivered to me. Everyone knew I was out, so they left it on my desk. Hell, we get deliveries all the time. I don't think anyone thought anything about it." Her tone pitches higher the more she talks, she's pissed off.

"Then tomorrow when you go to work, I'm the one who will sit in that reception area all day. Hugo can stay here," Dilan declares.

"No, you won't. You're staying with Deidre. Besides, Hugo does not sit in the reception area all day long. That's' for patients. I said the waiting room. Those are two different things. You're staying with her. Now that we settled that, I'm starving, my feet are hurting, and my friend is going to talk to me whether she likes it or not. And these," she points to the photos, "are being shredded."

"Damn. She's feisty when she's mad," Dilan states.

"She's not mad, man. She's just as upset as we are." I walk into the kitchen and grab us both a beer and a couple of takeout menus from the top drawer where I saw Deidre put them back the other night when we ordered out.

"You pick." I hand the menus and the beer to him. "I'm going to try Beamer, then take a shower. Get someone on those photos too. I want to know exactly where those were taken from. Obviously from the building next door. It's a sky rise apartment building. Get me what I need, then tomorrow you and I are paying someone a visit." I twist the cap off of my beer, take a swig, and make my way down the hall to Alina's room. It smells like her, sweet, innocent, and pure. No smell or sense of the hatred pouring out of me like a blood red orange. He wants me to know where those pictures were taken from. That piece of shit. I chug the entire bottle of beer down. Slam it on the counter top in the bathroom. If he thinks I'm going to barge into that building next door and fall into whatever trap he has in store for me, he is delusional. He could be over there right now. Watching. Waiting. I move toward the open window. Stand there in the dim light.

"Do you see me, motherfucker? If you do, I'm right the fuck here. Come at me." I hold my hands out wide. "Come at me, brother, just leave her the hell alone." I stay that way for several minutes, knowing he isn't over there. Hell no, he's gone. He thinks I'm crazy and that I would run right over there the minute she showed me. Maybe that's what he wants. To get me out of here and away from her so he can strike. Hell, I don't know what the hell he wants. I run my hands through my hair. Frustrated. Agitated. I can't even take my girl on a damn date anymore. This is bullshit. Reaching into my pocket, I pull out my phone and dial Beamer's number.

"Damn it, Beamer. Call my ass back now." I'm not about to leave him a shit ton of voice mails. That's the only message I'm leaving that prick. He can wallow in his self-pity for all I care. I take my shower, soap myself up, shampoo my hair, and when I step out, I stare at my gun sitting on the counter, my trigger finger ready to kill for the first time in my life. It's fucking time to draw my brother out. This game of his is over, just like his life.

"You sure you're okay?" I say skeptically. Alina is half asleep on my chest.

"Does it bother me that someone was watching us have sex? Yes, it does. Am I going to stop being with you or having anything to do with you because of it? No. Am I scared? Yes. I'm scared out of my mind, but one thing I'm not is a coward like him. I will not stop loving you because he decides I have to, or whatever the hell is running through his crazy mind. He ruined me at such a young age. Stole something from me that I can never get back. That I don't even remember him taking. So he can fuck himself to death for all I care." Damn. Dilan is right. She is feisty. This isn't funny, though. Not by a long shot. He's known to follow through with his threats.

"Don't treat me like I'm fragile, Roan. Not you." I lie there for the longest time, wondering if I should tell her family about this. I decide against it. Her breathing shallows as she slowly drifts to sleep,. As much as it pains me, I have to let her be herself.

Chapter Fifteen

Alina

"I'm fine, dad. Stop worrying about me." I roll my eyes as if he can see me. "Listen, dad, put mom on the phone so I can set something up for dinner with the family, please? I love you, too." I jerk my head and pull the phone away from my ear. Why does he have to be so damn loud?

"Hi, Mom. How are you holding up?" Chewing on the inside of my mouth, I know what she's going to say, better yet, what she's going to do. She's going to start crying, saying the holy prayer, and asking god why he took her son away from her. He's not the one who killed him. Oh no, we all know who did, and just like Roan said last time, it's time.

Calla is sitting across from me right now, talking on the phone to Cain. So much for our girl time. Both of us are on the phone while our food sits in front of us, getting cold.

"My sweet baby girl. God took one child away from me, but he did give me back another." I know she's referring to me and the fact that I've come to terms with who we are.

"Mom. I really think both you and dad should come and see Dr. Brown like I suggested. It will do both of you—"

"No, Alina. What will do both me and your dad good is when Royal Diamond breathes his last breath. Until then, nothing will do any good. Now, enough of this talk about a doctor." My eyes go wide at her abruptness. Calla gives me a concerned look from across the table, ends her call with Cain, and digs into her burger.

"I'm sorry, mom. I will never bring it up again. I'm worried about you, is all."

"And I'm worried about you. I worry about all of you. But I'm dealing, honey. The best way I know how." She sighs. I change the subject back to dinner. I really want her to get to know Roan better. After my conversation earlier with dad, I feel like he is coming around little by little, and that's progress when it comes to a Solokov vs. a Diamond.

Something has changed in my dad in these few short weeks since my brother's murder. He's still a hard core, demanding ass when it comes to ruling his empire, shouting out orders and I'm sure beating, or worse yet killing, those who cross him, but he wants what's best for me. And I love him all the more for not demanding me to stop seeing the man I love.

"Love you, too, mom." Disconnecting the call, I set my phone on top of the table.

"I'm so sorry." Reaching across the table for my hand, Calla squeezes it gently, her eyes filled with unshed tears.

It's so hard hearing the pain in her voice. It breaks my heart all over again. I wipe away a tear that escapes before it begins to trail down my face.

"I don't know what to say." Calla squeezes my hand one more time and lets it go. I pick at my cobb salad that sounded so good before. Now it looks like a pile of wilting blah in front of me.

"There's nothing to say. Just the thought of you thinking about me is enough, and especially after... well, you know." I don't want to bring up the fact she was the one who Royal decided to target, his sick way of letting us all know what he did to Alexei.

"Let's talk about you and the fact you're going to have a baby." Her beautiful face lights up, her sleeked back ponytail swings as she shakes her head back and forth.

"I still can't believe I'm actually pregnant. That's one of the reasons I suggested we have lunch today. Cain and I have our first doctor's appointment today. I wanted to check on you and see how you were holding up, if there is anything I can do?" She shovels more food in her mouth. I stifle back a laugh. Typical of a pregnant woman to eat like a starving horse. She's going to be the perfect parent. Cain will be too. They both care so much about others.

"Just keep you and the baby safe and healthy," I say in return. I appreciate her gesture, but there really isn't anything anyone can do. None of us will find piece or closure until we know the man responsible is dead.

"Thanks for lunch, even though I ate all mine plus half of yours," Calla exclaims, face glowing from her pregnancy. I have no doubt at all a lot of it has to do with how happy she and Cain are about having a baby. A flash of jealousy manages to sneak up on me. Visions of my belly growing with Roan's baby flashes through my mind. I snap out of it. It's way too early in our relationship to even think about bringing a child into this world, especially with the malicious, evil curse of Royal lingering about. We walk across the street to the hospital with Hugo ahead of us and her bodyguard right behind us. Even though I respect Hugo and care deeply for him, I'm sick of this. I would give anything to be able to walk around like a normal person, not fearing for Hugo's life or my own. He would go down dying for me if Royal or anyone else tried to do anything. It's a shame, really, that a nice man like him would sacrifice his life for another. It's also an honor to know a man like him.

Calla dashes in front of us once she sees Cain standing by the entrance of the hospital, dark aviator sunglasses on, feet crossed at the ankles as he is leaning up against the wall. The urge for me to ask him why he doesn't have a bodyguard or ten of them for that matter muddles around in my mouth. I snap it shut the minute I see Roan step out from the other side of him. Those two together are sinful in that sexy I'm-good-looking-and-I-know-it sort of way. Neither one of them even turns to check out all the other women walking past us in their high heels, tight skirts, and legs that go on for miles. Nope, not our men. They're both standing there with their glasses on, eyes penetratingly on the two of us. I can feel it, even though I cannot see their eyes.

"Hey, Doc." He's all smiles. His chin dips as he inspects my body. My nipples strain against my bra and scrubs. My panties are instantly soaked by his smoldering look I know has to be in his eyes.

"See you two later," Calla calls out before they slip through the door, Cain's arm protectively around her waist, tucking her close to his side.

"Damn, baby. Tell me something. Are those pink panties that match those scrubs you have on wet?" He slips his arm around me. A flush of the same color pink creeps up my neck. I can feel it, the blood pumping from my head to my core and back again with those sensual words.

"I took them off." I rest my palms against his chest, my tone seductive.

"You cougar, you." He smirks

"Ah. Teasing me about my age now, are we? Because the other night when I was sitting on your face and you—" He cuts me off with a demanding kiss. This kiss is brutal, almost angry. He's attacking my mouth with his tongue pummeling mine. I can't seem to move. I've never seen him like this before, it's as if he's punishing me for something I have no clue I even did. When we break apart, all the playfulness from moments ago is gone. Angry eyes stare at me.

"That's for not telling me you were leaving here and meeting Calla for lunch."

"Excuse me?" I take a step back from him.

"You heard me, Alina. After those photographs the other day, you stepped out without fucking telling me and that pisses me off." My eyes go wide. How dare he act this way towards me.

"Fuck. I'm sorry. It's just that I'm so worried he's going to come after you. He has to know we're serious about each other, and the one way he can torture my damn soul is to get to you. I told you, I've waited forever for you and the thought of—"

"Stop." I step in and place a finger on his mouth.

"I should have called you and I apologize for that, but I will not stop living my life because of him. It's broad daylight out. He's not going to try anything with a million people walking around in downtown New York." He has the nerve to scowl at me. Frustrating man.

"He's every damn where, Alina. He's like a ghost." What he's saying is true. We don't have any idea where he is or what he has planned. But damn it all to hell. I'm not going to stand outside of where I work and argue about this. Maybe I shouldn't be here, bringing unwanted danger to a hospital. It could be dangerous to everyone inside. But this is the only place that takes away my pain. I don't think about anything else here, except the fact that I have the ability to heal someone else's suffering. To make them feel better when they walk out of these doors. It's backwards in a way. When I walk in these doors, my misery disappears; when I leave, it hits me all over again.

Roan's right. I shouldn't be making myself an easy target for that bastard. The man has no conscience whatsoever. He's proven it with murder, the pictures, sending what he did to Calla, and kidnapping, drugging, and nearly killing her and the man I'm in love with. I sigh. This conversation is far from being over. I look down at my watch..

"I have to go," I say frantically. Ten minutes is all I have to get to the office, wash my hands, and look over the next patient's chart. "Pick me up at five." I don't have time to let him respond, kiss him goodbye, or even finish our conversation. I fly through the doors of the hospital. By the time I'm finished, I'm only two minutes late. Late for what I have decided is going to be my last day of work for god knows how long.

"Look, Alina," Dr. Ross steeples his hands under his chin. The wrinkles on his face are more prominent than I've noticed before. He's concerned, worried about me. I respect him more than anyone. He's lived in New York his entire life, he knows who I am. He also never brings it up. He's never had a reason to, and now I'm sitting here being honest with a man I work side by side with. Dr. Ross is one of the best Pediatric physicians in the entire state of New York. He's well respected, has patients like a saint, and a bedside manner like no one I have ever met. The man has taught me more in the few months I have worked with him than I learned while interning.

"I agree with you. I don't think you should be here. However, it's not because I think you're bringing danger into this hospital or into my office. I know you better than that. You're risking your own life by even being here. That, my dear, is what concerns me. Now, I implore you to please take all the time you need. Your job will be here waiting for you."

"Thanks for understanding. You don't know how much this means to me." He stands and comes around to the side of his desk where I'm sitting.

"Your heart is in the right place. And it's me who respects you more than you'll ever know. Now, go home. Always know I'm here for you. I'm only a phone call away." He bends and places his hand over the top of mine where I have it resting on my knee.

"Thank you," I say politely and truthfully.

A heavy burden is lifted by the time I climb into Roan's truck a few minutes after five. The silence lingers in the air the farther we go. Not the good kind of tension that I'm used to having with this man. Instead it's choking me half to death the way it pummels through the cab. We left things unsaid. And now here we are, driving back to his place, not speaking. I hate it.

"I'm not returning back to work until all this is over," I blurt out, hoping we can talk through this while we inch along through traffic.

"I know that must have been a hard decision for you." Both of us turn toward one another at the same time. His eyes holding guilt, mine showing sadness.

"Yes, it was, but I need to be honest with myself. The sad thing is I feel no pain there, no anger. Just peace. But you were right the other day when you said you thought it was too soon, and you were also right this afternoon when you said it was dangerous for me to be visible. It made me think I'm not only placing myself in danger, but the lives of others as well. If it's me he's after, he will stop at nothing to get to me, and that includes there. I wouldn't be able to live with myself if anything happened to someone because of me." Roan reaches across the console, takes hold of my hand, and brings it up to his lips, kissing across my fingers. His simple gesture means so much more to me than he will ever know.

"The way you care about others, Alina, is one of the million reasons why I love you. And coming to the hospital was a mistake. I apologize for that, but what I won't apologize for is getting angry because you didn't tell me about it. I'm not a controlling man at all. I respect your independence and the fact you've accomplished so much on your own. It's just if anything happens to you, Alina, I won't be able to survive. You're everything to me." The traffic starts to move. We drive with him still holding my hand, our fingers twined together on top of the console.

"I should give you your own spanking for showing up to the hospital the way you did," I say jokingly, hoping, though, what I'm trying to say comes across so we can drop it and move on.

"I agree. I acted irrationally when Cain told me the two of you were going to lunch. The first thing that ran through my mind was, *What the hell are they thinking?* I should have just called or waited until later to tell you. I knew Cain was going there to meet Calla. It still didn't stop me. Call me overprotective, call me an ass. I'll follow, wait, and do anything I have to, to keep you safe." The man knows how to hold my heart captive with the sweet things he says. He reminds me so much of my dad with the gentle way he talks to me, and his need to protect.

I remember every morning when all of us would wake up, the house a chaos with our entire clan getting ready for school and my dad trying to get ready for work. It didn't matter to him if he was late or not, or that my mom was a stay-at-home mother. He still helped her out, stole kisses from her in the kitchen, or gently squeezed her arm as he would stand by her as she was rinsing out our morning dishes and putting them in the dishwasher; on some days even driving the whole lot of us to school or surprising us by picking us up. It wasn't until I was a teenager and wanted to play soccer that I knew he did those things because he loved us and wanted to protect us from the danger of our world and the crazies amongst it. Even though I hated having one of my older brothers sit there during practice, deep down inside I knew it was because my dad loved me and he was only protecting me. I've been loved and protected my entire life.

Now that I'm old enough to appreciate it, have fallen in true love with a man who is also a protector, I see it so clearly. Earlier today, I told myself I would give anything to be able to walk down the street with no bodyguard behind me. That's not true. Not one damn bit. If it were, I would not be riding in this truck, holding hands with another man who wants to protect me, cherish me.

Even in this dark lifestyle of murder, drugs, hate, and deceit, a life I will loathe for the rest of my life, my destiny is right here with Roan, who has walked in my shoes. Grown up the same way I did. As much as I don't want to admit this to myself, it is my life, and I need to do everything I can to accept and embrace it.

Life can, and will always be, a fickle bitch. Trample all over you. Stomp on your heart. It's how you deal with the shit she throws at you that makes you into the person you are. I'm finally learning to deal.

Chapter Sixteen

Roan

"I thought you said you weren't controlling?" Alina says, heavy breathing coming out of her mouth, her chest moving up and down in a way that has her breasts begging for my mouth.

I have her spread out on my bed. Gloriously naked. Arms above her head. Legs spread so wide and that pussy of hers drenched.

We came back to my place tonight. Deidre left to go stay at her parents' house for a while the minute her parents returned from Japan, where her dad has been for the past three months with three of our other attorneys on a case gone terribly wrong. It seems half of our men cannot keep their damn dicks in their pants when they decide to go on vacation. Two of them got busted over there for being in the wrong place at the wrong time when a large prostitution ring was busted. Sons of bitches will never change. I should have let them rot over there. Taught them a lesson. But the idea of any of our men being in a foreign prison even scares me half to death. So what do I do? I send one of best attorneys over there to get them the hell out. The both of them will be shoveling shit for a very long damn time. The need for Deidre to leave their apartment so badly had me calling Dilan after she broke down once again. Only this time, she felt like she was being smothered inside of their place

I focus back on this perfection of beauty lying in my bed.

"This isn't controlling, baby, this is supervising over what's mine. I'm inspecting the goods, making sure they're in tip top shape and ready to deliver." I slip one finger inside her tight heat. Jesus, she's wet for me. Her ass flies off the bed. I love how responsive she is to me. How wet I can make her just by looking at her pussy.

"God, you're good with your fingers," she moans.

"Do you mean this finger?" I pull my middle finger out and glide my index finger in, curling it just so.

"Do that again." I quirk my brow at her demand, even though I do what she asks. She pants and presses her pussy into my finger more.

"That's my trigger finger, baby. And it looks like it's twitching to aim and fire." I rapidly start to pump my finger in and out of her. My cock is so damn hard right now it's fucking painful. There is no way I'm slipping inside of her without getting her to come once for me before I do.

I lean forward, my hand cupping over her, my finger still thrusting wildly. I tug one of her nipples in my mouth, craving for her to let go and come all over my hand. She's shouting out words I don't even understand. Russian, I think. Fuck me that turns me on even more. I bask in the glory of her perfect tits and her perfect pussy. I nibble, nip, suck, and bite, being as rough as I am gentle. The last time I feasted on her breasts, I left burn marks from my scruff she seems to love so much. The pain from them doesn't seem to bother her one bit, but me, I hate the fact of hurting her in any way at all, so I trimmed it down, made it smoother, softer and now, shit, I can suck those pink nipples as far into my mouth as I want and not worry.

"Roan." Her saying my name scorches my heart in a good way whenever she says it through ragged breaths. I am also getting to know her body and when she's about ready to let go. Not only does she clench herself around me, but she also screams out my name every time she's ready to come.

"Let me have this orgasm, Alina. Give it to me." I take her mouth with mine and stick another finger inside her. Then she does it. She explodes after a few faced-paced strokes all over my hand.

I draw my fingers out while still going at her mouth, her tongue matching my every stroke, wrapping itself around mine. Her mouth is deliciously sweet, and it's about to taste a whole lot better with what I have in mind. I pull away for a beat. Her mouth still parted open, I wipe her juices all across her lips and smooth them over her tongue. When she goes to lick her lips, I stop her by tracing my own tongue across them in a way that has her eyes going large, her tongue darting out, and fuck me, she's lapping up her sweet taste right along with me. Fuck, I need her. And I can tell she needs me. Her eyelids are so low I can barely see her stunning eyes.

"You may think I control you, but I'm here to tell you that's impossible, my beautiful lady. You control me. Your mere presence draws me close to you. And god, baby, you are my calm in this warring existing battle that my family and now yours has been suffering under for years. Destiny brought you and I together, and a much higher power put me here for you. I love you, and those three words right there are proof enough that you control every emotion instilled inside of me, but mostly you control my heart."

Tears form in her eyes. I wipe them away. Her next words have my heart shifting gears, rapidly speeding on an adrenaline surge.

"Then let's control each other together. I love you, too, so very much," she whispers, her lips trembling with the urge to cry.

I need her, to be deep inside of her. To show her how much I love her. To possess her. Always claim her as mine. To let her know I'm hers. God, I'm so hers.

I edge myself right where I want to be in between those magnificent legs of hers. Her lips part. Her eyes dance back and forth between mine. Slowly, I ease my way into the best thing I have ever felt in my life. Every time I'm inside of her feels better than the last. So tight. So sweet. So smooth.

She gasps, enclosing herself around me. I move slow and steady, swiveling my hips, driving as deep as I can go.

Her back arches high. I swing my arm around her ass and lift it, pressing her closer, begging to get as deep as I can with every thrust. Every touch.

"God," she screams. I capture her mouth, groaning myself, picking up my pace with the sudden urge to fill her. To take her where she needs to be.

"Fuck. I'm lost in you." Lifting away from her mouth, confining her lust-filled eyes to stay on mine, I want to watch her fall apart beneath me. To let her see what only she can do to me. I pump harder, faster, and thank god, deeper, and let go with her name on my lips. My body buried inside of my slice of heaven, my piece of mind, and the woman who without a doubt controls me.

Holding her close to me, our arms and legs tangled around each other. My thoughts drift to my friend, my brother Beamer. I hate pulling away from her. From the first time I held her in my arms, I love the way she feels. She was meant to be right where she is now.

"I need to try and get ahold of Beamer again." I say, dragging my body away from her.

"Of course." Propping herself up onto her elbows.

Reaching for my phone, I hit dial on his name, wishing he would pick up.

"Still no answer?" Alina asks. I drop my phone on the floor, not caring if the damn thing breaks. I have called everyone I can think of to see if they have heard from Beamer and no one has. Nothing. Not even our friends back in Michigan. This isn't like him at all. Something else must have set him off. What, though?

"No, and I'm starting to worry about him now. I have no clue where he could be." I pull her into me as tightly as I can get her. Her soft little body stays firm against mine as she draws circles around my chest. Her touch putting a dent into my dreary mind.

At first I was so damn angry with him. The way he spit those hateful words out to Deidre is not like the Beamer I know. He's usually so calm and collected, well put together. No. Something must have happened for him to go off on her like that. To spur that unforgiving flame under his sharp tongue. I have a feeling deep in my gut that Deidre knows what the hell is wrong with him and she's not saying shit. I'm going to have to pay her a visit in the morning, and if she knows something, she better fucking tell me.

Jesus, what if my brother got a hold of him? "Shit." I shoot myself straight up in bed.

"What is it?" Alina places her hand on my back.

"What if Royal got to him when he left here?" The words feel so damn bitter coming off my tongue.

"Don't say that. Don't even think it. He's more than likely blowing off steam somewhere."

I look down at my hand. The one missing a finger. The entire night my brother tortured me rages like a storm in my god damn head. He gets off on that shit, and when he's had enough, he makes you beg to kill him just to take away all the pain and suffering you're in. Then he taunts you a little more before he steals away your last breath. I inhale deeply, lay my head back on the pillow, and pull my sweet woman close to me. I know damn well sleep will be non-existent for me tonight.

"He'll come around, Roan. I know he will."

"Yeah. I hope you're right."

God. I fucking hope she's right. Those are the thoughts I have stewing away in my head while I listen to her breathing shallow, letting me know at least one of us will be sleeping tonight.

****

"Good morning," I call out to a half-awake, stunning woman spread across my bed, the covers half off her body, showing me those perfect legs of hers. Hell, even watching her lie there and stretch has my dick stretching right along with her.

"How long have you been up?" Tossing the covers off, she stands and scampers her messy bed-headed self into the bathroom. I walk towards the bed with two cups of coffee in my hand, waiting for her to do her business. I place one down on the side table and take a hefty sip of the other. I knew I wouldn't sleep last night. Finally somewhere around three this morning, I got up, opened up my laptop, and started setting things in motion with the plan Jackson and I devised.

After talking with Jackson yesterday, his wheels are in full swing, drugs coming in like he wants them to. All of Alina's brothers are on board. This is our only hope. The only way we know how to get him. He needs to hear on the streets that a heavy shipment of narcotics made it across the border and somehow managed to land in New York City.

Trusting and bonding isn't an easy thing to do with Chiko Vendoza, but somehow in a matter of a week or so, Jackson has done it, he's in. I'm sure the fact he just got out of jail was beneficial for him, moving as quickly as he did before the county had officially filed all the papers to completely drop all the charges brought against him. Very smart move on his part. Now Jackson is sitting on some very serious heroin. My skin crawls just thinking about how that shit actually feels.

"Not too long," I lie. I know she's worried. That's the type of woman she is. She also agreed to go see Deidre with me this morning and hang out with me at my office all day. The thought of her being out of my sight right now eats away at me every time we're apart, so having her around is a good thing. A damn good thing. My dick goes crazy once again, thinking about taking her on my desk. Over the arm of my couch or, hell, she can sit on me and ride me in my chair. But first, I need to find out what the hell Deidre knows, what she's hiding. I have a feeling I know what it is, but the words need to come out of her mouth.

"For you." I hand her the coffee when she comes towards me, her hair pulled back in some fancy clip, her face freshly washed.

"Thank you." She takes a sip and sets it back down.

"You know, I was thinking. If Deidre and Aidan—which I'm calling him from now on by the way. Not a fan of his nickname." She lightly chuckles. "If they really slept together like you think, then why would he say what he said and then just take off?"

"I really don't know. I'm going to find out, though, I can tell you that." I come across a lot angrier than I meant to.

"I'm going to shower, so give me about an hour and then we can go." She bends and kisses me, completely ignoring my nasty tone from a moment ago.

"Baby, wait." I need to tell her. Get this off of my chest. I've been feeling guilty about keeping the truth from her for this long.

"What's wrong?" She sits down on the bed. I hate the way she's looking at me now. She's trying to contain herself, to beat back the worry on her face.

"Shit, Alina. I'm just going to say it. I told both Cain and Anton what you told me." Hell. I can't even look at her. I keep my gaze trained to the floor.

"I know." My head flies up. How the hell does she know?

"How?" I ask her.

"Anton told me. I've known since the day before we left my parents'. I wanted to see if you would tell me yourself, if you would be honest with me." Holy mother of god. Is she a saint? I shake my head in disbelief.

"I apologize. I betrayed you."

"You did no such thing, Roan. You heard something that tore you up, you needed to tell someone, and I get it. I truly do."

"That's it, you're not mad? You're not going to throw things at me, call me names, chew me a new asshole?" She stares at the bathroom door for several moments, her expression difficult to read.

"No, I'm not mad, Roan. We've all been told things that tear us up so much inside that we need someone to talk to, someone who will listen to the anger building up inside of us. I told you because I trust you and I was falling in love with you, and because of that, I wasn't going to keep that part of my life to myself anymore. All of my brothers know. I've talked to each one of them. My biggest concern is I never want my dad to know. I couldn't bear the thought of him blaming himself, and he would. He's the one who took Royal in. Treated him like part of the family. He trusted him, and his betrayal to my father has done enough damage. I won't be the cause of any more pain to him."

"Come here, beautiful lady." I drag her across the bed until she's straddling my lap.

"This has been eating away at me for days. Every time I thought about telling you, something else would come up. I didn't mean to betray your trust." I nuzzle her neck, slipping my arms around her, pulling her body tight into mine. God. She's so strong. So sensible. I don't know what I did to deserve a woman like her. Christ.

"Thank you for understanding." I kiss her briefly. She climbs off my lap. And hell, I do believe I've fallen in love with her even more. She's known for weeks and she never said a damn thing. Fuck. With everything going on, I kept putting it off. Thank Christ she forgives me.

The water to the shower turns on. I would give anything to head into that shower with her. To work from home. I sit there staring at the blank wall for a long time. My phone rings. Digging it out, I look at the caller ID, hesitating briefly before answering it.

"Diamond," I say gruffly. Then my mouth goes as dry as the desert.

"Beamer, is that you?" No one answers. All I hear is heavy breathing and footsteps.

"Royal." I pop up off the bed and listen intently. And when the sound of the footsteps diminishes, I know damned well he's on the other end.

"Come and get me, pathetic coward," I taunt his crazy ass. "I'm right the fuck here. Right where you know I am. Waiting the hell for you. You pussy ass bitch."

Silence. Not a word. Only heavier breathing. I'm getting to him. I know I am.

"Only a coward would come after an innocent person. Only a little prick with no balls would kill a person who has nothing to do with this shit. You want me, motherfucker, then you come and get me. But so help me god, you spineless bastard, this time I'm going to fucking rip your heart out." I stop pacing, my heart beating so damn hard in my chest it's about to explode.

"I'll come after you, little brother, once I get my hands on that whore of yours. Before I take from you what's mine, I'm going to have a little fun with some of your friends."

Jesus. He has Beamer. Fuck. This is all kinds of messed up. No wonder my good friend hasn't answered his phone. He's got him.

"He has nothing to do with you, Royal. It's me you want."

"I'll get you. But like I said, I need to have some fun. I had to go into hiding because of you. I'm out of practice. I need to sharpen my skills if you know what I mean." He laughs that sick, fucked up, hackling laugh.

"Fuck you!" I yell into the phone. He says nothing, of course he doesn't, the fucker hung up.

Think, Roan, think! I cock my head toward the bathroom door. The shower is still running. Thank god she's still in there. The thought of her knowing about this is almost too much for me to handle. She's strong, but this will drain that strength out of her.

"Dad." My voice is shaky. My entire body is shaking with fear, all thoughts on my friend. Guilt kicks me right in the damn mouth. This is my fault, dragging him and everyone else into this. I should have known better. It should be me he has, not Beamer.

As soon as I hang up with my dad, I call Cain, and Jackson after him. We all agree to meet at the warehouse. With my eyes trained on the bathroom door, I call Dilan, tell him the entire story and ask him to get his ass down here as soon as he can. For the tenth time today, I thank god he's renting someone's apartment in this building and lives a few floors up.

The shower goes off and, fuck, she's going to be out here any minute. I pace the floor, my back to her, my shoulders lowered in defeat. I won't lie to her. I've betrayed her once already. She never even blinked an eye when I told her. No more hiding things from her. Right now, I have to be the one to crumble the woman

I love. To watch her fall apart with worry and blame, just like I'm blaming myself right now.

"Roan," she whispers. Her hand comes to rest on my shoulder. This time, her touch does nothing to calm me. The only thing it does is deepen the guilt, the pain.

"Royal has Beamer," I say softly through clenched teeth, spitting out the words that are eating me alive.

"How? What happened?" I look down at my phone. It's burning a hole in my hand. All I want to do is throw it, smash it, until there's nothing left of the damn thing.

'I had to go into hiding because of you.' Those words will haunt me.

Chapter Seventeen

Alina

I hate guilt. It's the worst feeling in the entire field of emotions. It will consume you, fill you with despair and shame from the evil that corrupts your soul.

Feeling content over our conversation we just had, I step in the shower, grateful he told me himself. I knew he would. I lean my head back under the spray, then jump, cradling my hand over my chest when I hear Roan yell.

Turning off the water, I dry off, throwing on my clothes in a rush. I swing open the door, bracing my hands up against the frame from the sight of Roan standing before me, his shoulders slumped over in defeat. "Roan," I call out his name. When he speaks those dreaded words, I want to fall to the floor. This is what he feared. It's true. Royal has Beamer.

Guilt consumes me, eating away at me from the inside out.

That's how both Roan and I are feeling right now, as if it's our fault. And it is. Royal wants me for some screwed up reason and he wants his brother even more. He needs to be found. If I really thought I could take someone else's life I would be the first one to do it. Even when I held the gun in my hands, shooting, imagining it was his life I was taking, deep down I knew I would never be able to pull the trigger. To kill him

I stand behind the man I love, who has yet to turn and face me. His entire body is trembling. A part of me wants to hold him, console him, and tell him we will get through this together. The truth is, I know all about his plan. He's shared it all with me over the past few days. It's a plan I hate. Anything that puts people in danger, I loathe. But nothing compares to the hatred I feel for Royal. How can one man single-handedly destroy the lives of so many others?

"What can I do to help?" I say quietly, knowing damn well he's not going to want me to do anything. I'm going to be stuck here worrying, feeling more guilt, while he's out there looking for him. Falling into his brother's trap. Royal knows Roan will come after him. He knows he will go to his death to save those he cares about.

He turns, and my heart aches from the torturous look of guilt and shame on his face.

"Dilan's on his way to stay with you. I've called my dad and Cain, but now that I think of it, Cain should stay as far away from this as possible. They were getting ready to leave for Michigan. I just fucked up. I should have never called him. He's going to be a dad. I'm not taking my chances when it comes to him. I'm going to call him back, tell them to get the hell out of here. Dilan will go with me. We'll work something out to get you to your parents' house or wherever you want to go. Just stay there until you hear from me."

The look in his eyes is tormenting my soul, crushing it into tiny pieces. He's rambling. I hate this for him, for me, for everyone. "You know Cain won't leave, Roan. Calla can come with me to my parents, we'll be safe there."

"Yeah. You'll be safe there." I go to him then. My defeated man.

"This is not your fault. Do you hear me?" He blinks rapidly. Vulnerability. Rage. Despair. I see them all in his eyes.

"Fuck. He has him, Alina."

"I know, baby. I'm calling my dad. Give me the address of where you're meeting?" I pull strength out of thin air, my tone firm and demanding. Roan needs time to pull himself together. He cannot leave here feeling defenseless. And he and Cain will not walk into this trap alone. He needs all the help he can get, and I know my dad will call my brothers. Whether they are family or not, to every one of them this is about revenge, closure, peace of mind for the crimes that bastard has committed on our families.

The muscles in his neck twitch. He's fighting against himself.

"Damn it, Roan. Give me the address. You cannot do this alone." Without even blinking, I snatch his phone from his hand and dial my dad's number.

"Roan?" My dad answers.

"No, Dad, it's me." My voice sounds panicky.

"Alina, sweetheart," he says as if he's surprised to hear from me.

"I need your help, dad."

"Alina, I know. Word travels, honey. I'm already on my way." I close my eyes. Of course he already knows.

"I want you to find him and kill him, dad. End this now." Silence greets me. I don't know if my words have shocked my dad or what the hell he is thinking.

"Alina, I want you at our house. Your mother needs you. And I need to know you will be safe. Hugo should be there any minute. And I need you to promise me you will stay there. Do you understand me?" His voice is raised. "Yes," I lie. I will go out there and make sure my mother is all right. I will stay, but the minute I have the opportunity to escape, I will. I don't care if I have to shoot someone or beat them over the head. This is my fight too, and this time I expect to win.

"I love you." Roan kisses me goodbye. Determination is all I see in his expression now. Revenge pouring out of him like an overflowing dam. Worry consumes me. I hide it. Seal it away. He needs to stay focused, not worry about me.

"Be safe." I kiss him one more time. All I want to do is drag him back inside, lock his bedroom door, and go back to where we were just a few hours ago. Loving, holding and promising each other a future. But I can't. He has to go and so do I.

I watch him climb into his truck. The man I love is leaving, and I hope with all that I have that he comes back to me. Just like those words he spoke to me the other night. I've waited my entire life for him like he has for me, and now that we've both found love for the first time in our lives, I will not let it be taken away from me.

Hugo closes the door after I climb inside, neither of us speaking the entire ride to my parents' house, the two of us lost within our own thoughts.

Plans have changed so much in the past half hour. Dilan is now with Roan. All of my brothers are now on their way. Every man I love is now in danger, caught up in the web of destruction caused by Royal Diamond. All of them except Cain, who agreed to come out to my family's home with Calla, which botches up my plan to escape. Now I wait and worry. Tears start to fall freely down my face. This burden is weighing heavily. The mixed emotions are more than I can take. I'm grateful Hugo is quiet and leaves me to shed my tears on my own. Words of comfort are not what I need right now. I need this nightmare to be over. I need my man back. I need to know my family will be safe. Until then, nothing or no one will erase the helplessness I feel. The guilt. The faith that is no longer there that I was finally finding happiness, and now why in the hell do I feel like it's about to be ripped away from me?

"Deidre." I jerk my head towards Hugo as we pull up to my parents' home.

Hugo looks at me as if I've gone crazy. Which I have while frantically digging through my bag for my phone.

I dial her number, then wait not so patiently for her to answer. "Come on, pick up." Voicemail. I hang up and dial again. It goes straight to voicemail again. I try again and again until finally giving up and dialing her mother.

"Oh thank god, you answered," I say to Beth, Deidre's mother. "Alina honey, what is it?" There is panic in her voice.

"I'm trying to reach Deidre and she's not answering."

"She's still sleeping, sweetheart. We stayed up late watching movies. Is everything all right?" I detect the dread in her voice.

"I don't have time to explain. I need to speak with her, please, Beth," I reply, my own voice dismayed. She must have fallen back to sleep after responding to my text a few hours ago, telling her Roan and I were coming over to talk. I knew I woke her when her simple response of "okay" came across my screen.

"Honey, you're frightening me," Beth says. The sound of her heels click on the floor, then her breathing accelerates as she starts to climb the stairs. They live in a three-story brownstone with Deidre's old room on the top floor.

"It's complicated. I—"

"Oh, my god. No!" she screams into the phone. I jump out of the car, my heart ceasing. "Be... Beth." I place my free hand on the hood of the car, my legs going weak. Something is terribly wrong.

"She's not here! My baby, she's gone!"

"Are you sure? I mean, she could be in the shower," I say.

"No. She's not. Her room is a mess. Clothes are scattered everywhere. It's as if she was in a hurry to get out of here. Where is she?"

I place my shaky hand over the receiver. "Hugo, go get Cain, please." His truck is in the drive so I know he is here.

"Noooooooooooooo!" She screams before I hear a crashing sound.

"Beth!" I yell and yell some more. I hear the rustling of the phone. She must have dropped it. What the hell is going on?

"He has her?" Is all she says before my legs do give out. I collapse onto the cement, my knees stinging from the hard impact. I don't know anymore if the screaming is coming from me or from Beth. All I know is this is the beginning, not the end of my nightmare.

BEAMER

"You sick fuck." Jesus Christ. Her screams are ringing in my head. My head is being held securely by some crazy motherfucker, while another crazy ass high on some shit has my eyes pried open and all I see is her. Deidre, strung up naked with chains around her arms. Her body limp as Royal slashes her back with a knife. Blood dripping down her body. Her violent cries and pleads for him to stop will never go away. How much more can she take?

Five minutes after I left their apartment, I was rammed from behind on my bike. Knocked off. And the next thing I knew, there were three men standing over me with guns pointed in my face. I fought them until they beat the shit out of me, cracking my ribs with every kick and punch to my stomach.

Tossed in the back of a van and brought here, I was ready to face my death. But god, seeing her up there and knowing I'm strapped down and can't do a damn thing to help her, makes me wish I was dead.

This is my fault. I should have never left her. Never spoken to her the way I did, especially after what we shared. The first time I saw her, I thought she was the most beautiful woman I had ever seen. And then she opened her mouth. And damn, did I want to shut her up. Her bossy attitude needed to be spanked out of her. We got on each other's nerves. The way she complained about being trapped in her apartment with the king of filth, the pig who left his shit everywhere, only inspired me to do it more. And then I couldn't take it anymore. Her brassy little attitude started to turn me on. I continued to tell myself it was because I was horny as hell. The first taste I got of her mouth told me it wasn't because of that, not at fucking all. And then I fucked her, hard, fast, and god, did she feel good, draining my cock and then fifteen minutes later, coming back for more.

And fuck, the fight we had. I should have never said what I did. It all started out as a joke. And now look at her. I can't take it anymore.

"Tell me where they've taken her, you fucking slut! I'm done screwing around with you. You tell me or I'm going to fuck you until you are so raw these slices on this pearly white skin of yours will feel like a gift from me compared to what I will do between those legs of yours."

"I'm te... telling you I don't know. I've been with my parents for days." I start to breathe heavier, listening to her stutter. *Hold on, baby doll*. I struggle against the restraints on my wrists.

"She's a pretty little thing, isn't she?" The crazy asshole holding my eyes gets right up in my line of vision. Rearing my head back, I head butt the prick. Watch him tumble backwards, his ass hitting the floor, holding his damn nose and screaming like the pussy bitch he is.

"Shoot that bastard up with enough to kill him. Or blow his damn head off. One or the other." The head pussy they call Scarface, known to all of us as Royal, bellows out from behind Deidre.

"Fuck off. Why don't you untie me and fight like a real man? Better yet, untie me and try to kill me yourself," I goad him to come at me.

"Shut him up." He points his knife in my direction.

I fight, squirm, and wiggle to try and get my hands or feet free. And then I feel it. The prick of a needle in my neck. I fight that off for as long as I can.

I'm drifting, the urge to keep my eyes open failing with each passing second. I hear him, though. Loud and fucking clear.

"Tell me what plans they have for me, bitch. I know you know something! You live with the fucking whore. Girls are tight. Now tell me!" My eyes fly open. Royal grabs her by a handful of hair, yanking her head back, and those blank half-dead eyes look right at me. *Hold on, baby doll*.

"She doesn't know a damn thing. But I sure as fuck do." I'll do anything to kill time. Anything to make him leave her alone. I heard him call Roan and I know with every breath I have left he will find us. That's all I know. After that, I descend into black.

DEIDRE

The most intense pain I have encountered in my life shoots up and down my backside. I'm shaking from the massive white spikes clawing at my face, like someone has thrown boiling water on every inch of my face and neck. I can't breathe. I can barely see, hear, or feel my arms.

My throat is raw. I'm shivering in spite of how hot my skin feels.

He slices me again and my mind drifts. I should have never answered the phone. I assumed it was Alina calling me after I texted her back with a one-word response.

I tossed my phone on the floor, sunk my face into my pillow, and screamed.

She and Roan wanted to talk to me. And I knew it had everything to do with Beamer not being around. After our fight, he left. It was all my fault. My life was put on hold with Royal on the loose, and I took my anger out on the man who risked his life to protect mine. I was a bitch, denying to myself he turned me on like no man has ever before. His dark hair, those damn abs. Those arms that are bigger than my waist. God, he's insanely sexy. But he's a damn pig, leaving a trail of a disastrous mess behind him everywhere he goes. Dirty dishes in the sink, leaving his towel on the floor after he showers.

And then he kissed me, pinned me up against the wall with his hard body. I melted. Gave in to my craving for him. We fucked. And I mean headboard-banging, body-smashing downright dirty fucking, and it was the most explosive orgasm I have ever had. That man knows how to work his dick and play with a pussy like a pro. And then he went and called me names. Started his bullshit again. Crushed me. And what did I do? I went for his jugular, said things I really didn't mean. Then he left. Somehow, I was wound up in the throes of the man he was trying to protect me from.

That call was not from Alina. It was from Royal. He told me if I ever wanted to see Beamer again to be outside of my parents' house in five minutes. I quickly got dressed. Tip-toed down the two flights of stairs, knowing damn well if my parents caught me leaving, they would put a stop to it.

The moment I exited the house, the black SUV was parked across the street, and like the stupid woman I am, I darted across, landing right in the arms of our worst enemy.

And now here we both are. Him tied to a chair. Me hanging by chains while this sick bastard gets his kicks by mutilating my body and making Beamer watch.

My eyes try to focus on Aidan, the man known as Beamer. After we had sex, I couldn't get his real name out of my mind, so I googled the meaning of it and it fits him so perfectly.

"Fiery one." And he's full of it. Confident. Secure. And I want to run to him so badly right now. To hold him and tell him I'm so very sorry for the way I treated him.

He's toying with them, smashing his head against the man now lying on the floor, holding his face. I want to laugh at him. To reach out and kick him. I'm too weak. The blood is dripping down my back, pooling around my toes. Every one of my limbs is fighting for control of the blood left inside my body. A prick of a needle, then a hot sensation seeps into my veins mixing with my blood flowing rapidly.

I watch as they poke Aidan with a needle in the side of his neck. His head lags to one side and then the other.

I'm going to die and I know it. I won't be able to tell him or anyone how much they mean to me.

"Did you hear me, you fucking slut?" Royal grabs my hair and places his knife to my throat. My eyes beg him to do it. To kill me, finish me off, so I don't feel a damn thing anymore.

My pain is slowly freeing my skin, leaving it with a tingly feeling.

I try to speak, to tell him to go fuck himself. I don't know a damn thing, regardless if I did, it wouldn't matter. He will kill me the minute he thinks he has the information he needs. And no matter what he does to me, I will not tell him shit. I know nothing anyway.

I manage to find some sort of way to speak, my voice hoarse.

"Fuck you," I say before I'm punched in the face. And just like that, Aidan's handsome face is gone and my pain is gone, leaving my world, my body, and my soul to nothing.

ALINA

I wake. My head is throbbing. My legs are aching. I'm in my old bedroom at my parents' house. Jumping out of bed, I halt when I see my mom and Calla sitting on the built-in daybed by my window.

"It's true, isn't it? He has her. He has them both, doesn't he?" I look from one to the other. Both of them have been crying. Their eyes are bloodshot and swollen. I feel sick. A roll of nausea manages to crawl up my throat. Dashing into the bathroom, I heave in the sink. The smell has me gagging, dry heaving, and crying. I scream. I kick. I claw my nails into the palms of my hands. My god. This is going to become a blood bath before it's all over. More innocent people will die because of me. All of this is because of me.

I slump to the floor, my entire body trembling.

"Alina. My goodness, honey." My mom with those sad eyes and soft voice enters the bathroom. She turns on the faucet. I hear her rinsing out the sink then handing me a warm cloth to clean up my face. I must be pathetic, sitting here on the floor with vomit on my face and blood on my hands from digging into my flesh.

"How long have I been out?" I look to see Calla now standing in the doorway. This isn't healthy for her or for her baby. That ugly thing called guilt moves at a snail's pace up my spine again.

"A little over an hour. You just collapsed. We had no idea he had Deidre until Cain picked up your phone and her mother was screaming and crying," Calla states. Even though I can tell she's been crying, her demeanor is calm. Her stance is strong. I wish I could feel like her. I don't. I'm weak and pathetic, and if anything happens to anyone, I will never be able to forgive myself.

"Where's Cain now?" My voice is barely above a whisper.

"He went to the warehouse where everyone is meeting." I shake my head after Calla's announcement.

"No. What if something happens? He should have stayed here."

"Alina. Listen to me." My mom bends down and hands me a towel to dry off my face, I assume. Her face is pinched in a frown.

"If it's us you're worried about, we are not alone. Hell, this house is surrounded twenty-four hours of the day anyway. There are more men out there than I've seen before. John and Cecily are here. Nothing is going to happen, and as for Cain, he knows what he's doing. He's been through this before." She glances up at Calla with an apologetic smile.

"Now, you stop this worrying, damn it. I need you to be the strong woman I know you are. The one who took care of herself for the last ten years. Those men out there," she points her finger toward the door, "are fighters. And let me tell you this, Roan loves you. I knew it when he stayed here in this home with you, a place that was once forbidden to him because we were the enemy. He had no idea then whether we would accept the two of you together or not. He didn't care. He will come back to you, just like your dad will come back to me, and Cain will come back to his wife and unborn child. Love, sweet girl, is the most beautiful thing in the world, and once you have it, you will do everything to never let it go. They'll come back, sweetheart. I promise they will." Tears fall freely down her face. They fall down mine, too, only these two strong women don't know the real reason why I'm feeling this way. Why the guilt is eating me alive. Why this is truly all my fault. I can't take it anymore. It has to stop.

I thought I was healed. That the love I found with Roan would close the gaping hole in my heart, and he did close it. But it's not sealed. It will never be sealed unless I tell them.

"I'm so sorry," I say through my cries, burying my face in the towel.

"It's not your fault, damn it. Do you hear me?"

"It is mom. You don't understand. It's all my fault. For ten years, it's been my fault. Ever since..." I hate to tell her this after everything she is gone through. It's heartless of me to cause her more pain. But they have to see, they have to understand that I need to go to him. Find him. I need to sacrifice myself to him in order to save the ones I love. And maybe if he thinks he has me, he will let them go. Leave everyone alone. And someday in the future when I think he trusts me, I will kill him. She just said once you find love, you will do everything to never let it go. I love Roan. I would take my last breath in order for him to keep on breathing.

"What on earth are you talking about?" She scoots closer beside me. My dear sweet mother. I pull myself together. Put a halt to those tears that threaten to spill again. And I talk.

"Do you remember the night before I left for England? How I wanted to go say goodbye to Royal?" She nods, her brows drawn together in confusion. Calla is watching on from the same spot in the doorway.

"Well, I went to seen him all right, mom. It didn't go like I told you all it did. In fact, it went somewhere I never thought it would go. He..." I turn my head away, ashamed for not telling them in the first place. If I had, he would be dead right now.

"He what?" She grips my quivering chin to look at her.

"He drugged and raped me that night, mom. Don't you see now why this is all my fault? I should have told you. I just, god!" Grabbing handfuls of my hair, I confess. I tell her everything. The whole sordid, disgraceful, worst night of my entire life. Him hitting me, drugging me, me blacking out and waking up to the pain between my legs. I hear Calla gasp. My eyes stay trained on my mom, who has more tears falling down her beautiful face.

"Dear god almighty. You've been living with this for ten years," she sobs, her words more like a statement than a question. I simply nod.

"Oh, sweet girl. Come here." And I do. I let my mom cradle me in her arms while I cry. I cry for the last ten years of my life. I cry for losing my innocence. I cry for the man I love. I cry for my friends. I cry for the brother I've lost and I cry for myself.

Chapter Eighteen

Roan

"Enough, Dilan." I stand here powerless, stripped bare, casting a shadow over this arrogant, self-serving, drug dealing cocksucker.

My dad gives Dilan orders to stop beating the hell out of this stubborn asshole.

He's the one. He knows where Royal has been living. He slipped and told Jackson all about some hotshot assassin who has been missing for a few years, and boom, out of nowhere shows up at his place of business buying his entire supply of shit, from pot to crack. And this asshole is supposed to be a top-notch drug dealer? And one of Ivan's men to boot. The entire world knows you don't talk jack shit about who buys from you, where you get your shit from, or even where you take a god damn piss. So what the fuck is his deal?

Thank god, Jackson snapped. Cold cocked him, knocked him right the hell out, along with a few of his men, and here we are in the middle of another cold, damp, empty warehouse with nothing but a piece of shit, who won't fucking talk. He sure could run his mouth a few hours ago, but now? Not a damn word.

Either this stupid fuck is so damn high he can't feel the pain or he is more scared of my brother than he is of a dozen men standing around, watching Dilan beat the ever loving hell out of him. My guess is both. He's half way dead. How the hell he could talk now is beyond me.

Eyes swollen shut, every damn finger broken, arms dangling limp by his side, he's a mess. And Christ, his nose, that bitch won't stop bleeding, which means if he doesn't talk and talk soon, he's going to hell a lot quicker than I want him to.

"Look, man," I bend down to talk in his ear. Hell, he's even bleeding out of his ears. Good lord. I'd hate to see what Dilan would do if you really pissed him off. This dude is all kinds of fucked up. "I'm going to ask you one more time. That's it. If you don't answer me, I'm going to turn you over to that man standing in the corner." I laugh in his ear.

"I forgot you can't see him. You're all kinds of fucked up, Chico. Let me put it this way. His hands are twitching to get to you. And do you know what he's holding in one of those hands?" He says nothing. His head lifts and he moves it around to the best of his ability, sniffing like a starving dog.

"A very long machete. Now, I've heard some really bad things about him and his machete. He doesn't play nice with his toy." I swear in that second, he stops breathing. What I said is true. Sinclair, as they call him, does some pretty sadistic shit before he ends your life. This bitch would be screaming for his mom.

"Let me put it this way. Either way, you're going to die tonight. You know this, so help us out here. Just tell me where my brother is. I mean, come on, man. It wasn't that hard for you to spill your guts and tell my buddy here all about my brother re-surfacing. I know for a fact you've been one of his suppliers for years. So which is it? Have you been helping him out all this time? Hiding him away? Feeding his addiction? You set us up, man. Lied to my friend over here. That's not cool. Now, innocent people could be hurt. You fucked up in more ways than one. " I stand and wait.

Everyone remains quiet. He knows his time is up. We all know it. Either he talks now or he's dead.

Then we hit the streets, hunt down every damn drug dealer we know. Which we've done so many times before, coming up empty-handed. Not this time, not when he has both Beamer and Deidre. If they don't talk, they get a bullet to the head.

Every god damn thing we planned has been blown to shit because this fucker set us up. I should have known it couldn't have been that easy for Jackson to gain this fucker's trust.

When Cain called me, telling me about Alina passing out when she called Beth only to find out Deidre is missing and we all know for some unknown reason he has her, I lost it. Went bat shit crazy. Sick to my stomach. I know first-hand the hell he will put you through before he kills you. I wouldn't be standing here right now if it weren't for Cain's expert eye when Royal videotaped the torture he put Calla and I through. I'd be dead, and so would Calla. Cain knew exactly where we were. And John saved us. Now it's my turn to save my friends. To seek redemption and to return home to the woman I love.

"I don't know where he is," he sputters out.

"What was that?" I grab hold of his hair.

"I said, I don't know where is he is, but I have a name of someone who might." He stops. Goes on a choking fit. Coughing up blood. Yeah, this idiot is so close to drawing his last breath.

"Name." Ivan comes forward and stands within a few inches of the man whose hair I'm still holding firmly in my hand.

"Rayna Carruso. She lives in Newark. All I know is she doesn't have a damn clue who he is. She's innocent. I can swear to god on that. She has no idea who he is. I'm begging you not to hurt her." I let go of his hair.

“You better be telling the truth or I won’t end with you. I’ll have every person you care about killed. Every single one. Get this filth out of this warehouse,” Ivan spits out.

The dirt bag fights, he actually has the gall to start begging, screaming for us to let him go. Every single one of us ignores his pleas to spare him his life. The last words spoken as we all walk out the door are from Ivan

“Kill him.”

“I get why you’re here, Cain, and I appreciate your loyalty to me and our family. However, I want you to leave, go back to Ivan’s. If this Rayna knows anything and we locate Royal’s whereabouts, I don’t want you anywhere near this. We all know he isn’t going to go down without a fight. You’ve been through enough. I won’t allow it to happen again,” my dad commands, then he turns his attention to me.

“Fuck no. I’m not leaving. This is my war, too, dad, and I’m not going anywhere.”

“You will not argue with me, Roan. You will go and that’s the end of it.”

Son of a bitch. I run my hands through my hair. No. I’m not going anywhere. I have waited way too long for this day. I can feel him near. I feel his threats, his demands for me to come and find him. He still thinks of me as the weak little brother who would cowardly hide from him, scared of what he might do to me. Not anymore. I will not back away from this. I want his blood on my hands, not on my dad’s. Not on Ivan’s. MINE!

“You listen to me, dad. I’m going nowhere. You may be the boss still, but above that you’re my dad, and I will not stand by and watch him destroy you anymore. What kind of man would I be if I let my dad walk into the hands of a psychotic killer? Huh? You didn’t raise me to walk away, you raised me to fight, to believe in myself, to honor and protect. You and I are together in this. Do not ask me to walk away from you, dad. I can't and won't do it." I stood there for a minute in a stare down with the man who could make me leave if he really chose to. His features show his conflicted emotions. Then I see it, the moment he agrees with me, grateful he is going to let me stand by his side.

"I give the orders, Roan. You're not in charge, yet. Do you hear me?" I nod my understanding.

"As for you, Cain. Get your ass out of here." My dad turns and walks away without another word. Stops at the passenger door of the black SUV were Ivan has been for the past half hour. I watch him enter and shut the door, the black tinted windows concealing him from me. I feel his stare, his struggle within himself, his worry over the possibility of losing both of his sons. He underestimates me. No way in hell am I going to lose this battle. I've lost too much blood, sweat, and even tears over this.

"Don't keep me in the dark," Cain calls out from my side.

"Don't let anything happen to my girl." I turn to face him.

"Never. Be safe, man." He pats me on the shoulder, steps up into his truck, and peels away.

I pinch the bridge of my nose, lean back against my own truck, and pull my phone out of my pocket, finding her number and smiling when I hear her say hello.

"Hey." I glance up to the heat of the late afternoon sky and close my eyes, letting the sweet sound of her voice seep into my skin.

"Please tell me you're coming back. You've found him and it's over." There's something in the way she speaks that has me cocking my head back down. Her chipper sweet voice is gone. Sorrow to the point of being broken reflects from her end of the call.

I clear my voice, careful not let on that I'm concerned for her.

"Getting close," I say softly and confidently.

I'm not going to fuel her fire and worry her any more than she already is. She has to be going out of her mind with dread over the fact that Deidre is with him. She knows first-hand the devious unthinkable things he can do.

"How are you?" I ask her.

My speech is low, waiting for that dreaded answer. *You know damn well she isn't fine*. No one is fine and to be honest, I'm so fed up with no one being fine. This is the time in both of our lives where we should be happy to the point of shouting it from the rooftop of the Empire State Building. We're in love. Newly in love. And instead of spending as much time with each other as we possibly can, being able to learn from each other, to give as good as we get, to indulge, make memories, she's there fretting over this shit and I'm here wishing like hell I weren't. We need a break in this. Someone has to know where in the hell he is.

"I'll be better once this is over and everyone I care about is safe."

She's so quiet. This isn't like the Alina I know. Did something else happen that she's not telling me about? No. If anything happened, John would have been the first one to call my dad. This is about her. She's trapped inside her past right now. The memory of what he did do her. This angers me even more, not towards her, but towards my brother.

"I'm better. Worried about everyone. Especially Beamer and Deidre. I know what he's capable of and it scares me to death. He will stop at nothing to get what he wants. He's proven that." Her tone is serious, but not as stable as she's trying to make herself sound.

We think so much alike, her and I. All I want to do right now is wrap myself up in her sweetness. To smell her innocent fragrance and to kiss away her fears.

My curiosity gets the better of me. If I don't find out what's troubling her, I won't stay focused like I need to be. One small slip up from anyone and we could all die.

"You going to tell me what's wrong with you or wait until I see you so I can spank it out of you?" I chuckle, trying to make light of this dark situation.

She sighs. And fuck me, what she tells me next, not only makes me proud of her, it also makes me want to hold her all the more.

"I broke down a while ago and told my mom and Calla everything that happened to me the night before I left for England." She sighs then sniffles.

"I'm proud of you, beautiful lady. That couldn't have been easy," I say it with enthusiasm to convince her I'm more proud of her for finally telling her mom.

"It wasn't easy. I cried like a baby. The funny thing is, I feel so much better. I know I will never erase the past. I just wish for once I told them sooner. None of this would be happening if I had just told them." Her voice harbors more sadness.

"We all blame ourselves. The truth is none of us are blaming the one person whose fault it really is. Once you do that, you'll really be able to let go and move on, babe. You know I'm right." I grind my teeth, bend down, and toss a rock into the woods. I speak the truth. My parents blame themselves. I blame myself. John blames himself for not being able to kill Royal. It's not our fault. Not a single one of us turned him into the person he is. He brought all this on himself. The only things he loves are drugs. Drugs are the love of his life.

"I love you, Alina," I say quietly. My focus suddenly steers away from her, the crunching sound of tires over gravel indicating someone is pulling around the back of the warehouse in this shit part of town.

"Baby. I have to go. I'll call you when it's all over." Crouching down on the side of my truck, I tuck the phone between my neck and shoulder so I can pull out my gun. I glance around. Everyone else is crouched down, hidden from whomever the hell is pulling back here.

"I love you, too, Roan. No matter what, always remember that. You saved me, Roan Diamond."

"Alina. Hello!" Damn it. *What the hell is she up to?* Something is not right with her and it's a hell of a lot more than just her worrying about the safety of everyone else.

She hung up. I jerk my head back and stare down at my phone. That almost sounded like a goodbye. Panic skims across the back of my neck. A sinking feeling that something is about to go terribly wrong punches me instantly in the gut. I can't seem to put my finger on it. Fuck! I look to the ground as if the answers are right there under my feet, anger boiling, bile rising to my throat. Am I being paranoid? I'm not with her to see with my own eyes whether she's all right or not. Maybe she needed to reassure me of her love. That's her way of keeping my mind where it needs to be. To know she will be waiting for me when I return.

The deep rumble of the vehicle gets louder.

I look up, point my gun, and then heave out a heavy sigh when I see it's Dilan's truck. *What the hell?* Asshole knows better than to pull up here unannounced.

"Yo. We got her. She's scared out of her mind, man. This chick doesn't know a damn thing," Dilan calls out.

Of course, she doesn't. No one does. I'm not into beating a chick or even threatening one, but this time, I will do anything I can to get answers.

Jackson hops out of the passenger side, opens the back door, and pulls out a very skinny, unkempt, long-haired blonde. You can tell right away she was once an attractive woman, but the drugs have eaten her alive. She's nothing but bones. Jesus H. Christ, what the hell is wrong with people? We all have an addiction to one thing or another, but to slowly kill yourself by poisoning your body with chemicals? To tear the hearts out of people that love you? For them to stand by and know there is nothing they can do to help you until you sink so deep into the hole of despair, or worse, wind up dead with a damn needle shoved in your arm? I know firsthand what that feels like. I watched what it did to Calla when they drugged her. You have no control over your body. Your mind. Nothing.

"Why didn't you call, idiots?" I leap from my crouched position, tucking my gun safely in the back of my jeans.

"We did. About ten minutes ago. I called your dad." Dilan strolls my way like the badass he is. Fuck. My mind is not in the right place. I need to stay focused or I'm the one that will end up killed. I've waited too long for this day to come. The day when I can end his pathetic excuse of a life. The day justice will finally be served for all the wrongs that maggot has done to my family and to the woman I love.

The woman who did not in her own way tell me goodbye. God damn it. What the hell does she think she's going to do? This is exactly what I mean about not controlling your mind. I should be thinking about this woman who may be my last chance in finding out where Royal could possibly be.

"Take her inside." I nod towards the warehouse.

Angrily, I slide my finger over my phone. "You have news already?" Cain says when he answers the phone. I need to be reassured Alina stays put and doesn't try to do something crazy, like go after him herself.

"We have the woman. Getting ready to talk to her now." My boots crush the gravel as I strut with purpose towards the back entrance.

"Do me a favor. I just hung up with Alina. She's acting weird. Do not let her out of your sight. You get me?"

"I got you, Roan. I'm almost there."

I hang up. It's time, god damn it, to find out where this motherfucker is.

"I'll make a deal with you?" I question Rayna. This woman has a chance to get out of the mess she's in. If we can be the ones to give it to her, then by god I will. If I can save one person from fucking up their life any more than it already is, I'll do it.

She's so scared. Just like every other person who comes in contact with my brother. Whatever he has threatened her with, has her not talking. I can see it in her eyes. She knows something.

"W...what?" her mousy little voice squeaks.

"If you tell me where you think he is, I will not only spare you your life, but I'll get you the help you need to get yourself clean." I kneel down in front of her and wrap my hands around her skinny ankles. Christ, I could wrap them around twice. That's how underweight she is.

Her slanted eyes scan everyone in the entire room. Hell, this isn't normal protocol to leave a witness alive. I can't seem to tell anyone to kill her. Will I be making a mistake? At this point, I don't give a shit. I need to find him. The rest of the bullshit I can deal with later.

"You promise you'll keep me safe? He... he said he would kill me and my entire family if I told anyone where he was." Her bony little body starts shaking uncontrollably, tears rippling down her face. I want to tell her she will have nothing to worry about because he'll be dead. I don't, though.

"You have my word," I simply say.

"He's been renting a house in West Nyack."

"Do you know the address?" I ask calmly, even though I'm furious inside. That area is populated with families. It's more a residential area.

"20789 Mayfield."

"Thank you, Rayna." I remove my hands from her ankles, stand, and look at both my dad and Ivan. I need their reassurance I'm doing the right thing here with her. Her death on my hands would haunt me for the rest of my life. They both nod in unison.

"Wait. There's more." I quirk a brow at this little mouse of a woman sitting here shaking so badly.

"He... he's not there. I mean he was, but he's not now."

"And how the hell do you know this?" It's Ivan now who makes his presence known by standing directly in front of her.

"Look. I'm telling you what he told me to tell you. I don't know how he does the things he does. He gives me what I need and... and I don't say a word. But tonight, he called me and told me to tell you your friends are at that address. Then he told me to tell you that he won't be there. He said you would know where he was." She looks right at me when she says it.

"Aric, get her out of here, drop her off at the best rehab you can find," Ivan states.

****

"This doesn't add up," I voice my opinion to everyone.

"You need to think, Roan. Where could he be?"

"I'm telling you, I don't know. I have no fucking idea what the hell he means by that. Fuck." I start pacing the floor. It's been a damn hour since Jackson and Dilan took off to the hospital. Cain and Ivan went back to their house to check on the women. He has us scattered all over the god damn place.

For the first time in my god damn life, I'm thankful for who we are. That we have cops on our payroll. They swarmed the house in West Nyack, and sure as shit, there they both were.

Deidre was hung up, and hanging on by a thread. Beamer was drugged and unconscious. He's playing some sick game of cat and mouse with all of us.

And this shit of me knowing where the hell he is. Nothing. None of this adds the fuck up.

"You're setting us up, Royal. I can feel it."

Just like that, my phone rings. I glance at the caller ID.

"It's him." Unknown number again.

I place my finger to my lips, indicating for everyone to remain calm and quiet.

"Royal," I state.

"God, she's fucking beautiful, isn't she?"

"Stay the hell away from her," I roar into the phone.

"Aww, come on, brother, don't you remember when we were younger how we used to share everything?" Heat pools under my skin. Fuck, he has her. Jesus Christ.

"This isn't a game anymore, man. Don't do this. Tell me where you are."

"I'm right where I'm supposed to be, little brother."

Chapter Nineteen

Alina

A calming, peaceful sensation makes its presence known after telling my story to my mom. I should have told her the minute I returned home that night. Her soothing words, the way I felt with her loving arms wrapped around me, stroking my hair, kissing my face. Repeating how sorry she was for not reaching out to me all those years ago when I left.

I will never get rid of the guilt. This I know to be true. He has my best friend and Beamer. The things he must be doing to them right now are killing me.

Everyone else is downstairs, dealing with this situation the best way they can. I simply cannot climb out of my bed. There's something soothing about being in my childhood bedroom, where I would play all day, be a carefree child with not a single ounce of worry on my mind. The dolls I used to play with lie in a small baby crib my dad and older brother Alexei put together one day for me. I remember Dad coming home with this big surprise for me, telling me my dolls needed a place to sleep too. All three of them are tucked under the blankets exactly where I left them.

I should get up, grab one, and hold her, remembering times when guilt was an emotion a young child couldn't begin to comprehend, yet I cannot seem to get my legs to uncurl themselves from the fetal position. So I lie here with my phone in my hand, praying Roan will call me. If only to hear his voice.

I jolt when my phone rings. I smile wide, knowing it has to be him. Finally calling me back an hour or so after we hung up. If they found him and he's gone, I won't have to try and find a way to find him on my own.

"Roan," I say, not even bothering to check to see who's calling.

"Wrong Diamond, Alina." Hurdling out of my bed, my body stills. I recognize this voice.

"Do you miss me, beautiful?" My ability to form any type of coherent sound at all has vanished. What does he want? Where is Roan? My family? I need answers and still I cannot speak.

"I bet you didn't think you would hear from me again. Let me put it this way. Wherever you are, leave now. Meet me at the warehouse on 27th and West Hill. And Alina, come alone. If I even smell you've told anyone, I will start killing people. The gift I will send to your family this time won't be near as nice as the last."

The line goes dead.

Anger signals a trigger to my brain. I dash into my old closet, clawing through boxes, looking for any sort of weapon I can find. There's nothing. I panic. I need to somehow get into my dad's office undetected and get his gun.

Slipping on my tennis shoes and tucking my phone in my back pocket, I run out of my room, down the hall, lightening my steps as I descend the stairs. I have no clue where anyone is or how the hell I'm going to get out of here without anyone knowing. Scaling along the wall like a criminal until I reach his office, I turn the knob, slowly opening the door then shutting it softly behind me. I scramble to the desk and open every drawer. Nothing. His gun he always leaves is missing. Of course it is, he took it. He's on a mission to kill.

“What are you doing?” I snap my head up to Cecily, Calla’s mother, standing in the doorway.

“Shut the door, please,” I whisper.

She does so silently.

“I need help,” I plead her with my eyes.

“What kind of help?” She remains up against the door, her voice barely above a whisper.

“I need to get out of here. I need a gun.” Her eyes go wide. She shakes her head.

“Alina, have you gone mad? You cannot leave here. Its way too dangerous for you.”

“Listen to me. He called me. Royal called me. He wants me. I have to go to him,” I cry out.

“We have to tell John.”

“No. We can’t. He’ll kill them, he said he would.” Those words strangle me to even say.

“Sweetheart. This isn’t how things are done. There is no way I will allow you to risk your life. If I let you leave here, knowing where you’re going, I might as well sign my own death certificate as well as my husband’s and my daughter’s. Do you get what I’m saying? He’s playing us all. Cain, your dad, and Ivan are on their way here right now. Deidre and Beamer are at the hospital, and Roan and your brothers are still at the warehouse. Trust me when I say you’re safe here.”

I crash to the floor, curl my knees up to my chest, and cry. I scream for someone to help me. This was my plan all along, to somehow, someway come into contact with Royal. For me to sacrifice my life for everyone else’s. To convince him that I would be with him, if he would just stop his vendetta against our families. If he stopped killing and hurting others, I would go. I would give up my life for those I love.

"Thank you, god. Thank you. Thank you." I repeat over and over. Deidre and Beamer are safe. Everyone is alive.

I'm losing my mind. What kind of game is he playing here? Are his intentions to drive me insane? I rub my temples, the urge to scream lodged in my throat.

I continue to rock myself back and forth, my mind flipping round and round.

"Let's get you back upstairs sweetheart."

"Okay." I manage to squeak out, or at least I think I do. My judgment is so tattered, so lost. I feel as if I'm in a nightmare. Clawing, clinging tightly to anything to try and wake me up. For someone to tell me this is all a bad dream.

I don't even know who brought me to my bed. It had to have been Cecily, she's the last one I remember speaking with. Startling, I sit up with my Dad, Cain, and John sitting on the daybed across from me. This is like a big giant 'fuck you' from the déja vù gods. The three of them are sitting exactly where Calla and my mom were earlier.

"I have to go." I scramble out of bed.

"Alina, stop. Damn it, stop." Cain grabs my arm and swings me to face him.

"Don't do this. I need to save them, damn it." I try to jerk free of his hold.

"Calm down. Just tell us where he said to meet him," Cain asks.

"You can't possibly be going there? I don't understand why everyone doesn't just come here. I'm calling Roan." I start to panic.

"It's a long story. Now listen to me, god damn it." I snap my mouth shut.

"Deidre and Aidan are fine. They've been found." I know. Cecily told me. I whisper, "B..but where's Roan?" I shake my head to all three of them, my mind whirling like the beginning of a hurricane in the middle of the Atlantic.

"You need to tell me now where he wants you to meet him." John steps up in front of me. There's something going on. They're hiding something from me.

"Where's Roan?" I demand.

"That's why you need to tell us where HE.SAID.TO.MEET.HIM." My dad gets right up in my face.

"I'll tell you in the car." I stand firm and toe-to-toe with all three of these men.

"You'll tell them now." My body goes rigid at my dad's the firm command.

"I won't. If you want to know where he is, then I'm going too." Cain drops his grip on my arm. I turn defiantly, standing tall against my dad.

"You know nothing about how these things are done. You demand to withhold information from me, information that might spare the life of the man you love." His words are a slap to my face.

"What are you talking about?" I say.

"You want the truth? Here's the truth. He's contacted Roan, he said Roan would know where he is. Now god damn it, Alina, you wanted it, now there you have it. If you want this hell we're all in to be over, then you tell us now."

I shake my head. This isn't how it was supposed to go. I have no choice. Through begging tears, I tell them.

Falling to my knees, I cry, long and hard. What if something happens to Roan? To another member of my family? To his dad? After what seems like an hour of my mind racing, strumming up the worst possible scenarios, I refuse to be weak any longer. I lift my head and remove my unstable body from the floor. It's in that moment every hair on my body sticks straight up. A terrorizing shiver strikes through my heart. A cool breeze soars into my room. I feel his vile existence behind me.

"Hello, Alina." I should have known he would try to get to me. He set them all up. It is me he wants. They've all fallen into his trap. Every single one of them.

"How did you get in here?" I whisper.

"It doesn't really matter how I got in here. What matters is I'm here with you. Now, turn around."

"No." Damn it. I pound my fist into the side of my legs. My throat tightens and more tears fall from my eyes.

"Don't defy me, Alina. The consequences will be much worse if you do."

I wipe my eyes then slowly with nothing left inside of me to hold on to, I spin on my heels and come face to face with Royal Diamond.

Chapter Twenty

Roan

I sit in my truck. The night is crisp. I welcome the cool breeze flowing through the darkened cab, the moon underneath the clouds. Blackness surrounds me everywhere.

This shit is so fucked up. So out of our control. I have no clue who's coming or going. My clever manipulator brother has us all in a tailspin. Some of us go left, the others go right. And here we are, stupid enough to split up, the promise of leaving no stone unturned.

I needed time to think. To gather my thoughts after he called.

And now he does have her. He has the woman I love.

The minute John, Cain, and Ivan walked out her bedroom door, he took her. Calla went to check on her and she was gone. Vanished.

How in the hell could one person cause so much destruction? Kill ten men and make his way into their house and back out again undetected? We all know the answer to that. He obviously had someone on Ivan's payroll working for him as well.

The corruption, deceit, and betrayal will never stop. No matter who dies, it will always be there.

People will always want more than what they have. Their greed turning to need. It's all fucked up and it's times like these when I feel helpless. I would give anything to not be the man I am.

I've failed her. My promise to keep her safe means nothing. I have no control over the man who has her. God, what she must be feeling right now. Scared and all alone.

He said I would know where he was. I have no idea where in the hell he is. He's the one who's been here for years. Not me. I let my mind drift as far back to my childhood as I can remember.

And then... Wait? I sit upright in my truck. He couldn't have taken her there. He hated that place when we were little. Hated it more than I did.

"Son of a bitch." I lift my head, my gaze training on Anton standing outside of my truck. "Follow me, I know where they are."

I'm distressed on this drive, merging in and out of traffic. Memories I've buried so deep come tumbling back to haunt me.

"I hate this beach house. It's boring." I throw another rock into the lake, watch it skip... one...two... three times over the water.

"I hate it here too, little brother." I watch my big brother pick up a flat rock, place it in his hand, and flick his wrist smoothly. He always beats me at skipping stones.

"You're so good at doing that. I wish I could be as good as you." I try again, only this time, it plops right down into the water.

"You have to keep practicing, Roan. Practice makes perfect. That's what dad says anyway."

"Yeah. He says we can do whatever we want when we grow up. What do you want to do, Royal? I mean, when you get to be big like dad?" I look up at my big brother. His long, shaggy hair is hanging in his eyes. He's such a cool brother. When he's not being mean to me, that is. When he's mean to me, I hate him. I tell him that too. I don't know why I tell him that, because every time I do, he laughs and then hits me more. Sometimes he hits me so hard my skin turns purple and it hurts really badly when I touch it. I never tell on him, though. He said if I do, he will kill me. Cut my head off and throw it in this lake. That's why I never go in the lake past my knees, which isn't very far. Or else I stand on shore and watch my dad and brother swim. The water scares me.

But not today. Today he's being nice.

"I want to work for dad. To rule the world like he does." Royal tosses in another stone.

"Dad doesn't rule the world." I scrunch up my nose at him.

"Yes, he does. He has men who do whatever he tells them to do. And they carry guns and knives too." He looks down at me. My eyes get really big.

"You've seen a gun before? Like a real gun?" I stop watching his stone skip. I want to hear all about the guns.

"Oh, yeah. I've held one too. But what I really love are the knives. The knives John has."

I like it when John comes over. He always brings candy. He even brought me a present for my fifth birthday last year. It wasn't a knife or a gun. It was a truck. A big, cool truck.

"You better not let mom know you held a gun or that you like knives, she'll be mad." I mean it. I hear her yell at dad to put his gun away when he comes home or when he walks out of the room in our house that we can't go into.

"I'm not scared of mom or dad," Royal says.

I don't want to fight with my brother. He'll hurt me if I keep talking about mom. He was happy when he talked about knives. Yeah! I want to talk to him about knives, and then we can keep skipping stones and he will stay outside with me.

"How big of a knife do you want?" I whisper.

He looks at me really weird.

"Why are you whispering? You're stupid?"

"I'm not stupid. And that's a naughty word. I was whispering so mom doesn't hear us talking about knives. She's still under the tree reading her book, you know." I don't like him calling me stupid. Mom says that is a really bad word and not nice to call people that. She said no one's stupid.

"And I have a knife."

"You aren't supposed to have a knife. You're only seven." I don't want him to have a knife. He could hurt himself. I should tell on him. If I do though, what if he hurts me with his knife? Oh, man. This is bad.

"Shut up, you idiot." He pushes me down, only I don't fall in the sand. I fall in the water. I go under. It gets in my nose. In my eyes. I cough. Cry and scream for my mom. She saves me. My pretty mom saves me. She carries me out of the yucky water and grabs hold of my brother by his arm. "How many times do I have to tell you to keep your hands to yourself, Royal?" She yells at him really loudly.

"He started it." I didn't start it. He always says that.

"You're not going out on the boat with your dad tonight." Mom keeps walking and yelling at my brother. And he's mad. He loves going out on the boat with my dad. They spend the night out there because my brother says it's like a small little house. I want to see it, but I don't like the water.

I'm so scared now. He's going to hurt me badly. I hold on to my mom tightly. When I look down at my brother, he looks up at me with scary-looking eyes. Then he takes his hand and does what it always does when he's mad at me and says he's going to cut my head off. He takes one of his fingers and draws a line across his neck.

I don't think I like my big brother anymore. He's not stupid, because no one is stupid. No. I think he's those words that Sonja from school calls him. She says he's evil and crazy. I don't know what those words mean, but whatever they are, I think she's right.

"Roan, do you want to play Frisbee?"

"Heck yeah!" I jump off my small little bed and follow my big brother outside. He's ten now and I'm eight. He's also still really, really mean to me. They call him a bully in school. Mom is always coming to get him from the principal's office, because he and his friends like to punch Tommy Broderick.

I've never been to the principal's office. No way, man, Principal Miller scares me, plus I want to get good grades so I can be smart like my dad and my Uncle John.

"Come on, you chicken shit. Get in the water." I stand on the edge of the shore, shaking my head no. I won't even go in up to my knees anymore. Not since that day he pushed me in a few years ago. I don't like the water. I don't even know how to swim. That's why I still won't go out fishing on the boat with my dad and Royal. The boat is not very far out. But my dad has it far enough out that you either have to swim to get to it or paddle out in the little canoe. I told my dad if he brought the boat all the way up to the shore, I would go. He said he couldn't. The people who owned this place before we did, made the boat so it doesn't move. It has to stay right where it is, which is silly to me because all boats move. I don't understand what he means by that, I really don't care anymore when Royal and my dad go out on the boat, me and my mom play games and she always lets me stay up as late as I want.

"I can't swim and you know it. If you want me to play, then we can play on the shore." I really do want to play. It can be so boring here.

"Come on, I'll teach you. It's more fun in the water."

"No. Just forget it." I turn and start walking back up to the house.

I start to scream when Royal throws me down on the ground and grabs my hair. He starts dragging me down the shore, away from the house. "Royal, stop. Stop, Royal."

"Shut up, you idiot. You need to learn how to swim. You're such a pansy ass."

"No, Royal, stop, I do... don't want to learn to swim. Stop."

The water is so cold. He drags me farther and farther out. I'm choking, kicking my feet. Every time I open my mouth to try and scream, I swallow more water and then I choke some more.

I'm scared. So scared. I cry so hard. He keeps going. Yelling and calling me naughty names.

Then he lets go of my hair. My head hurts so bad. I don't care about my head hurting, because all I'm trying to do is keep it from going under the water. I can't. It keeps going under. I swing my arms, kick my feet, and I keep going up and down. My chest hurts. My eyes hurt. Royal looks like he's getting farther and farther away.

Is that my dad? It is my dad and he's running into the water. I can't see him anymore. I see nothing. Everything is so dark, like the color black.

I never played with my brother again after that day. My mom saved me from him again. He never asked me to, either. Instead, he punched me and hit me every chance he got, just like he did Tommy.

"Roan. Are you sure this is the place?" Anton knocks on my window, bringing me out of my recollection. I've pulled into the driveway and don't even remember doing it. Shit, I dredged up so much the entire drive here. He used to always say this place would be the death of one of us.

"This is the place." My hands grip the steering wheel tighter.

"It's abandoned. What the hell is this place?"

"This is my family's old lake house. We haven't been here in years. We both hated this place." I find my eyes traveling over every detail of the outside of this small house. The lights from my truck shine brightly on the peeled white paint. The grimy windows, half boarded up. I was sixteen years old the last time I came here with my dad. We boarded the house up. Swore we would never come back here again. Dad couldn't come here alone. He had too many memories with our family here. Little did he know I fucking hated this place. I came that day only for him, and only because he swore it was the last time he would come here. I laugh at the audacity of that bastard having her here. I could count the steps it will take me to get exactly where he is.

"What the hell's so funny?" Anton's boisterous, angry tone ricochets throughout the secluded forest.

"Nothing's funny. It's ironic. He tried to kill me here when I was eight years old. We used to come every year. It was so boring. But my dad loved it. He loved to fish and do absolutely nothing. This was his place to relax. Very few people know of this place." I talk as if I'm in a trance and, fuck, who knows? Maybe I really am.

"Fuck, man. This is some fucked up shit. I would love to sit out here and reminisce with you, but that crazy fucker has my sister."

"They're not in the house." I twist to face him. "They're in the boathouse."

Chapter Twenty-One

Alina

"You won't get away with this." I stare at the man I loathe more than anything. The last time I saw him I feared for my life, not this time. I stand tall. My trembling dissolving. I won't give up, though. I'll do everything in my power to escape him. To get back to the man I love and the family I finally have back in my life. He may have stripped my innocence away from me years ago, but he's meeting a different woman now. A woman who found true love.

"I already have. You've sent them several hours away from here. Now, come here." He points to the floor directly in front of him.

"Fuck you." I spit, then spin on my heels, dodging for my bedroom door. My hand is stretched out to grab the handle when I am jerked back by my hair. I try to scream for help. I get nowhere when his hand covers my mouth.

"I will kill your mom. Do you want that?" He tugs harder. I shake my head no.

"I swear to god, Alina, if you even breathe until I have you out of here, I will kill her. Do you understand me?" I nod.

This is what I wanted, to be the one he came after, to be the one he wanted. To sacrifice myself for everyone else. Now that he has me, everyone I love is safe. He pushes me out of my bedroom door. The upstairs of the house is quiet and dark.

I feel a blade pressed up against my neck. It all happens so fast and yet at the same time feels like it's taking forever. We slink down the stairs quietly. I know I'm breathing heavily. My throat is tight. My heartbeat accelerating with each step we take. We slip through the front door undetected. My eyes dart around for help. I thought there were guards out here. Men protecting us. There's no one. Nothing.

The farther we walk away from my family home, the more I realize there isn't anyone around to help me. My life as I know it will be gone. My hopes, dreams, and finally finding peace within myself to love are demolished. Destroyed. Over what? A personal vendetta? A man who has fallen over the edge of sanity, he has no remorse for the crimes he commits. The innocent people he slaughters.

I can't do this. I refuse. You told yourself you would fight. Now fight!

I rear back my elbow and connect with his stomach, the shock loosening his grip just enough for me to break free.

Instantly, I run.

You just have to make it to the gate. Make it to the gate and you're free, Alina.

"You fucking bitch!" he calls out angrily, grasping at the back of my shirt.

I'm nearly there when I feel my body lunging forward, tumbling into the grass just a few feet from the gate, from my freedom.

The crushing weight of his body over mine sends me into a full-fledged panic. Immediately, I use every ounce of fight in me to pull away from him, but it's no use.

"Don't fight me, Alina," he growls in my ear, his hot breath sending a sharp chill up my spine.

"You won't get away with this. My parents have security set up everywhere," I manage, pushing up to fill my lungs with enough air to call for help. "*Nikky!*"

"He's fucking dead!" he cuts me off, pushing me back down against the damp grass beneath us. "He needed to die anyway, the guy was getting too old to stand guard at the gate," he continues, his voice holding a sardonic edge that has my skin crawling. "They're all dead," he husks into my ear, his lips turning up into a smile against my neck. "Do you honestly think I don't know my way around this house? That I don't know where every man stands guard or where every camera is?"

"No..." I whimper, defeat slowly filling me.

"They're dead, Alina," he croons darkly, tightening his grip on me. "Every single one of them. No one is coming for you," he continues, somehow leaning in even closer, his lips skimming my ear as I fight the tears that threaten. "Now, if you don't move your ass, you'll be joining them."

"You're an animal," I spit, trying my best to buck him off of me.

He outweighs me. He doesn't budge.

"Get up," he orders, pushing himself up slightly as he takes hold of the back of my shirt, nearly choking me as he yanks me to an upright position. "Now walk."

He begins pushing me forward. I will myself to hold it together, be strong, but the minute we walk past the booth by the gate, I lose it.

Nikky's lifeless body is lying face down outside of the gate.

"Oh my God..." I sob, taking him in.

"Get in!" he demands, popping open the trunk of a dark-colored car. Reality hits me and immediately, I begin shaking my head, trying to contain my sobs. "Goddamn it, Alina! Get the fuck in there!"

My body won't move. It remains still.

"Fuck it."

****

I remember nothing until I feel a foot lodged right between my legs, pressing the tip against my core.

"That a girl," Royal smirks.

I look down to where his foot is and a sigh of relief escapes me.

Thank God, my clothes are still on.

"Where are we?" I ask in a raspy tone I don't recognize as my own, trying to shake the grogginess from my head.

"This place?" he asks, throwing out his arms like we're in some famous mansion... someplace sacred.

I glance around the small, musky-smelling room. The tiny windows are broken out, shards of glass littering the concrete floors. The remains of what was once a tiny kitchen at one end and a small mattress on a rusty frame at the other are the only signs that this place was ever inhabitable. A bright light steals my attention, causing me to squint at its harshness as it sways over me.

"This is my family's old boathouse," Royal announces. "It's a piece of fucking shit, isn't it?"

He takes a few steps back, taking in the decay surrounding us before his voice fills the room again.

"My dad loved this fucked up place. He made us come here every summer. A whole entire week of doing nothing. I hated this god damn place. And you know what?" he asks, an inch from my face. "So did your *lover*. He hates it more than I do," he whispers.

He stares down at me, his features full of vengeance. His gaze transcends into an eerie lingering gaze that stretches to a vindictive smile.

"Roan?" I whisper.

"Don't say his name!" he roars as his hand comes up and comes crashing across my face.

Scorching white lights flash before my eyes. Instinctively, I try to move my hand up to cup my burning face. They're tied to the chair.

Although panic sets in, I try and remain calm. I have no idea what this crazy man has on his mind by bringing me here. I will not surrender to him. He will most definitely not see any fear.

He begins to rub the backside of his hand across my cheek, slowly. I feel sick from his touch, my insides internally cringing. He's taunting me... tempting me, and I hate it.

"Do you know how long I waited for you?"

Oh God. He's delusional.

It's so hard for me to think rationally when he's touching me. All I can think about is how many people those hands have killed, if they have raped or beaten more women. The color red is flashing before my eyes.

"You need help!" I cry out, the stinging tears forming in my eyes.

I refuse to cry. If I cry, I will feel like I'm giving up hope that someone will find me.

"You *were* my help, Alina. This beautiful, sweet, and innocent young woman was all the help I needed," he whispers, his voice softer than I'd heard it in so long before something flashes in his eyes and his fingers slide down, gripping me firmly around my throat. "Then you started fucking my *brother*!" he grounds out, his voice returning to near deafening levels. "The both of you up and ruined it all. Did you really think I would just let you walk away from me? Leave me with no one? With *nothing*?"

"Please, don't do this," I shake my head, my voice pleading. "If you loved me at all, you would let me go."

I watch him frantically grind his jaw back and forth. His angry eyes scorn into tiny slits.

"That's the problem. I *do* love you. But you see? You're in love with someone else. And that makes for an even bigger problem. Do you know why?" He doesn't let me answer, he grips my neck even tighter, shakes my head back and forth. "You're fucking the enemy. *My* enemy. Out of all the cock-sucking men in this world, you choose him? The one man who stole my fortune from me? That kingdom should have been mine, but no! Ever since that punk could talk, he had my parents wrapped around his finger. He's fucked me in more ways than one his entire life and now he's taken the woman I love," he continues, shaking his head. "No, Alina. I'm done letting him take from me. It's time I take from him."

His eyes go wide. He releases his hold on my neck. In and out I breathe in the damp air, gasping air back into my lungs.

Adrenaline races through me. I watch him move to a small table behind him. He grabs a knife. The face of the man I love flashes before my eyes.

This is it. He's going to kill me.

I will never be able to tell Roan I love him again. I will never hear him call me beautiful lady, taste his sweet lips. Hear his deep voice.

My heart stops in that instant when he walks around me and slices through the rope with his knife. He lifts me up and throws me onto my stomach on the dingy, smelly mattress. The chair I was sitting on falling to the floor makes a loud clanking noise.

"No!" I shriek, desperately clawing my way up the mattress.

Not again. This is not going to happen again.

"Come here, Alina," he croons.

The calm in his voice is terrifying. Still struggling to get away from him, I'm pushed back down against the floor, only to be lifted, my back against his front.

I try to let out a scream, but it's no use. My mouth is immediately covered with his putrid hand.

"Don't fight this. It's going to happen," he threatens calmly. "I'm going to take what's belonged to me all along and this time? You're going to watch me. I'm going to fuck you, Alina."

I can't say what my mind wants to say. The moment he removes his hand from my mouth, he stuffs a cloth inside. I plead with my eyes for him to stop. I want to tell him I will disappear with him if he will stop. I will do anything he asks me to if he will stop. I claw at him, my nails dinging into his jagged scar on his face. He shows no fear, no pain, as my nails dig into his skin. The blood. *Oh God... I've drawn blood*. This time, I welcome the color red.

It's all short-lived. I feel my wrist snap. I scream under the confines of the cloth in my mouth, tears staining my cheeks as I'm thrown onto the bed then flipped roughly onto my stomach. My hands drawn behind me are taut. I hear him breathing heavily. The sound of my wrist crackling. My bones splintering in half.

Tears soak the mattress beneath me. His hand grabs my legs to keep them still. And then he's gone. I lift my head and my eyes go frantic with panic. I mumble incoherently for him to stop.

"So beautiful," he speaks calmly. He sets the chair I was sitting on moments ago upright, his eyes hard as steel.

I watch him, completely at his mercy. He lifts his boot-cladded foot on the chair. Pulls the leg of his pants up. God, what is he doing?

My body trembles as I watch in utter horror as he pulls out a syringe from the inside of his boot.

"Don't worry, Alina. This is for me," he sneers. "I want you to remember everything we do tonight."

I'm still as stone, watching this unhinged man flip his arm around, push up the sleeve of his thin, black t-shirt. Without even blinking, he shoves the needle into his already track-marked, bruised flesh. Royal closes his eyes as the euphoria of the drug works its way through his system. The dirty syringe falls to the floor.

"God," he shakes his head, sighing in delight. "That shit is wonderful."

He fixates his glassy eyes back on me and slowly, begins to step back toward me.

My breathing ceases.

God. Somebody help me.

I crane my neck when he moves to the end of the dingy bed. He bends and runs his hands up and down my legs, sending chills over my skin, making my stomach lurch.

Please, I pray, my shoulders shuddering as I close my eyes.

If he is going to take me, I refuse to watch.

I stiffen when his rough hands come in contact with the skin on my ankles. He wraps his hands around them and forces my legs apart.

"Hold still, Alina," he whispers, tightening his grip on me as something cold runs over me. "I would hate to tarnish this delicate skin."

My eyes snap open. A long jagged knife, serrated on both sides, is in his hand. Small, sharp angry points stare back at me. *God, he's going to cut me.* My body stiffens.

"You know, I think I want to hear you scream... beg me to stop," he croons before giving me his eyes dancing with dark amusement. "I won't," he snickers. "No, you need to feel the pain. I want to hear you scream. The only thing better than listening to you beg would be if my little brother were here to see this. For him to watch me take what he thinks is his. Speaking of watching, do you know how much it killed me inside to stand in that window and watch my brother fuck you? To see him touch you, taste you? If only I loved guns like my family does, I would have killed the both of you that night. I had the perfect shot from that penthouse across from yours."

His words pull at the last strings of my sanity, and I can no longer hold back, the sobs leaving my heavy chest as he continues his torment.

"I wanted to kill him and you both. Instead, I had to kill the woman who lived in that building across from yours. Never again, Alina. I'm going to make you scream," he promises. "And when my brother gets here, he's going to watch me fill you up with my dick over and over and again before I slice his fucking throat."

I try to dig deep into my soul, chanting repeatedly that Roan is safe.

Everyone I love is safe. Not a single person knows where I am. Royal is testing me, teasing me into believing Roan is coming here. I refuse to believe it.

"Let's take this out, shall we?" he asks, tugging at the cloth he forced into my mouth.

I suck in several gulps of much needed air, but I'm sobbing so hard now, it's taking everything out of me.

"Don't cry," he whispers, running the back of his hand over my cheek. "I'll be gentle."

In the next moment, I feel his palm move back down to my legs, the steel gliding over my skin, and hear the sound of my pants being shredded with the blade of his knife.

Throbbing pain shoots up my leg. With every nick of the knife in my skin, my sobs of agony heighten.

"You need to stay still, Alina."

"How can I stay still when you're slicing my leg?"

"I told you I didn't want to ruin this perfect skin. You wiggle, you get cut. Simple as that," he says, his words starting to slur, the drugs taking effect as I freeze in place. "Perfect." He chuckles deviously.

I lie still, praying for him to slip and accidentally cut right through my femoral artery. End my life. The pain is overwhelming; the blood is trickling down my leg. He repeats the same thing on the other side. I hold completely still as he wedges the knife between my jeans and my leg. In one rapid slice, he sears through my jeans, all the way up.

He rips my jeans clean off my body. I continue to lie still, my body shutting itself down without me even trying.

"I'm not sure which one I want first. Your ass or your pussy?" His vulgar, sick words tumble out of his mouth as his grubby hands begin kneading the cheeks of my ass before flipping me over onto my back. "Open your eyes, god damn it!"

I feel the tip of the knife penetrate through the skin right above my pubic bone, and my tearstained eyes fly open.

"You fucking *watch,*" he orders. "If you move those eyes away from my knife, I will slice you all the way up."

I swallow and hold my breath as he glides the tip of his knife slowly up my stomach, over my belly button.

Unhurriedly, like he's dreaming, fascinated with his design across my skin, he circles, lines my flesh, not once penetrating my skin.

"Your skin would make the perfect canvas. Did you know that?" he looks into my eyes. His hands continue to carve lazy, unscathed circles across my skin.

I don't think I've breathed since he started moving his knife.

"I'm going to carve a gift for everyone to see onto this canvas, Alina."

The knife keeps moving upward.

The blade disappears under my shirt, scraping across one of my nipples before it moves up to the collar of my shirt. Just like my jeans, it's ripped down the middle.

I'm laid in front of him in just my bra and panties.

My lungs burst open. I cough and gag, collecting air into my lungs.

He drops the knife to the floor, standing over me as it clanks against the concrete. Keeping his eyes locked on me, mesmerized at the sight, I watch his hands go to the waist of his jeans.

My eyes plead silently once more with him. Desperately, I wiggle my fingers, trying to escape the confines of the rope around my hands and wrists. I squeeze my eyes shut, muffle the scream threatening to tear through my throat when an excruciating angered jolt of pain shoots through my wrist.

Immediately, I know.

I'm not going to be able to get free.

I'm defeated.

I'm dead.

Chapter Twenty-Two

Roan

The first thing I smell as Anton and I run through the knee-length grass is the damp earth, the sweet smell of pine from the trees, and the swampy, stagnant, and stale stench of Lake Thomas.

We move like lightening around the side of the boarded-up house, the flicker of the light from the houseboat up ahead.

More recollections than I care to count flicker through my mind faster than the speed of light. Years of pent-up anger, hatred, and the determination to save the woman I love give me the strength to trudge through the murky dark waters of this lake that has invaded my dreams for years.

My body shakes and my stomach churns when the water makes contact with the bare flesh on my arms.

Growing up, Royal had threatened me many times about cutting me up into small pieces and feeding me to the sharks he said lurked in this water, the one and only reason why I never learned to swim. While his mind may be living in the past, he has no idea my uncle taught me how to swim the very same way he taught me how to kill. How to sneak up on a person without them even knowing it.

It took John two months of drilling into my head that fear is what will get you killed. The only thing I fear now is what state I will find Alina in when I reach this damn boat.

"Fuck," Anton barks, when the sound of Alina screaming tears across the dead quiet of the night. My arms pump faster, my legs kick harder, the sludgy water scaling across my skin.

"How the hell did he get her out here?" Anton gasps out, his shortness of breath evidence in itself that he swam just as hard as I did to reach the edge of the boat.

"There used to be an old canoe that my dad would use to get himself out here. The damn thing is anchored down." My arms pull myself up onto the front part of the boat. I kneel down, extend my hand, and drag Anton up beside me.

Another piercing scream slices through my heart. What seems like forever only takes five seconds for us to climb down the few stairs, and the sight before us brings us both to a sudden halt.

As if he was expecting us, Royal is leaning up against the wall on a small makeshift bed, Alina spread out between his legs, her eyes wide, and her chest bobbing up and down, splotches of blood all over the floor and mattress, and a damn knife to her throat.

"Your timing has always sucked, little brother." He slinks the knife further down her body, the tip drawing a straight line, blood mixed with the long-lasting, toe curling pleads of her cries.

"You son of a bitch." Anton takes two steps forward. "Stop right there or the knife goes deeper. Better yet, I may just cut her beautiful little head off."

Anton stops. My eyes lock dead with the man who has the same blood as mine coursing through his veins. Brothers, two men who hate each other. Brought into this world by the same two people, and yet we are nothing alike. His entire life, he has been so full of anger and hate. A chemical imbalance missing from his warped state of mind.

"Roan." My name falls from her lips like Royal just stabbed me through my heart with his knife.

"I told you not to say his name, Alina." He presses the knife into her stomach more forcefully. Her screams are excruciatingly loud. Jesus. This ends now.

Faster than a speeding bullet, I pull the knife from my back pocket and fling it through the air, hitting my target dead on, into his shoulder. The knife drops from his hands. Anton sweeps in, scooping Alina in his arms, her body limp from relief, or exhaustion.

Her agonizing whimpers are a clear indication she's alive. None of this is about me anymore, it all has to do with the woman who means everything to me. She's my happy, my heart, and this fucker hurt her.

I know she's safe as I grab my target by his throat and squeeze.

"Baby, are you all right?" Her cries rip through my chest. "Yes." Her one syllable word scathes the tiny surface of my anger.

"Take her up top. The minute everyone else gets here, find a way to get her to shore safely. I'll be at the hospital as soon as I get rid of this filth." Relief washes over me knowing she's going to be fine.

"Don't waste your time on him, he's not worth it." Out of the corner of my eye, I watch the two of them disappear.

"Just you and me, brother," I snarl.

All these years, I've done so much dreaming of torturing him. Teasing him like he did me. Now that Alina is hurt, all I can think about is her. How she needs me. How I need her.

"Did you know that five minutes of squeezing the carotid artery is all it takes to kill someone?" I crush down more on his pulse point, the fast paced throbbing from his racing heart a necessity to my desire to finish him off.

"Any second now, that rapidly beating heart is going to spiral downward. Every thump slower, your blood is going to stop pumping and you are going to fucking die," I seethe.

"Fuck you." His voice is shallow.

"You'd love that, wouldn't you? You would love to be able to pick that knife up off the floor and carve me up. Cut off my head and throw it in this lake like you told me so many times. It isn't going to happen. I'm not going to give you the satisfaction of hurting me anymore. What I am going to do is kill you in the one way that will haunt your soul while you burn in hell." I begin to apply more pressure. My free hand comes up, taking hold of the knife lodged in his shoulder, yanking it out. Blood is oozing out. He brings his hand up, wraps it around mine, his eyes bulging. Losing oxygen with every second that slowly ticks by.

"You're not strong enough. You're weak. You've always been weak, Royal. How does it feel to be helpless, to know any second now you're doing to die?" I plunge the knife into his leg. He cries out. I draw it back out and like a man who has no control over his way of thinking, I stab him over and over. The entire time, he gasps, his eyes slowly losing focus.

I would love nothing more than to squeeze the life out of him. He needs to suffer before he comes to his demise. I release the hold I have on him, his body slumping to the floor like the sack of rotten shit he is.

Automatically, his tainted hands cover up the gaping hole in his leg. Blood is pouring out of him like out of a water hose with holes scattered throughout.

"You don't have it in you to kill me." His voice sounds unaffected from the pain he has to be in.

"That's where you're wrong, motherfucker. I've been waiting for this for years." I turn on him, knowing he's bleeding out like a god damn sieve, my eyes scanning the room for anything to torment him further.

"What the fuck are you doing?" He screams when I pick up an old can of gasoline from the corner, twisting my body back around, and kneeling on the floor in front of him.

"Playing, brother," I say with no compassion, no feeling at all.

"You pussy ass mother fucker," he cries out.

I laugh, unscrewing the cap.

"Ouch," I say as I begin to douse him with the gas. He starts screaming, begging for me to stop. I stand directly above him, the gas penetrating my nose.

"How does it feel to be tortured? To know you have no control? I'm going to rule the world just like dad. It's all mine. Everything is mine. I'm coming out unscathed. Your dream of killing me was just that. A dream. A fantasy. But mine, my dream has come true. Even though I would love nothing better than to torture you, to cut you little by little, to stay here all night and slowly kill you, I have a woman who needs me, loves me." I drop the can by his side, my stomach churning as I watch the gas eat away at his skin.

"Always remember I had her first." His words strike me as if he carved my heart clear out of my chest.

I refuse to let him goad me, to give him the satisfaction of knowing what he did to Alina, that he destroyed her trust in men for the last ten years. He wants to die playing dirty. His time is up. I'll play as dirty as this scumbag wants me to play.

"Let's talk about Alina, shall we?" His eyes go wide as he tries to keep his shit together, trying to conceal the pain I know has to be coursing through his body.

"Go to hell." I laugh at the irony of those words. Why is it that when a person is about to die, the one thing they tell you is to go to hell? This seems to be a pattern. Fuck, I love this shit.

"You know," I grab him by his chin. Forcing him to look at me, "let me tell you the same thing I told Mac and the other people who died recently. They all told several of us to go to hell too. Calla started this nice little saying. It seems to be a trend. I'm going to have to thank her for that." His half-dead eyes look at me like I'm the one who's about to die.

"I may be going to hell, but you'll beat me to it." I laugh while he scoffs.

"I should have killed you when I had the chance," he says.

I reach over, picking up his knife. He's going to die by my hands using the knife he hurt Alina with.

"Let's get back on track here, brother." I snatch the blood-covered hand he has over his gaping wound and pin it under my knee, disabling him to be able to move it, and reach for the other hand, circling my hand around his wrist.

"Just kill me already, you chicken shit," he croaks out.

"I'm about to. I have a few more things to say first." I take his pinky finger, slicing it right off. "That was for Calla," I lift the next finger. "Dad. Mom. Alina. Me." I slice every single one of his fingers off his hand. I've never seen so much blood in my entire life. It's pouring out of him like water out of a broken faucet. My stomach nearly lurches up and out of my throat, his loud, shrilling screams deafening my ears. With the little strength he has left, he tries to wiggle his good hand free from underneath me. I don't budge.

"Alina and I love each other. While you rot in hell, remember this. Every morning I will wake up to her beautiful face, her body wrapped around mine. Every night, I will make love to her. Hold her. Kiss her. One day she'll marry me. I'll plant my seed inside of her, watch her have my babies. She's mine, brother." I bring the knife up, ready to plunge it into his heart. The coward closes his eyes. Fuck him. I would love nothing more than for him to watch me suck the last breath out of him. But I don't care anymore. This needs to be done. I need to see my girl.

"Roan, enough." I spin to the sound of my dad's voice. Alongside him stands my uncle John, both of them dripping wet. Jesus, they must have swum through the murky water.

"What the fuck?" I stand. Royal falls over, his screaming turning into low cries.

"His death will not be on your hands, son. Leave. Go to Alina. We've got this from here." My uncle never once takes his eyes off of Royal, who is squirming on the floor.

"Go now." John stalks over to me and takes the knife right out of my hands. As much as I want to stand here and argue with the two of them, I won't. The plan all along was for Royal to die.

I walk up beside my dad, stopping next him.

"I'm fine, son. Now go. After this night, there will be no more talk of this. Go."

I place my bloodied hand on his shoulder, firmly squeezing. His eyes are full of unshed tears. I leave him there. No more words need to be spoken. No more lives need to be slain, except the man's who deserves to die.

I walk away from the one and only person who has bullied, scared, and fucked with my head my entire life, and as I jump back into the deep dark water of this shit lake I hate and swim to the shore then run to my truck to get to the hospital, the only thing I can think of is he's finally gone. He will no longer be able to hurt the people I love.

Revelation 20:10 "And the devil who deceived them was thrown into the lake of fire and brimstone, where the beast and the false prophet are also; and they will be tormented day and night forever and ever."

EPILOGUE

One year later

"You like that?" I growl like the starving man I am as I wrap my mouth around Alina's clit, sucking her sweetness into my mouth.

I've been gone for four days. Four damn days too long to stay away from this beauty. With my dad not ready to give up his reign yet, I work alongside Cain and now Dilan. We rule this fucking gun-stealing community. I love it.

It's been almost a year since we were dragged through hell. The moment I walked into her hospital room looking and smelling like I lived in the sewer, I saw her sleeping peacefully in her bed. Her entire family surrounding her while she slept.

Fuck. The sight of her lying there safe had me fall to my knees. The outcome of what could have happened to her if Anton and I hadn't shown up would have had my body floating at the bottom of that lake, just like I know that's where John and my dad left him.

Not one word from anyone about what happened to Royal has been spoken, except between Alina and I. She needed to know I wasn't the one who killed him. Am I grateful for being stopped before I did? Fuck if I know. I'm glad he's gone. That's the only thing that matters to me.

All her scars are healed. Thank Christ. The ones on her leg were mostly surface cuts. The one on her stomach not so much. Twenty stitches and a five-inch scar he left behind. My lady's a trooper, though. She dealt with it all. Told me straight out he may have put a few scars on her body, but the one that was on her soul was healed by me. God, I fucking love her.

"Don't stop." Alina brings me out of my shit thoughts and back to this glistening pussy in front of me. I inhale and fuck her wild with my tongue until I have her coming all over my face while she screams my name. I will never get tired of hearing her say my name full of need.

"I missed you, now kiss me." I crawl up her body and plunge my tongue into her mouth. This incredible woman has turned into one kinky, wild, and beautiful lady. I'm not complaining one damn bit. She nibbles at my bottom lip.

I flip her over onto her stomach, her sweet round ass begging me to take it. I run my hands down the spine of her back to the globes of that ass. I'll take her ass later. Right now, I need inside her pussy.

I hiss the minute the head of my cock enters her.

"Mother. Fucker!" I yell. Our doorbell rings. *Who the fuck is here?*

"Shit," Alina hisses. Both she and I jump out of bed, snatching our discarded clothes off of the floor.

"Calm the hell down." I scream at whoever the hell is behind that door.

"What the fuck?" I yank open my door. My mouth falls open at the bundle of pink staring me in the face. I calm right the hell down. The sight of Cain and Calla's four-month-old daughter brings a smile to my grumpy face.

"Hey, pretty girl." My arms instantly go under hers, stealing her from her dad.

"You're damn lucky you have her with you. I just got home." I glare at Cain, my brows raised in the you-get-what-I-mean sort of way.

"What the hell ever. Give her back. We're not here to see you anyway. Where's my little princess' doc?"

"I'm right here." Alina comes around the corner, her hair pulled back. Damn, she's hot. She needs to keep that ponytail in. The minute they leave, I'm tossing her ass right on this couch, pulling the hell out of that hair and fucking her until she screams.

Cain spins around toward Alina while I smile at little miss drool face.

"Sorry to barge in, but Calla is in court all day and Justice will not take her hand out of her mouth and she's drooling all over everything." Cain's tone sounds panicked.

"She's teething, you dumb ass. Even I know that," I say between laughing.

"What?" he calls out like he can't believe people actually have teeth.

"Give her to me." He reaches for her. I hand her over with a little wink. She's a damn doll. Too bad she looks exactly like this fool standing in front of me.

"He's right, Cain. Look at her." Alina points to Justice, who has her hand shoved in her mouth.

"You mean she's going to have teeth?" he says.

"Uh, yes. And she's probably going to get fussy the minute it starts breaking through her skin too." Alina rubs the baby's hand and starts talking to her. My mind on the other hand drifts to her stomach, on images of her belly keeping our baby safe. God she'd be hot with my child. Fuck. There goes my cock. Hard as a brick.

"Hey, where did you go just now?" A snap of a finger in front of my face brings me back out of another dream.

"Did they leave?" I scan the room for Cain and Justice.

"Like two minutes ago. You've been standing there staring into space."

"I was thinking how I need to get you back into our bed so we can continue what we started before dumb ass showed up." I pull on the back of her ponytail, drag her to me, and lick the soft skin on her neck.

"No need for the bed. Fuck me right here." Her hand cups my dick.

"Yes, ma'am."

"You have got to be kidding me." This time it's her turn to start throwing words around as she struts to the door and flings it open to... "Oh, my god. Deidre," Alina's sweet voice cries.

We haven't seen or heard a word from Deidre since that dreaded night. After Alina came to the next morning, she demanded to see Deidre. By the time we went to her room, she was gone. Discharged herself in the middle of the night against doctors' orders. For an entire year, her disappearance has been a mystery to us all. Her parents claimed she needed time to heal.

Alina has taken her absence hard. The not knowing is what has torn her apart for an entire year. A few times a week, she would call Stefan and check on Deidre. Only to be told she's fine and coping the best she knows how. Everyone knew something was off. Things weren't right. However, we respected their wishes. And now that I round the corner to see her for myself, I see why.

Deidre is standing in our doorway, holding a small baby boy who looks exactly like Beamer.

Acknowledgments

I acknowledge you the reader. Every time you read a book, no matter what, you deserve all the recognition in the world! Many kisses and hugs to all of you!

Other Books by Kathy Coopmans

The Shelter Me Series

Shelter Me

Rescue Me

Keep Me

The Contrite Duet

Contrite

Reprisal

The Syndicate Series

The Warth of Cain

The Redeption of Roan

The Absolution of Aidan

late winter of 2016

The Deliverance of Dilan

Spring of 2016

Made in the USA
Middletown, DE
05 May 2022

65215011R00137